THE
PIECES
WE
LEAVE
BEHIND

CONTENT WARNING

This book is meant for a mature audience and contains content that may be triggering or inappropriate for some readers—including graphic sex scenes, profanity, mentions of sexual assault (off page, not involving MCs), bullying, violence, a MMC with a filthy mouth, depression, drug and alcohol use/abuse, dubious consent, and the death of a loved one.

To all the lost souls.
May you continue wandering until you find yourself content
and continuously wrapped in love.
And if you ever find that you aren't, I hope you look for more.

ONE

MADISON

I watch as they lower the dark wooden casket into the ground. It's a beautiful day. Late May, and the California sun shines brightly and beats down oppressively on my bare shoulders. It's hot—too hot for this time of year in the Bay Area. But it is beautiful, and it's a beautiful final resting place, with the mountains to the north and San Francisco Bay at my back. It's not what she would have wanted, though. Or, at least, that's what the argument was about last night and maybe why my aunt sobs with abandon into my shoulder, her arm nestled in the crook of my own. Not because she's gone. My grandma suffered in the end, and we should be glad that it's here now, or at least that's what they told me. Whatever waits on the other side, whether it's paradise or nothing, is better than existing the way she was before—with both her mind and control over her body completely gone.

Death, from what I understand, can be a mercy. There are far worse things. Things that I'd know nothing about. Maybe that's why my mother watches the way she does, stoic and unmoving beside my father, not reaching for comfort at all. Maybe. But there's something else, too. Something between these three women that I don't quite understand. Something unspoken, but it feels like resentment.

"I can't believe you wore that dress, Madison," my mom tells me as my dad pulls the car onto the interstate. "I told you how it makes your hips look."

I don't respond. I glance over at my aunt, who just shakes her head.

"You need to practice with your violin when you get home. At least for an hour. It's been days," she adds.

"We're getting drunk when we get back to the house," my aunt replies.

"Not her. You keep forgetting she's only eighteen, Emma."

"Jesus. You've changed," she shoots back.

"And you haven't. That's the problem."

"One day," my dad says as he rolls down the window and punches in the code for the gate at the end of the driveway leading up to our home. "You two have one more day together. You just buried your mother. You're both adults—let's spend the rest of the day honoring her, not fighting."

Mom sighs and waves him off, leaning against the passenger side window. Emma crosses her arms in front of her and rolls her eyes at the woman in the side-view mirror before we pull into the garage.

As we head inside, I send my boyfriend, Ethan, a text telling him that I hope he is feeling better and that we are just getting home. He wanted to be there for me today but came home for the summer from Stanford sick and was spending the day in bed instead.

Upon entering the home, my dad grabs a glass from the cabinet and fills it halfway before sliding the bottle of gin down the counter toward my aunt and pulling out three glasses. My mom shoots him a look that says, *'no fucking way,'* but he just shrugs his shoulders and heads up the staircase, presumably to his office. He doesn't take off days, either. My aunt fills her glass, then adds two fingers of gin to another and sets it down in front of me. I bring it to my mouth and take a long, hard sip, meeting my mother's eyes when I do—despite her cautionary glare. It's not like this is my first drink. She appears to give up when I set it back down, then pours her own and heads to the refrigerator.

"What do you guys want to eat?" she asks. "We have so much food in here. I could put the lasagna Ethan's mom sent over in the oven."

"No one is hungry," Aunt Emma says, throwing back the rest of her drink and pouring another. "We're just thirsty."

"For god's sake, Emma," my mom says, turning on the oven and tossing in the lasagna anyway. Emma is right, though. I'm not hungry, either. With her back to me, I add more gin to my glass as well.

"An apt tribute," Emma says. "Mom would have appreciated it. And you know what? She wouldn't have wanted us sitting here moping around, either. She wouldn't have wanted to see us fighting. She'd want us celebrating...*dancing*. It's the least we can do after burying her here."

"I'm not doing this. Not again. I'm not having this discussion; it's over with. I paid for the funeral. I paid for the burial plot and the headstone in the same beautiful cemetery where my husband and I will be buried. And you, too. If that's what you want, Emma."

"And I'm the one who was there. Every day. Taking care of her when she was sick. Feeding her, bathing her. Watching that disease eat through her brain. But you're right, Mel. It's over. It's finally fucking over." She pulls her phone out of her purse and connects it to the living room speakers, and Bonnie Tyler's voice fills the room. "That's more like it," she says, hiking up her skirt and swaying her hips to the music, the clear liquid in her glass threatening to slosh over the side.

Sometimes, it is hard to believe they were raised by the same woman—that they grew up together—though I suppose my aunt was ten years younger than my mother, so maybe they didn't really grow up together at all. At least, that's the only way I can rationalize it as I glance back and forth between the two women. One composed, operating by a rigid set of self-imposed rules. The other seems to operate solely on impulse, with no rules at all.

And me—I'm more of the former, though I'm not sure if it's more by nature or nurture. Sometimes I feel like there's someone else buried inside who's dying to get out. But I don't know her. And I don't know what to do with her. And she only knocks every now and then—at times like these. For the most part, she's quiet, and I'm content. Why wouldn't I be? On paper, my life is perfect. I have nothing to complain about...nothing that anyone would want to listen to, anyway.

"Ugh, can we listen to anything but this?" my mom pleads.

"What are you talking about? You love Bonnie Tyler. And she was one of Mom's favorites; you know that."

"I can assure you that though I'm well aware she was one of Mom's favorites, I do not love Bonnie Tyler," my mom replies.

It's hostile—more than it needs to be—and it's confusing. Again, everything about these two women confuses me.

"Come and dance with me, Maddie," Emma says.

"Her name is Madison," my mom corrects.

"Come and dance with me, *Madison*. You should, too, Amelia."

"Yeah, right," I tell her as she pulls me out to the middle of the living room floor. "Mom doesn't dance."

"Your mom," she replies, "can move. *God*, can she ever. Don't think that she can't. I've seen it with my own eyes. She can dance and drink and sing with the best of us."

She lifts our joined hands over our heads and twirls me before leaning in and whispering in my ear, "Don't let the stick she's got up her ass now fool you."

My eyes dart nervously toward my mother to ensure she hadn't heard what she said before I allow myself to laugh.

"Someone has to be the adult around here, Emma," she says before leaving the room to answer a phone call. "Clearly, it isn't going to be you."

"Clearly not," she says to her back as she leaves the room.

"I'm sorry, Aunt Emma," I tell her.

"About what? About your grandma?"

"Yeah, that. But also—her."

"Oh, don't be sorry about her. Do you know what her problem is? It's not me. It's that at some point in her life, someone told her that to be a person of a certain age and a certain status, you had to stop dressing a certain way and stop doing things like singing and dancing and fucking up, and she believed them. And she's mad about it. And that has nothing to do with me—or with you. Fuck. I shouldn't have said that. I shouldn't be telling you things like this. I'm sorry, Madison."

"It's okay," I tell her.

I hate that they fight. I hate that it's like this and that I never really got to know her or Grandma because of whatever this is, but if there's any day when someone should be allowed a free pass, I guess it's the day they buried their mother.

In a place she didn't know. In a place she wouldn't have wanted—according to Emma, anyway.

She twirls one last time and throws herself down on the sofa. "The truth is your mom was always just...better than us. Wanted better than what we had. Bigger. And look around—she got it." She pauses, gesturing at our surrounding home. "She got what she wanted, didn't she? I'm glad for her for that. If she's happy, then I'm happy. But..." she trails off, "...no, I'm sure she's happy."

"Are you happy, Aunt Emma?" I ask.

"Oh, sweetie, I'm thrilled. Don't worry about me. I got what I wanted, too. I have enough," she says, reaching out and tucking a stray lock of blonde hair behind my ear.

And I believe her. I think. She has a smile that always reaches her eyes. She brings with her an air of contentment and ease, I guess. I don't know how else to describe it, but I know whatever it is, it isn't something I'm used to feeling in a room with my parents and my peers. Maybe they do have everything they want, but they aren't content. They aren't at ease.

"You look just like her, you know."

"Yeah, I do," I reply. I've heard it so many times before. I've seen it in photographs. The same pale blue eyes. The same stick-straight blonde hair, though mine is more than halfway down my back, and hers falls just above her shoulders now in a cut that is as sleek and sophisticated as she is.

'*As cold, too,*' I think, then wonder where it came from. The last couple of days have had a weird effect on my mood. I'm off, I guess.

When my mom returns, she pulls the lasagna out of the oven, and the three of us eat or at least feign to do so, mostly pushing the food around on our plates. Eventually, I excuse myself to my room, leaving the two of them alone and hoping they'll be okay without me as a buffer. I close the door behind me, collapse onto the bed and pull out my phone, finally checking my texts and social media notifications, which are primarily condolences for my loss.

And one that is something else. Something I wasn't expecting.

Harper: Isn't Ethan supposed to be sick?

She sends me a picture of my boyfriend at a crowded house party with a beer bong in his mouth.

Yeah, he was supposed to be sick.

Me: Where are you?

I strip off the dress that my mom said made my hips look too big and pull on a pair of shorts and a tank top that's party-appropriate instead. I'm relieved when I go downstairs and find that everyone seems to have retired to their respective rooms for the night. It makes it easier. Not that I can't come and go as I please, I'd just rather not have to answer any questions right now. I enter the four-car garage and climb inside my white Mercedes, pushing the button on the opener before typing the address into my phone. I've been to Weston's place before for parties, but only a couple of times, and I don't trust myself to find it on my own now. I am directionally challenged as it is; I wonder if it's a curse on my generation or if it's just me who has maybe had things a little too easy and is maybe a little too used to having the way paved or pointed out ahead of time.

I pull up to the house and park, then make my way on foot down a driveway that's as long as my own, the vibrations from the music inside hitting me before I'm in the door. I open it and scan the packed room, but I don't see Harper. I send her a text, and she replies that she's out back by the pool, but she lost track of Ethan a while ago. I wonder if he's still here. I haven't texted him. I was too angry that he lied and made me think he was at home sick in bed. I don't get angry very often and hate confrontation, but today, my nerves are fried. Still, I begin to regret coming here as soon as the door closes behind me. I don't want to make a scene, so what is my plan, exactly?

I make my way toward the back door that I know leads out to the pool but run into Weston and Blake before I make it outside.

"Oh, shit," Blake says when we make eye contact. "I mean...hey, Madison. What's up? You want a beer?"

"No," I reply. "I don't want a beer. Where's Ethan?"

"He's not—" he starts.

"He's upstairs somewhere," Weston finishes.

Blake shoots him a cautionary look. "Dude, what are you doing?"

"What? Fuck him," Weston says. "You're too good for him, Madison."

I almost leave. *Almost.* In fact, when I turn, barely hearing the last words he says, I'm not sure if my feet are carrying me toward the staircase or the front door. I could go home. I could let him explain what happened and why he lied to me tomorrow, and that'd be easier—better even. But I'm already making my way up the staircase, my heart hammering in my chest. I walk down the hallway, past a bathroom with a line in front of the door, and continue down the hall, peeking into the rooms with open doors before stopping in front of a closed one and holding my breath before reaching for the handle. I think I know what I'll find—every cell in my body is screaming at me not to open the door. Still, I need to see for myself. I crack the door open just enough and find him with his back to me and his pants around his ankles.

"What the hell are you doing? Get out!" the girl on her knees shouts at me.

And I do. Like a robot, I close the door and head downstairs while the image seers itself into my brain. And I do it without saying anything, without him even knowing that I know, and without any words to describe the new feeling welling inside my core.

I didn't make a scene. That's a good thing, right? I'm not crying now as I descend the staircase, even though my cheeks burn hot. I make it to the front door without anyone else stopping me and pull it closed behind me, letting go of the breath I've been holding when I do.

"Madison," Weston says after it closes behind me. I look over and see him leaning against the railing on the front porch, smoking a joint alone. I wonder why. I wonder if he knew what I'd find, too, and if he's out here waiting for me. "Did you find him?"

"What do you think?" I say, shrugging.

He holds the joint out to me, and I take it. I hit it hard, feeling it burn the back of my throat, and remember that I hate it. I never smoke. I don't like how it makes me feel. I need something to dull whatever I'm feeling now, though. Not sad, not hurt. I think I'd know better what to do with that. It's rage, and I need to shut it down. I hand the joint back to him and ball my fists at my side.

"Fuck him," he says again.

Yeah, someone was probably fucking him. It wasn't me. Not anymore, anyway.

"I mean it. You are way too good for him, Madison." He's drunk. Very drunk. And high. And one of Ethan's closest friends. We'd all gone to East Side Prep together, and he graduated last year with Ethan. "If I had a girl like you—smart, pretty—fuck, I'd be home every night. Not running around on campus fucking anything that moves."

Yeah, I doubted that. I barely know the guy, but I know him well enough to know he isn't the relationship type. He is gorgeous, though. Fuckable, but not datable. I wonder if I'm the opposite—if that's how they see me. Maybe I'm boring. Maybe I'm bad at it. Maybe that's why my boyfriend was "running around campus fucking anything that moves." The reality behind those words crashes down on me, and I feel sick to my stomach. But, of course, I'm not an idiot. Naive, apparently, but not stupid by any means. This wouldn't be the first time he's cheated on me. He wouldn't choose a crowded party down the road from my house, surrounded by all our friends, if it was the first time. I would have pieced that together once I got home and had time to think about it.

He offers me the joint again, and I shake my head. "I need to go home."

"I hope you're not mad at me. You know, kill the messenger or whatever," he says. And I'm not. I don't even know him well enough to be mad at him. I realize now that maybe there are other people I should be mad at—closer, mutual friends who smiled in my face while they knew what was going on behind my back.

Fake. Fake. Fake.

Fake smiles, fake friends, fake happy. I think about the weekends I spent with him at Stanford and how he'd introduce me to his female friends who were always so kind and smiled when they met me and told me I was so lucky to be Ethan's girlfriend. I wonder how many of them were lucky when I wasn't there.

Speaking of fake smiles, I instinctively shoot him one now. "I'm not mad at you, Weston. I'm...grateful, actually. For your honesty. And I won't tell him, either."

"Don't care if you do," he says.

"See you around," I tell him.

I turn and make my way down the driveway toward my car. On the way home, everything feels surreal—too quiet and like I'm not exactly in my body. I can't stand it, but I also can't imagine drowning out the silence with any type of music right now. I'm not sure how much of it is from the weed, as I'm certainly not used to smoking, and how much of it is because I just realized my relationship was a one-sided sham. I wonder how long that's been the case. I wonder if it started when he moved in at Stanford or if it was true when we were in school together, too.

I'm a goddamn joke.

Once inside, my heavy limbs tell me they won't make it up the staircase. I grab the gin left out on the counter and drink straight from the bottle before collapsing on the couch and sinking into a light, barely-sleep.

It doesn't last long.

It's still dark when I hear someone shuffling around the house. It startles me—both because I'm not expecting it and because I'm confused for a moment about where I am and what I'm doing there. I take in my surroundings and reorient myself, and once I do, the rest comes flooding back.

"Aunt Emma?"

"Oh, shit! You scared me, Madison."

That makes two of us.

"What are you doing? What time is it?" I ask.

"It's almost five. I can't sleep. I'm ready to go home. This is just..."

A fake place full of fake people?

"I'm going with you," I tell her.

"To Lost Hollow? Oh honey, you can't. Your mom won't like that."

She is right. She won't like it. I'll miss violin practice, and my parents had gotten me a job interning for a state representative my dad works with for the summer. I'm supposed to start in three days.

"I'm an adult," I tell her. "I can make my own decisions. I want to go."

"I don't know, Madison."

"Take me with you, Emma. I can't be here right now. I can't *breathe*."

A knowing look washes over her, and she must realize that I need this because I see the moment she changes her mind, even if she doesn't say it aloud.

"Give me five minutes," I tell her.

I take the stairs two at a time, then run to my room, throw open the closet, and pull out my suitcase. I don't know exactly what clothes I pack, but I know I stuff it full, so there has to be more than enough inside. I top it off with some toiletries and makeup and hurry downstairs. I still have over an hour before my parents will be up for their Sunday morning tennis doubles at the country club, but I need to play it safe. If I wasn't gone before she got up, I wasn't gone. Period.

I head out the front door and hop into the old silver sedan in the driveway.

"Wow. You actually made it in five minutes. I'm impressed," she says. "At seven, I would have left."

"Yeah, I'm glad I made it, then."

Before we're out of the valley, my mom starts calling. I don't answer. Once we're outside of Redmond, Ethan starts texting. I don't answer those, either.

And once we cross the border into Oregon, I email that state rep's office and regretfully decline my internship. Then, I toss my phone out the mother fucking window.

TWO

MADISON

It's past noon by the time we finally pull up to the old cabin in Lost Hollow, Oregon—the same house where my mother grew up and where my aunt lives now with my grandmother or, well...had. I guess now she lives alone. When I step out of the car, the chill in the mountain air shocks my system, causing goosebumps to erupt on my skin. I'm still wearing the same shorts and tank top I had worn to the party last night and the same makeup I'd put on for the funeral that afternoon. I'm not sure what it looks like now, and I'm not eager to find out. Still, I take a moment to revel in its beauty—to breathe in the cool, crisp air knowing the moment it fills my lungs that it's different than what I'm used to. Not just cleaner and clearer, but thicker somehow, and I'd swear I could even taste it. Something a lot like spruce and burnt sycamore settles on my tongue before each breath fills my lungs.

"You coming?" Emma says from the front porch.

"Yeah, sorry. I just...forgot what it was like here. I forgot how beautiful it is." I turn away from the house and can just barely spot the blue-green waters of the lake in the distance.

"Well, it's been...how long has it been?"

"I was only eleven," I tell her. "So, around seven years, I guess."

"Seven years? That long?" She shakes her head. "I guess that makes sense. The last time you were here, I think you still wore bows in your hair."

Yeah, I guess I probably did. I grab my bags from the back and follow her inside.

"It's changed a lot since then," she says, looking back at me and smiling over her shoulder. And yeah, that's an understatement. I expect to be greeted by the same old, orange sofa set that had probably been there since the 70s and the same kitchen that was probably there for even longer, but I'm not. Instead, the first floor has been opened up—save for a couple of wooden beams that were probably necessary for support in an old cabin like this one—and the kitchen completely updated with modern chandeliers that somehow complimented the old bones of the place perfectly.

"I had the first floor remodeled about five years ago when the store took off, and then had the bathrooms updated when Mom started to get bad and needed them to be more accessible. I had the ramp in front put in for the same reason. Now, the upstairs is still pretty much the same. You can stay in your mom's old room. Do you remember where that is?"

"Yeah, I do," I tell her.

Top of the stairs, first door to the left. Not that it was possible to get lost in this place.

"We don't have very good signal up here, but we do have wifi. The password is on the fridge. Oh, but I guess...you don't really need that anyway, do you?"

"Nope," I tell her, remembering my phone. She didn't say a word about it when I chucked it out the window. "I guess not."

"Do you want to tell me what that was about?" she asks.

"No," I say. "Well, probably. Eventually, but not right now."

"Okay," she says with a shrug. And then, she just lets it go. Just that—that small gesture—makes me glad enough that I came here. "Do you want something to eat? Drink?"

"I think I just want to sleep," I tell her, heading toward the staircase.

"Madison?"

"Yeah?"

"Your mom hasn't called yet. That means she probably hasn't figured out where you are."

"No, probably not."

She probably thought I spent the night with Ethan. Even though I don't say the name out loud, thinking it makes me wretch. I don't think I will be hungry for a very long time. It occurs to me that I haven't cried yet and still don't want to do it now. I'm just...angry. And I don't know what to do with it. There's nowhere for it to go.

"Once she does, she's not going to be happy," she says. "And you're going to have to talk to her; I'm not going to lie to her. I can't hide you, but you can stay as long as you want."

"Okay."

"Do you have a plan, Madison?" she asks.

Yeah, I did. I *had* a plan—past tense. Make perfect grades. Go to the best school I could get into and excel academically. Immerse myself in as many extracurriculars as possible so that I'd look better on paper. Make friends with the right people. Date the right guy. Get a degree and then keep going and then, once I'm finally done, marry that guy, live in a house like the one I grew up in, have a kid, and repeat the cycle.

Isn't that *the* plan? The one everyone has, what everyone hopes for?

It feels pretty empty now...like a fucking joke. I think of my mom standing emotionless at her own mother's funeral, upset instead about the dress I wore and the violin practice I skipped out on the past few days. I think of how she's stopped singing and dancing and—now that I think about it—laughing, too.

And I think of how I didn't cry or scream and how maybe I'm the same.

"I don't have a plan," I tell her and smile sadly. "I just...need a break. I think I need a long one. I'm so...*exhausted.*"

And there's so much behind it. Mentally, physically, and emotionally, I'm drained. I've been in the red for a long time; I'm unsure exactly how long. I just need a break. Just a few weeks, maybe, to clear my head.

"This is the exact right place for that," she tells me, returning my smile, but hers is sincere and reaches her eyes like it always does.

Without saying anything else, I head up the staircase, take a left, and turn into the first bedroom. My mother's childhood bedroom hasn't been touched in a couple of decades, and that's obvious now. There's a full-size bed with a white, lacy duvet pushed up against the back wall of the small room, a bulky, dark wood dresser to the left, and matching built-in shelves lining the wall to the right. The porcelain dolls are still there. They frightened me when I was younger and aren't much better now. There must be fifteen of them sitting there, watching me with the kind of eyes that seem to follow you around the room. The rest of the shelves are filled with trophies, ribbons, and sashes. I never paid much attention to them before, but I do now. They're from cheerleading and dance competitions; I guess my aunt was right. My mom could, at least at one point, move. It'd be safe to surmise that she still could. Like riding a bike, I'm sure your body remembers even if you think you forget. It's in your bones, maybe even deeper.

I make my way to the other end of the shelf, running my fingers down one of her beauty pageant sashes before pulling it over my head. I add a crown to complete the ensemble and turn toward the vanity to asses the absurdity of it all.

"I'm Amelia Walker-Ridgeway," I tell the girl in the mirror, raising my voice a few octaves. "Queen of the Country Club Bitches. And a whole lot of other shit that doesn't matter at all. Aren't I impressive? Don't you want to *kiss my ass*?"

I pause for dramatic effect and for the answer that doesn't come because, of course, there's no one else here. I remove both the crown and sash, not bothering to return them to the shelf, then collapse on the bed. The sheer curtains on the room's sole window do nothing to keep the light out, and usually, that'd be a problem for me, but for whatever reason, it isn't now. While I expect to lie restlessly for hours, I instead sink effortlessly into a deep, dreamless sleep.

When I wake up, the room is dark. At this time of year, I know that means it's late; I must have been asleep for a while. My stomach instantly reminds me how long it's been since I've eaten, my appetite apparently returning much sooner than I anticipated.

I head downstairs to the kitchen. The lights are on, but I don't see Emma—not that I'm super worried about it. She's a 32-year-old woman and is free to come and go as she pleases; I'm an adult, and I don't need her to hold my hand while I'm here and monitor my every move—not like they do at home. I open the fridge, not entirely impressed with my findings. I pull out a bag of carrots and some hummus and devour almost the entirety of the nearly-full container before Emma's phone starts to ring on the coffee table.

I pick it up and stare at the screen: Incoming call from Mel.

Oh, right. That's my mom. She said I was going to have to talk to her. I guess now is as good of a time as any.

THE PIECES WE LEAVE BEHIND

"Hello?"

"Madison? What the hell do you think you're doing?"

"Nothing! I just..."

"I've been calling you nonstop. So has Ethan! Harper said the last time she talked to you, you told her you were on your way to a house party. I called hospitals. I was about to call the police, Madison."

"I'm sorry," I tell her. Not that I left, but about all of that, I guess I am sorry. Now that I think about it, I can't blame her for having that reaction.

"And you can't even pick up the goddamn phone?!" she shouts. She rarely shouts, never curses. I think I even hear a hint of a rural accent that used to be there.

"It broke," I tell her. I've never been good at lying, but that wasn't necessarily a lie. More than likely, it did break. "Look, I'm sorry I didn't say anything. I just needed to get away. I had to get out of there. I need a break, Mom. That's it."

"I am going to..." she starts. "Emma *better*—"

"It's not Emma's fault. She wasn't even going to tell me she was leaving. I made her take me with her."

"Well, how do you plan on getting home? You have a job to start on Wednesday."

What's your plan, Madison?

"I don't, actually. I quit."

"You *what*?"

"I quit. I'm not going home on Wednesday, Mom. I don't know when I'm coming home. Like I told you, I just need a break. I'm tired, Mom."

"A break from what, Madison? Tired from *what*, Madison? Your perfect life and everything coming easily to you all the time?"

Yeah, maybe.

"A break from lounging by the pool with your friends and your boyfriend?" she continues. "From designer clothes and everything I've worked so hard to give you?"

She does this. Throws the things we have—these luxuries that should have made everything about my life nice and easy—back at me as if I'd asked for them, required or demanded them in some way. Like I knew what it was like to live without them. I didn't, and maybe that's why they meant so little to me. Our house is just a house. My car is just a car.

My boyfriend is just a piece of shit.

But she knew what it was like to have less. Way less. My grandmother raised Emma and my mom on her own, working at a cafe in the village and often living on whatever they were going to throw out that day. It wasn't an easy life, and I'm constantly reminded of that. She wanted bigger, and she wanted more for herself and for me, too, whenever I came to be. Like Emma said, she got it, too. She got those things, and she collects them voraciously, both clinging to them for validation and holding them out for everyone to see so that they all know how hard she's worked, how far she's come, and—most of all—how happy she is.

If she still feels as empty as I do, she does a good job hiding it.

"I brought plenty of clothes," I tell her. "And I don't have a boyfriend."

"Really?" she questions. "Does he know that? Because the guy who has been texting me all day—who has been out looking for you all day—sure as hell seems to think he's your boyfriend."

"Well, he should know better. If he's really that stupid, someone should let Stanford know. Get the poor guy some help."

Yeah, about that. He got in, and I didn't. And I'm *better* than him. Am I a little bit bitter? Maybe. None of that matters now.

"Is that what this is about? You're fighting with Ethan? Oh, honey. Trust me, spending a few weeks slumming it in Oregon isn't going to make you feel any better. And I would know—I did it for years. Just...come home and deal with it. Whatever crisis of character you're having, I can assure you the answer to your life's perceived problems is not in Lost Hollow."

"I'm not fighting with Ethan; I'm done with him. And I don't think I'm looking for answers either, Mom. I'm just tired."

"Your dad hired him to work at the firm this summer."

"Sounds awkward," I reply flippantly.

"Where's Emma?" she asks.

"She's not here; she must have left her phone. I found it on the coffee table."

"Did you check the garage? Her *studio*?" she asks with a condescending tone.

"Of course, I did," I tell her.

Lie. That one was a blatant lie.

"Tell her to call me when she gets back," she says. "And she's sending you home."

"No, she's not," I say. "You might be able to get her to kick me out, but she can't send me home. You can't make me come home."

"Are you sure about that? I've got a great deal of leverage that says otherwise."

"That stuff means more to you than it does to me."

"Let me talk to Emma. I know she's there."

"She's not. I'd give her the phone if she was, but she's not."

"Just make sure she calls me back," she says before hanging up.

I shrug and set the phone back down where I found it. That could have gone worse.

Did you check the garage? Her studio?

I cross the living room to the garage entrance, open the door, and step inside. 'Studio' is an accurate description. The back wall is covered in local landscape prints—many of them are of old buildings I recognize from the area they call the village. It's Lost Hollow's version of downtown, but not quite enough to earn that description. It's basically just a few streets with restaurants, bars, and stores. That's where Emma's store is, too. Wood etchings and handmade signs rest on palates on either side of the space, and Emma is leaning over a table running down the middle where, apparently, she makes her jewelry. She doesn't notice when I walk in, and I don't want to startle her and ruin whatever she's working on, so I sit on the step and watch for a while, waiting for my moment.

Eventually, she turns off the tool she's working with and picks up what looks like a bead, turning it and examining it in her hands. Appearing satisfied with her work, she sets it aside and reaches for another.

"Hi," I say before she can get started again.

I still manage to catch her off guard; she shrieks before turning to me, her hand covering her heart.

"Jesus, Madison. You scared me. I guess I'm a little too used to being alone out here," she says.

"Sorry. I didn't want to interrupt. It's just that....what was that anyway?"

"What? Oh, this?" she asks. I nod when she holds up the tool she's been working with. "It's a woodburning pen. Do you want to see? Come here."

I cross the room to the table, and she holds the bead up for me to see, the letter 'A' in flawless calligraphy etched into the surface.

"These are for some bracelets I'm working on," she tells me.

"Wow. That's...impressive. You do those all by hand? Is it hard?"

"It isn't hard to use, but it takes time to hone the ability—and talent, too, I suppose," she says.

"You *suppose*? Look at this place. You definitely have talent, Aunt Emma. I'm impressed. Do you sell all of this at the store?"

"I sell most of it in the store. I take orders and requests online, too. Sometimes, more than I can handle, and I have to shut it down for a while so I can catch my breath...and catch up with the orders, of course."

"That's...insane. I mean, sorry. I'm just kind of blown away. I knew you had the boutique in town, but I had no idea about any of this. Mom never mentioned it."

"Really? Huh..." she says, looking off to the distance now. That truth didn't just surprise her, it wounded her, too. I consider, for a moment, apologizing, but somehow think acknowledging it would only make it worse. Remembering why I came looking for her in the first place, I change the subject.

"She called you—my mom. I answered it and spoke to her. I told her where I was, that I quit my job and broke up with my boyfriend, and that I wanted to stay."

"How did she take it?" she asks.

"How do you think?" I reply. She laughs, and I add, "But she conceded...for now."

"So, you're staying?"

"If you'll have me," I say. "You mentioned you were a little overrun with your work. I could help—not with this stuff, of course—but I could help out at the boutique."

"Really? You'd do that? I could definitely use the help."

"I would love to do that," I tell her.

"It doesn't pay well," she laughs.

"I'm okay with that."

"Do you want to tell me what happened? With the boyfriend?"

"He was cheating on me. Not once, but all the time...at least over the past year, and maybe longer than that. We started dating when I was 15; he was the only real boyfriend I ever had and...."

I'm not sure how to articulate the rest of what I am feeling. Maybe because my reaction surprised even me.

Emma tries to help by filling the silence. "I get it. First loves hit hard. That kind of heartache—everyone has felt it, and you'll likely feel it again—but that first dose is particularly nasty. I think, maybe, because you're not prepared for the way it incapacitates you."

"Yeah," I say. "I wasn't ready for that."

But that's not it—not quite, anyway. It hurts, but not the way I expected it to and not the way Emma described it, either. I'm not incapacitated. I don't even know if I'm sad. I'm just angry. I'm angry because I was the last one to know and because they all just smiled in my face. Like I was a joke or I didn't matter or, even worse, like what he was doing to me was normal, and it was totally fine.

Fake.

It was all fake, and I now find myself contemplating what else falls into that category. It occurred to me in the car that I was more upset about the lost time and feeling like I was behind somehow now than the lost person. I keep waiting for it to hurt like she says. I keep waiting to cry. I even tried to this afternoon before I fell asleep, but I couldn't.

Maybe I had been faking, too.

"Everyone processes things differently," she says, and I wonder for a moment if she'd read my mind or if I'd said it all out loud. "Some people...they like to be alone, quiet...still. If that's you, take all the time you need. But, if you need to move and keep busy, you can start tomorrow morning."

"I think I'm the second one," I tell her.

"Well, get some sleep," she says. "We can leave around 9:00 AM tomorrow."

But since I did get some sleep, this time when I head upstairs, I do lie awake. Alone, quiet, and still.

I don't think about all of the things I'll have to do the next day or how I'm going to usefully fill every minute of my time like I normally would. I don't scroll through social media or worry about what everyone back home is doing without me. I don't think about what I'm missing.

I like that, too.

THREE

MADISON

T he next morning, we make the short drive together up to the village. Since I was just a child when I experienced it before, I wasn't able to appreciate Lost Hollow for what it is, but I do now. I can see why people flock here in the summer. The village bears the bones of its original structures with a modern flare, overlooking the lake and its impossibly clear blue-green waters with the still snow-capped peaks of the Cascades as the backdrop. It's already bustling, with people pouring into and lined up outside restaurants for brunch, and all of the inns on the strip have hung their 'No Vacancy' signs at the end of their walkways. I can see the ski lift already moving in the distance, but there won't be any skiing at this altitude this time of year. Now, people are just along for the ride, trying to grab the best photos and videos for their social media posts. My friends would be all over that.

'You don't have any friends,' my inner voice replies. I'm not ready to worry about whether or not it's right.

Once we get to the storefront, there's another girl who looks to be about my age waiting for us. I assume this must be Ava—the girl Emma told me I would be working with and who would be training me this week. She isn't what I expected, but I'm not sure what I expected. I guess maybe someone simple, someone that fits more with my small mountain town assumptions, but Ava doesn't do that at all. She looks impossibly chic—her yellow sundress compliments her coffee complexion perfectly, and her shoulder-length straight dark hair blows in the breeze. Suddenly, I feel underdressed in my cut-off shorts and off-the-shoulder tee, with my hair pulled up into a top knot.

Tomorrow, I'll do better.

"Ava, this is my niece, Madison—I told you about her," Emma says, unlocking the door to the shop. "She's going to be working your schedule this week, so you can show her the ropes."

"Yeah, of course. Nice to meet you, Madison," she says.

"Nice to meet you, too," I tell her.

We step inside the shop, and I stop for a moment, admiring the whimsical decor and the beautiful, eclectic collection of art and clothing inside.

"Do you like what you see?" my aunt asks, smiling.

"Yeah, I do. This is impressive."

"I'm sure you recognize a lot of my stuff, but the rest of it is all from local artists and designers, too. We've got a good thing going on," she says. I smile and nod in agreement. "I have a couple of things I need to get done in the back, and then I'm going to take off if you guys think you will be okay without me."

"Oh, yeah. We'll be fine," Ava says. "We can handle the summer people—one scowl at a time. Plus, Chloe will be here at noon."

The summer people? One scowl at a time?

"Come on," she adds, turning to me. "I'll show you around and teach you how to work the register and the iPad to take payments before the store opens."

She shows me around like she said she would, telling me the proper way to ring up each item and where to find the prices for art, and how to place print orders with various artists. She shows me a book that contains each artist's various wait times and tells me the ones with red stickers are currently too backlogged to take additional orders.

"And the dates are hard dates, and they know the red stickers mean no—it's stated clearly on the sign—but you can still expect people to come and ask for them and ask for exceptions, thinking the rules don't apply to them for the right price. We don't do that here."

"Okay," I say. I try to make it sound confident, but just the potential for confrontation makes me nervous. "Is it pretty busy, then?"

"It comes and goes with the seasons, but yeah. In the summer, we are slammed."

"By the summer people with their scowls?" I ask. "What did you mean by that?"

"You know...the rich people that come up from wherever, mostly California, to escape the monotony of their boring, privileged lives. Don't get me wrong, it's great for our local economy, and we are all happy to take their money, but we're happy when they go, too. They just...take. And look down their noses at us—treat us like servants—while they do it."

Oh. People like my family. *'People like me,'* I think, remembering my own assumptions about Ava before I met her.

We open the store at 10:00 AM, and when Chloe comes in around noon, we're slammed like Ava said we would be. Though the job isn't necessarily difficult, once the pace picks up, so do my nerves. I fumble too slowly through my orders and get more than my fair share of scowls, heavy sighs, and eye rolls. I begin to wonder if Ava's wardrobe selection is more strategic than fashion. They treat me like I'm less, and I feel like it, too. After a particularly hostile encounter, I can't help but think of my internship at the state rep's office—of how much prestige comes with the position despite how much easier the work would be.

And yet, no college would be impressed by the fact that I spent my summer working retail. Funny how that works.

At 4:00 PM, when we wrap up our shift, my feet ache, and I'm mentally drained. My aunt's assistant manager comes in and introduces herself to me before we leave for the day. I realize how little energy I have left to give when I'm met with her own.

"You must be Maddie!" she says. "I'm Lisa."

I resist the instinct to correct her. *It's Madison.* My mother had been correcting people since I was a little girl, making sure the nickname never stuck, and at some point, it became a reflex for me to do the same. Hearing it now, though, in her soothing tone accompanied by a warm smile, I'm not sure why. I didn't really mind the name. In fact, it sounds...nice.

"That's me," I tell her.

"Wow. Look at you. You look *just* like your mother. How is she doing?" she asks.

"She's fine," I say, not really sure how to answer the question. My mom is the same as she always is, which is fine, I guess.

'*Fake*,' my brain screams again, but I ignore it—put it away somewhere else until I'm ready to deal with it.

"You know, we were good friends in school. Cheerleaders together, if you can believe that. I lived just a couple blocks away from Emma and Amelia. Still do, actually. God, I'd love to see her. Of course, I understand why she doesn't come back to visit. I've seen pictures of your *mansion* in Palo Alto on Facebook; I've read all about her foundation. And I've seen your dad," she says, wagging her eyebrows.

I'm not so sure it's a mansion. Also—my dad? *Ew.* Not sure what to say, I only smile.

"I'm so sorry about your grandmother, by the way," she adds.

"Thank you," I tell her. "We are just glad she isn't suffering anymore."

"Of course," she says. "Well, I won't keep you any longer; you two should get out of here while you still can. It was so, so nice to meet you, Maddie."

"You, too," I say, and head for the door with Ava.

"Hey," she says once we step outside. "I feel like an idiot about some of the stuff I said about the rich summer people from California. I really had no idea—"

"That I was one of those assholes?" I finish. "It's okay. You weren't wrong."

"I hope I didn't offend you. I mean, you don't seem like one of them. You seem cool," she says. "Shit. I don't know if that was a compliment or not."

"I'll take it as one."

"Hey, have you heard about the festival?" she asks.

"No," I tell her.

"There's this huge music festival on the beach this weekend. It's a crazy excuse for us locals to get drunk and act like idiots with the tourists, and we fully take advantage. The rules are lax here in the summer because everyone wants to make sure the tourists have a good time spending their money. You should come with me and my friends."

"Yeah, that sounds great," I reply, surprised. I didn't expect to make friends while I was here, and I definitely didn't expect an invite after I'd been outed like I was, but I am grateful for it.

"Cool. Give me your phone; I should give you my number," she says, holding out her hand.

"Oh, I'm kind of...between phones right now," I say.

"Well, that's okay. I think I'll see you almost every day between then and now. We'll figure it out. Oh—do you need a ride back to Emma's?" she asks.

"No, it's fine. I can walk. Thanks, though."

"I don't blame you. It's a beautiful day for it. We have a lot of those around here."

"Yeah, I bet," I tell her. "I'll see you tomorrow. Thanks for everything, by the way."

"You're welcome. See ya, Maddie," she says. She heads in the other direction, and I start to make my way down the hill toward Emma's neighborhood.

The walk back to the house takes a little less than half an hour. Once inside, I kick off my shoes, throw myself down onto the sofa, and flip on the TV. I'm relieved to see that Emma has a variety of streaming services; I don't have a phone, I don't have plans, and I'm not quite sure what to do with myself. Having reached into my pocket for the phone that didn't exist on several occasions today, I am starting to regret that now.

I settle on a reality show I've heard Harper going on and on about. I keep telling her I'll watch it, but I never have much free time at home between school, music, volunteering with my mom, and getting dragged along to the country club for whatever event or dinner they have going on that week. I'm only a few minutes into it before Emma comes down the stairs, speaking into the phone.

"Well, maybe she's predisposed to it," she says. "I would have thought you'd understand better than anyone what it feels like to want to escape for a while. A long while, in your case."

It must be my mom. I shake my head and move my arms in a distinct 'no' gesture, hoping she won't hand me the phone.

"Actually, you know what? I thought I heard her come in, but you know how this old house is. Looks like she's not here after all." Pause. "Yeah, I'll tell her." Pause. "You know, I think we've talked more in the past two weeks than in the past two decades. We should do this more often, Mel."

Her brow furrows, and she pulls the phone away from her ear and looks at the screen before shrugging. Ah, she hung up on her. She does that.

"Sorry about that," I tell her. "Thanks for covering for me, though."

"No problem," she says. "I'm starting to get the feeling you don't normally have a lot of free reign, do you?"

"No, not really."

I had the illusion of freedom. I could do what I wanted as long as I did what she wanted. As long as I stayed in line, stuck with the plan, and ran with the right crowd.

She let me go spend weekends at Stanford last year because it was Ethan and it was Stanford. I could do whatever I wanted with my weekend nights if she hadn't already committed me to something else. I've only been grounded for partying once, and it was only because it was in the wrong zip code.

"You don't understand! Something real could have happened!" she yelled at me. I didn't get what she meant then, and I still don't get it now.

"She said you could stay, though," she tells me. "Not that you really need permission...you know that, right?"

"Yeah, I do," I tell her. "It'd be nice if she'd catch up."

She laughs. "She did say you had to have a phone, though. And you need to answer her calls and texts. She's having insurance send you a replacement with same-day delivery. Though, up here, same-day does sometimes mean the next day."

"Great. I'm not looking forward to whatever happens when I turn it on."

"You may have to answer your mom, but you don't owe anyone else shit, Madison," she says. "Are things okay with you two? With this and the stuff she was saying about your outfit the day of the funeral, I just don't know what to think. She's different, you know, than the person I knew. I mean, she was always very opinionated and liked to get her way, don't get me wrong."

"It's not bad," I tell her. "We get along, but maybe that's because I always do what I think she would want me to do."

I haven't really pushed back, even about my clothes or food or whatever, because I know she's just looking out for me and wants what's best for me. Now, I don't know. It feels different.

"I think I may have...fucked up somewhere. Bad. And I don't know what to do about it."

"Well, you're still just getting started. There's plenty of time to fix it," she says. "Scoot over. What do you say we order Chinese food? Overdose on MSG and reality TV together?"

"Sounds good to me."

FOUR

MADISON

O ver the week, working at the store became easier. I was
comfortable enough now that I told Emma I felt like I'd
be okay working on my own during the slower, morning week-
day hours. Ava and the other girls seemed to like me enough
and appreciated my help—I wasn't slowing them down or just
making things harder for them like I worried I would in the beginning. But I've always been smart, a fast learner. I've always
taken pride in my work, and this was no different.

Dressing in my nicer, designer clothes and taking more time
with my hair and makeup did seem to have a direct effect on
how I was treated by the clientele. Still beneath them, but not
quite worthless. It made me want to scream that my family had
money, too—that we had two vacation homes and that I went
to one of the best prep schools in the Bay Area, and then I'd
realize that was, and maybe I was, part of the problem.

None of that should have mattered. But it did.

My phone, with its same-day shipping, arrived the next day like Emma said it would. It was late only by a couple of hours, but next-day nonetheless. When I turned it on, my texts were filled with messages from my mom and Ethan, who, at first, had simply been asking where I was and then later, once he figured out that I'd been there on Saturday, flooded me with excuses.

It was only the one time.

Don't give up on us. I love you.

Are you really going to throw away three years over one stupid, drunk mistake?

Please don't tell your dad.

I must have read them all a million times, thought about replying a million different ways, but in the end, said nothing.

Now, it's Friday—the day of the festival. I head down the hill toward Emma's after closing the shop at 8:00 PM, exhausted from the long day but grateful to be walking back at a time when the sun hung lower on the horizon. It had been hovering around 90 degrees this week, and I was thankful for the reprieve. Once inside, I head upstairs and change into short jean shorts and a cropped black tank that my mom would have said showed far too much cleavage. I tie a flannel around my waist, then finish it off with a small woven satchel and a pair of yellow-tinted shades. My hair hangs stick straight down my back like it always does as it is almost impossible to get it to do anything else.

While I sit and wait at the shuttle stop, I pull out my phone and start scrolling Instagram. I've gone four days without it and thought maybe I'd just be done with it all, but it's easy to fall back into those old habits. It's hard for me to be quiet and still.

I look through pictures of my friends back home partying together and camping on the beach, lying in the sun by their pools, and I miss them. And that makes me angry, too. Aside from a message I received from Harper while I was between phones about how she heard about Ethan and how crazy it was, I haven't heard from any of them. It doesn't feel good. It's not like I expected the world to stop turning without me in it, but I did expect someone to notice—at least save a space for me for when I returned. Maybe even worry about me a little.

What if they all knew? Would I still want that space? And if they didn't, did I not want it anymore anyway?

The shuttle pulls up, packed to the max, and I find a place to stand near the middle and hold on. It's even hotter, the air even thicker, inside this tin can. There are two more stops before we get to the beach area, and even more people pile in.

When I get there, I text Ava, who tells me to come to the main stage to meet her and her friends. It takes a while; I maneuver through the masses of people, one of the most eclectic crowds I've ever seen, before spotting Ava and Chloe down toward the front-left of the stage. They're standing with another girl and a group of guys, all of them bare arms, tattoos, and muscles.

I wasn't expecting them. She didn't mention guys. I've never been with a guy with a tattoo. I mean, fuck. I've only been with one guy *ever*.

And it has been so long. I'm staring long before I reach the group.

"Hey," I say once I do manage to get to them.

"Hey, girl!" Ava says. I freeze when she brings me in for a hug, a beer in each hand. She must be drunk—we're friendly, but we aren't that friendly. And I've never been much of a hugger, anyway. "You found us! I got you a beer. Elijah won't serve you, but he'll serve people he knows."

"Thanks," I say, draining half of the cup in one go. It is hot, and I needed it. I've needed this for a while.

"Hey, everyone—this is Maddie. She's Emma's niece," she says.

"Wow," one of the guys says. "You are not what I expected."

"What are you talking about?" Chloe asks. "You asked me what she looked like. I told you—hot blonde with huge tits. She's exactly what you expected."

"Okay, you got me," he says. "I'm Ben."

"Nice to meet you," I say.

"This is my older sister, Ariana," Ava says, putting her arms around the shoulders of the girl next to her. "And that's Ryan, Liam, and Ezra. Liam and Ezra are brothers, too."

I say hi to them, too, but only Ariana and Ryan say hello back. Liam and Ezra stare through me with eyes almost the same blue-green hue as the lake to my left and likely just as cold. One—Liam I think—has sandy brown hair, and the other's hair is much darker with dark eyebrows to match, making his light eyes pop even more.

I wasn't used to this kind of reception, especially from men. I wonder what I've done to piss these guys off. My instinct is to smile anyway, say something nice, and try to earn their approval. I question where it comes from and just barely stop myself before I do. I glance back and forth between the two of them for a minute, and when neither breaks away, I turn back to Ava, downing the rest of my beer.

"Looks like you need a refill," Ben says. "Let me grab that for you, Maddie."

"That'd be great," I tell him, and this time, I do smile. "Thanks."

Over the next couple of hours, I sing and dance with the girls and finish off my third beer. The band finishes their set, and I'm getting ready to head back to the shuttle and to Emma's, but Ben and Ava insist I join them for a bonfire on the beach. We walk about a mile or so along the east side of the lake, past the vendors to an area that isn't part of the festival, and sit around a firepit. A couple of the guys open the trunk of a nearby car and pull out a cooler filled with alcohol. Ben comes back with a container of lighter fluid and empties what seems to be the entire contents onto the logs.

"Oh my god, Ben!" Ariana shrieks. "Are you insane? You're going to burn the whole town to the ground!"

He lights the match and shoots her a shit-eating grin.

"GET THE FUCK BACK!" Ava yells.

The four of us seated around the fire pit backpedal toward the vehicles, then Ben throws the match and does the same. With a loud whoosh, the flames jump at least ten feet into the air before settling at a more reasonable height.

"You fucking idiot," Liam says, shaking his head. "Fucking pyro with a death wish."

"I'm a fucking pyro living his best damn life," he shoots back. "If I die, I die."

Only a couple of them laugh, the rest just shaking their heads as they walk back over to the fire pit. Ben sits down next to me and throws his arm around my shoulders. Liam sits down next to Ryan and does the same, planting a kiss on his lips. *Oh.* They're a couple. I don't know how I didn't notice that earlier. I thought I noticed just about everything about all of these guys, especially the two brothers. Their immediate, unwarranted dislike for me hasn't stopped eating at me, and I couldn't stop myself from glancing at them the entire time we were talking and dancing.

Especially the one passing out beer, whose eyes I refuse to meet again.

"Hey, you skipped Maddie," Ben says.

Ariana shoots Ezra a look similar to one I've gotten from my mother when she's cautioning me to behave. He doesn't react and sits down on the log next to her. Ryan reaches down into the cooler and pulls out a can.

"Heads up," he says to Ben, tossing the can to him from across the fire. He catches it and opens it before handing it to me.

"So, Maddie," he says. "What's your story?"

"I don't know," I say. "I don't really have a story."

"She's a trust fund kid from Silicon Valley," Ezra says. "And that's what she's doing here—looking for a story. Just like the rest of them."

"Ezra, shut the fuck up," Ava says. "Maddie is cool. She's not like them."

"Then, what are you doing here, Maddie?" Liam counters.

I don't really know. I don't have a good answer for that. I'm not looking for a story...or am I? I wasn't lying when I said I didn't have one—not a good one, anyway. I *am* a trust fund kid from Silicon Valley, and my life has been overscheduled and micromanaged for as long as I can remember, and for whatever reason, I never thought to question it until I walked in on my boyfriend with his dick in some other girl's mouth.

I couldn't exactly say that.

"My grandma passed away recently, and I came up here to keep Emma company and help her out at the store," I say instead.

"I'm so sorry about your grandma," Ariana says.

"Thank you," I tell her.

I'm grateful when Chloe changes the subject, mentioning that a guy they all know texted and asked where they were hanging out; she asks the group if she should tell him or not. They all answer with a resounding 'no' and start picking him apart. I pull my phone out of my pocket and am met with an onslaught of messages from my mom. Feeling uncomfortable as it is and not wanting to read them in front of Ben, I excuse myself and head back toward the treeline.

Mom: Where are you?

Mom: Where is Emma?

Mom: Why aren't either of you answering your phones?

Mom: If you can't be mature about this, maybe it's time for you to come home, Madison.

Maybe she should leave me alone for more than 24 hours. Now is as good of a time as any to get used to giving up control over my life, Mom. I'm starting college in two months, and you won't be able to control me there, either.

In my current inebriated state, I close one eye and actually start to type out something to that extent instead of giving her what she wants, but my gaze shifts to a woman about 30 feet into the woods lying across a picnic table with her skirt hitched up around her waist while a man thrusts into her. I'm frozen there for a moment, unable to tear my eyes away until I realize I recognize that skirt. I recognize the head of wavy, blonde hair and even the turquoise rings on her fingers. The woman is Emma.

Holy shit. I immediately avert my gaze.

"Oh, fuck. Enjoying the show?" Ava says from behind me.

"Um, no," I reply quickly. "Should we...do something?"

"Like what? Join? I didn't realize you all were that kind of family, but...I'll try anything once."

"No, I don't mean *join*," I say.

"Oh, you're *worried* about her," she says. And yeah, I guess that's what I was thinking. I guess when I saw what I saw and realized it was Emma, my instinct was that something was wrong and that he must be taking advantage of her. "Um, I don't think she needs help, Maddie. She looks like she's having a great fucking time. I'm a little jealous."

"Um, yeah. I guess you're right. We should...leave her to it."

I don't like it. It upsets me, even. But I start to think I may be a little jealous, too. That was something I'd never say out loud. She was right, though. Emma was a very enthusiastic participant. My cheeks burn, and I'm grateful for the cover of darkness, hoping it isn't too obvious.

Once again, my reality surprises me. Among these people who I would have thought to have been sheltered by their small town, I was the one who was apparently rigid in mindset when it came to sex.

It's not like I'm entirely inexperienced. Ethan and I probably had sex hundreds of times. I thought it was good. I usually came...at least half of the time.

But my experience *was* limited. And it didn't look like that.

"I just wanted to check and see if you were okay," she says on the way back to the beach. "Ezra and Liam can be a little rough around the edges, but they're good people. Just kind of...hard to get to know. It's not personal, Maddie."

It feels personal. I don't say that.

"It's fine if they don't like me," I tell her. Even though it does bother me, I'm not going to let them ruin this for me. "I'm still having fun."

"Okay, god...I was so worried you were pissed. I'm so glad. Ben and the girls all seem to like you, though."

"Yeah, I like them too."

"Come on, let's go back. Unless you want to see how it ends," she says, gesturing toward the woods.

I don't look over.

"I really don't," I tell her, and we make our way back to the fire.

"No, I'm 100% sure they're leaving tomorrow morning," Chloe says. "My mom has the address on the calendar for a deep clean later that day."

"Well, good. I'm glad they're leaving. I hope they drive off a goddamn cliff on the way home," Ariana says.

"How can you be glad they're leaving? How can you be glad that the fucking piece of shit gets to just go home and keep being the same frat boy bitch he always was like nothing fucking happened?" Liam says.

"You know it's not the first time he's done something like this," Ben adds.

"Are you talking about—" Ava starts.

"*Don't* say his fucking name," Ryan cautions. "Don't."

"The Warrens?" she asks instead.

"It won't be the last either," Liam continues. "And he'll keep getting away with it—hiding behind his family's fucking money for the rest of his goddamn life. We should do something."

"Yeah, like what? Rack up assault charges for the four of us? Give him something else to laugh about?" Ryan asks.

"He should be in jail. The cops should do something," Chloe says.

"Wake the fuck up, Chloe. Were you born fucking yesterday? They aren't going to do shit," Ezra says.

"They might. If we give them time," she says.

"No," Ryan says. "They won't. They came to my house. Told my parents themselves that they were sorry, but their hands were tied."

"How is she, Ryan?" Ava asks.

He shakes his head. "She's...messed up. Still doesn't want to leave her room. Won't talk, won't eat."

"We *could* do something," Ben says. "Chloe said they're leaving tomorrow, right? The house will be empty."

"Yeah, but not for long," Ariana says. "You know renters will be there the rest of the summer. *They* didn't do anything...yet."

"Not tomorrow, though," Chloe replies. "My mom's schedule said 6:00 PM. If she's starting at 6:00 PM, no one will be checking in until at least the next day."

"So it isn't long, but there's our window," Ben says. "We could—"

"Not in front of her," Ezra cuts him off. "We shouldn't be talking about this in front of her. She's not one of us; she's one of them. One of those fucking privileged assholes that have never had to face consequences for anything in their lives. We can't trust her."

Something real could have happened!

"Fuck you," I spit out, only because I'm drunk. "I don't know what your fucking problem is with me—"

"Really? Because I think I was just pretty fucking clear about what my problem is with you."

"We could light it up," Ben says. "Burn it to the fucking ground."

"No," Ryan says. "It's too...obvious. Someone else could get hurt but...I think we should go over there. Fuck the place up. I'll bring my golf clubs. It'll make me feel better."

"It sounds like my kind of good time, babe," Liam says. "But no. Not after we said it in front of her. Ezra is right. We can't trust her. She's not one of us."

"I'm not going to tell anyone shit! I don't even know who or what you're talking about. You know what? I'm sorry Ava, but I'm done. I'm out of here. I'll catch the shuttle back, and I'll see you at work."

I throw my bag over my shoulder and push up off the log.

"No, we're doing it," Ezra says. "We bring her. Force her to participate. Then she can't say shit."

"I'm not doing that. I'm not going anywhere with you."

"I think he's right, Maddie," Ava says. "I think you have to go with us."

"What? You're doing this, too?"

"We're all doing it," Ariana says. "You, too."

"I...don't even know what you guys are talking about. I really didn't hear anything. I won't say anything. I don't even know who I'd tell."

"Oh, I'm sorry—did you think you heard a question in there?" Ezra asks. "I wasn't offering you a fucking choice."

I look around the fire at Ava and her friends, waiting for someone to be reasonable and give me an out or—at the very least—an explanation. I don't get either one.

I guess this is it. I'm still learning the dynamic here. I don't quite understand the teams, where I fit, or if I even fit at all. But I do understand that this is my chance to prove that they can trust me and that I'm not *one of them*, whatever that means.

"Okay," I tell them.

"You sure? You're not going to shit the bed? You won't feel bad for the fucking sociopaths?" Liam asks.

"I'm going to feel bad for Chloe's mom," I say, earning puzzled looks from them all. "She's going to waste her whole evening cleaning that house for no fucking reason."

"To Chloe's mom and her sacrifice," Ben says, raising his beer.

"YES! TO CHLOE'S FUCKING MOM!" Ariana yells.

The rest of them shout, and I join them, laughing while we drink to Chloe's fucking mom. I mostly stay quiet for the remainder of the night, sitting between Ava and Ben, watching them all and observing their mannerisms. In some ways, they seem a lot like my own group of friends back home, but in some ways—important ones, I think—they don't. I can't quite put my finger on it.

I think, maybe, it just feels real. Everyone is easy, too, now that no one is paying any attention to me. It's kind of like I'm not there. Maybe that's why I drink too much.

By the time we leave, it's late, and the shuttle had stopped running a while ago. I get into the backseat of Ariana's car, drunk enough that I'm not sure I'll remember any of this. Wondering how much of it was real, and what would really happen tomorrow night.

"See you tomorrow, Maddie," Ava says when I get out of the car.

Wondering who the hell I think I am. And eager to find the answer.

FIVE

MADISON

"Hi, Emma. I'm here to pick up Madison," a deep voice bellows through the open front door.

My heart drops into my stomach. I didn't hear from any of them, so I assumed maybe they'd forgotten about it all or changed their minds. Or they'd only been joking about forcing me to come along as collateral. I certainly wasn't going to reach out and ask.

In fact, I was so convinced they weren't going to go through with it—that they maybe even made it all up just to scare me—that I was sitting on the sofa in my pajamas now, an open bag of pretzels in my lap and my jaw probably on the floor.

I was just about to go to bed. I don't have to work tomorrow and planned a morning hike to a nearby waterfall. I even packed a bag. And now, this.

"Madison," Aunt Emma says, looking me up and down, "I didn't realize you were going out tonight."

"Umm...."

"Did you forget we all made plans to go to the movies?" he asks. "Are you that much of a lightweight that you don't remember?"

He leans against the doorframe and smiles kindly at Emma, an entirely different face and tone than the one I knew from last night. His eyes, though, aren't any different. They challenge me. I return what I hope is a similar icy glare.

I'm new at this.

I have no doubt he and his friends will make me regret it if I don't go with them. I have no doubt I'll regret it if I do.

"Let me go change," I say, rising from the couch on unsteady legs and heading toward the staircase. Where was the girl from last night who stood up for herself and agreed to this shit?

Probably at the bottom of a bottle, if I'm being honest.

Shit.

Is there any chance this is *still* just a prank?

"Make it quick," Ezra says to my back. "I like the previews."

I grit my teeth as I walk up the stairs to my room. It takes a lot of control not to slam the door behind me when I get there.

He likes the fucking previews.

I flip through my wardrobe, trying to find the appropriate outfit to wear to commit a crime. Nothing really jumps out as fit for the occasion, but why would it? I'm a first-time criminal.

I come across Ethan's black Stanford hoodie; I must have packed it on accident when I was haphazardly tossing whatever I could fit into my bag. I pull it over my head now, then pair it with some black yoga pants, pile my hair into a messy bun, and look in the mirror.

I look like a cat burglar. Damn it.

I strip off the yoga pants and pull on a pair of shorts and my hiking boots instead. Once back downstairs, I find Ezra and Emma laughing in the kitchen. It makes me angry—jealous, maybe even. Not in the typical, possessive type of way; I'm not interested in him like that. I'm angry to see him so...easy. So different than he was with me last night with Emma now. Ava told me that it wasn't personal—that he and his brother were good people, just a little rough around the edges.

He doesn't look so rough around the edges now. And I know it's personal.

"Are we going or what? I like the previews, too," I sneer.

"After you," he says, opening the front door for me.

"Nice to see you, Sweetheart," Emma calls after him. Sweetheart? *Him*? "Tell your dad I said hi."

"Will do," he says, ushering me out with a hand on my lower back. For a moment, I don't breathe.

"Turn off your phone," he says, his tone changing the moment the door closes behind me. "And get in the truck."

Liam and Ryan are seated in the front, Ben in the back. I climb into the back seat next to him and move over to make room for Ezra.

Where are the girls?

I swallow hard.

They turn down a dirt road, heading in the opposite direction of town. My pulse picks up. I shouldn't have gotten in a truck with these four men, two of whom were overtly hostile and one of whom was neutral at best.

"You need to calm down," Ben says into my ear, quiet enough that the others shouldn't have been able to hear it over the music. "They can smell fear."

They can *what*? That was a joke, right?

But he's not laughing, and neither do I.

"Where are we going?" I ask him.

"Picking up Ava and Ariana. Then, it's a long, winding drive up to Veil Falls where all the rich people live. If you're going to puke, let me know."

I exhale a small amount of relief. At least I wouldn't be alone with them.

I think I might actually puke, though.

"And Chloe?"

"No. With her mom, we thought it was better if she didn't."

So, we're really doing this then.

We pull into a gravel driveway in front of a cabin where the sisters are waiting on the front porch swing. The two of them walk around to the tailgate and hop in without saying a word. I glance back and see a set of golf clubs and a couple of baseball bats, too, and my palms start to sweat.

Ezra turns around, reaching past me to open the back window. "Hey! Turn off your phones."

"We're not fucking stupid," Ariana says back, rolling her eyes at him.

Ben wasn't kidding about the road. It is a long, painstakingly winding drive up to the falls area. I expect that when we get there, we'll pull into a neighborhood or a driveway, but we don't. Liam turns off the headlights, pulls the truck off into the woods, and drives about fifty feet back before parking.

No one says a word, and Ryan hops out of the truck, lugging a pair of bolt cutters with him. The rest of them stay put.

Sensing my confusion and perhaps my fear, Ben leans into me. "They'll have an alarm. He's going to get into the breaker and turn the power off."

I nod, silently.

"Stanford, huh?" he says. "You are fancy."

"Uh, no. Not really. It isn't mine, I mean. I actually...didn't get in. It's my boyfriend's."

"Oh, you have a boyfriend?"

"Um, no. I mean...it's complicated."

"Will you two shut the fuck up?" Ezra growls. "I need to focus. You can flirt with her later."

"Jesus," Ben replies. "Sorry, man."

"*Shut the fuck up, Ben!*" Liam says from the front seat.

Ben shakes his head and leans back against the bench seat. We sit in silence for a few minutes before Ryan reappears and gives Liam a nod.

"Let's go," he says, and we all pile out of the truck. Liam throws the golf clubs over his shoulder, and the other two guys grab the bats and follow Ryan. I fall behind, walking with Ava and Ariana, my legs like jello.

"Fuck," Ava says, shaking out her hands and audibly exhaling. I'm glad I'm not the one who is a nervous wreck. "I'm kind of freaking out right now."

I open my mouth to express a similar sentiment, but nothing comes out.

"I'm not. I'm not scared," Ariana says. "I'm too angry to be scared."

We walk up behind a large, modern home, and hop the gate. The backyard has a pool with both a slide and waterfall, and a complete outdoor kitchen. Even I find it a little excessive, given how rarely the weather would permit its use during the year here. Liam pulls out a club, then heads to one of the sunroom windows and swings, breaking it easily. Everyone freezes for a minute—I assume waiting for an alarm—and when it doesn't come, he clears away as much glass as he can, climbs in, and moves through the house, letting us inside through the back sliding door.

"Grab a club," he says, extending the golf bag to us as we step inside. Reluctantly, I follow Ava and Ariana's lead, indiscriminately selecting a club from the bag and taking in my surroundings. This could just as easily be my family's vacation home, and we were doing this for what? I don't even know, but here I am, unsure of how I even got here or what the hell I am doing with any of them. These aren't my friends; they're practically strangers. I shouldn't have gotten into the truck. Hell, I probably shouldn't have gotten into Emma's car.

For the first time since I got here, I want to go home, but it's too late for all of that now. I'm already culpable, aren't I? Just like they wanted.

"You first, Princess," Ezra sneers. "Take a swing."

And if I'm not culpable already, I'm about to be.

"I'm not a fucking princess," I tell him through clenched teeth.

I steady the club in my hands and approach a mantle lined with crystal and glass sculptures that probably cost a small fortune and take a swing, sending the works of art flying and shattering against the pristine marble floors.

It's...satisfying.

"Not bad, not-a-fucking-princess," Ben says. "Let's break some shit."

The other girls grab a club, too, and the space fills with the sounds of cabinets cracking, glass shattering, and the thud of golf clubs against drywall.

I swing again, taking out a lamp and a framed wedding picture sitting next to it in the process. I expect to feel bad when I watch it shatter but, although I still think I might later, I don't right now. Instead, I feel a rush; the unmistakable frenzy of adrenaline hits and it feels so fucking good. It feels good to feel something.

My lips turn up into an involuntary smile. Ava looks over at me from the wall she's swinging at and laughs.

I make my way around the room, destroying anything that looks breakable just like everyone else, chasing the high I wasn't anticipating. Again, this could just as easily be my family's vacation home, and instead of deterring me, I use it as fuel. I forget that I don't know these people or what they've done to offend my accomplices and swing, lashing out at my own mother, at Ethan, at my friends. I destroy and destroy and imagine that, in doing so, I'm breaking out of my own cage—my over-scheduled and micromanaged existence, my lack of freedom.

The plan.

I bury the club into the wall and picture the figurative wall that came down when I started to see things for what they really were.

Fucking fake.

I think about the fact that I haven't cried, that I haven't wanted to talk to Ethan at all—not to make up and not even to bother breaking up. I don't even want closure. I think about the friends I haven't missed and who haven't missed me either. And I don't fucking care about any of it.

I haven't cried because he didn't hurt me that day.

He woke me up.

I laugh and make my way up the staircase, turning into the first bedroom I come across. And I wake up again.

Two beds with pink comforters sit on either side of the room, the names Winslow and Harlow above the respective beds. They're covered in baby dolls and stuffed animals.

They were just kids—young kids. They didn't do anything. And they didn't deserve this. They didn't deserve to be afraid in their own home, no matter what their brother had done.

Shit.

I backtrack out of the room and down the staircase, stuff the golf club back in the bag, and storm out the back door. I don't know how I am going to get back, but it doesn't really matter.

"Hey! Where the fuck do you think you're going?!" Ezra calls out, following me past the pool and into the woods.

"I did what you wanted. Now, I'm getting the fuck away from you guys...like you wanted," I say, moving deeper into the woods.

"You're going the wrong way, dumbass! That's not even the way back to the truck."

"Little kids live there, you know that? They don't deserve this, no matter what their brother said or did to any of you, which I should have questioned from the beginning. Did he offend you by existing like I did? I bet you guys started whatever this was, didn't you?"

"He raped Ryan's little sister," he says.

I stop in my tracks. "What?"

"You fucking heard me. He raped Ryan's sister, and then, when he knew he was going to get away with it, even went around town bragging about it—making fun of her. His family slandered Ryan's family. She went to the hospital; went to the police. They said there wasn't enough evidence to do anything about it. But...you know that's not true, don't you?"

I know well enough that women are often dismissed in these situations—that these cases were too often not brought to trial. But I only knew in the abstract. I've never been close to it.

"You know what happens when one of them is a rich white guy, and the girl's family is fucking destitute, right? Surely, you aren't that sheltered by your parents' income bracket."

I swallow hard and nod, feeling small and stupid before the quiet is broken by the sound of sirens in the distance.

"Fuck!" Ezra yells, turning back toward the house and breaking into a run. I run after him and find the lower level of the house engulfed in flames.

"FUCKING BEN. FUCKING PYRO IDIOT!" he yells. He turns toward what must actually be the direction of the truck and breaks into a run again, bat in hand, I suppose assuming the others had gotten a head start when the fire started. I follow behind as closely as I can, but lose my footing and fall hard on the ground, twisting my ankle in the process.

"What are you doing? Get up!" Ezra says, panic in his voice. I do, and the minute my weight hits my left ankle, I scream in pain, and it gives out.

There's no way I am going to be able to run anymore. I'm fucked.

"Let's fucking go!"

"I can't. I can't walk."

"Fuck!" he yells again. "Okay, come on."

I climb onto his back, and he starts to run again, stopping when we get to a clearing. He sets me down and runs his hands through his hair, frustration dripping off of him, anger in his eyes when he turns back to me.

"God damn it!"

"What's wrong?" I ask. "Are we lost!?"

"No, we're not fucking lost. They left us."

"What? Why? Why would they do that? Why would your friends...your brother—"

"Because they had to! It's what I would have done, too. And it's *your* fucking fault!"

"My fault? I—"

"Shut up!" he hisses. He brings his hand down over my mouth and slams my body up against the tree behind me, pressing up against me. "Shut...the fuck...up."

I panic, thinking he's about to hurt me, and struggle futilely against his imposing 6'2" frame. Then, I hear radio static followed by a voice in the distance saying something about checking the parameter.

"I hope you're happy," he whispers, his mouth impossibly close to my ear, warm breath causing me to shudder. "We're going to get caught. And you're going to get to go home just like Jonathan and laugh about it while I face real consequences and rot in jail."

Even in a whisper, his tone is dripping in rage. He looks at me like he wants to rip me apart with his teeth.

"Don't...move," he says, and this time, his lips brush up against my ear. "Don't even fucking breathe."

And, not for the first time today, my body reacts in a way I don't expect. Maybe it's the rush of it all—what we'd done to the house and knowing we're about to be caught now; I'm not really sure. Maybe it's just that it's been so long. But a tingling sensation builds in my lower body, and heat floods my core. I feel desperate to rub up against him, and if he wasn't so effectively pinning me against the tree, I don't think I'd be able to resist.

What the fuck is wrong with me?

I think maybe he notices—sees it in my eyes or senses it in my body language, because something flashes in his own eyes, and he backs off a bit. Suddenly embarrassed and uncomfortable under his gaze, I look away, hearing the footsteps closing in on us now. Even Ezra looks panicked, and I can see the wheels turning in his head, likely trying to decide if he should make a run for it without me and risk being chased down or stay put and risk being found.

He was right. This is it.

Something real could have happened.

I think I understand what my mother meant now.

My eyes zero in on a trail sign not far to my right: Veil Falls, 2.5 miles.

I push Ezra back with enough force that, having been caught off guard, he stumbles away from me.

"Stay down," I hiss and limp onto the trail.

"HELP!" I start to yell. "HELP! Is anyone there? Help me!"

SIX

MADISON

"Ma'am?" A police officer says, his hand on his holster. "Ma'am, I need you to calm down. Put your hands on your head."

"What?" I say, doing as he asks. "Aren't you...aren't you looking for me? Aren't you here to help me?"

"Just put your hands on your head, don't come any closer."

I do as he says.

"My ankle," I say. "I got hurt on the trail. It took me all day to get back down here. I'm pretty sure I missed the last shuttle. My phone is dead. I can barely walk. Please, help me."

"That's what you're doing out here? You...got hurt hiking? Why didn't you ask someone else to help you on the trail?"

"It was empty. It rained all day. And after I got hurt, I tried to cut through the woods to get back down faster. Why are you questioning me? What's going on?"

"Where's your bag?"

"It got to be too much—I had to ditch it."

"You see anyone else out here?" he asks.

"No," I say. "Not at all. Why? What's happening?"

"Nothing you need to worry about," he says, an obvious change in his demeanor. *He believes me.* "What's your name?"

"Madison," I reply. "Walker-Ridgeway."

"Walker, huh? No shit?" He flips on his flashlight and aims it directly at my face. "You Mel's daughter, then?"

I squint and shield my eyes with my hand. "That's me."

"Oh...sorry," the officer says, lowering the light and approaching me. "Go ahead and lean on me; I'll get you home. You staying with Emma?"

"Yes," I say. I don't want to touch him, but I really have no choice at this point if I want to get out of this. I did need the crutch.

I hobble back to the house with the officer at my side, relieved when we finally get there and I can release him. I lean against the cop car, surveilling the scene. There's a fire truck, an additional police car, and an ambulance.

"Oh my god!" I say, feigning shock. "There was a fire!? Is everyone okay?"

"Luckily, no one was home," he says, then eyes me with suspicion. Did I not sell it? I know I'm not a good liar. It was easier out there in the dark. His eyes drop to my shoes, and I'm suddenly grateful I'd chosen them.

"Hey, Brenda!" he shouts. "Need you over here for a second."

"Yeah?" she asks as she approaches.

"Let's see that ankle," he challenges.

But the injury is completely real. Not worried, I remove my left boot and pull down my sock, revealing a swollen ankle that's already started to turn purple.

"Ouch," the woman says. "Looks like a sprain—a bad one. I don't think you need X-rays or anything, probably just RICE it. I can bring you in if you want, though."

"No," I tell her. "I'm sure you're right."

"The swelling should start to go down in a couple of days. You're young and healthy; you'll just need to go easy on it for a couple of weeks."

"Thanks for taking a look at it," I say.

"You find anyone?" she asks the officer.

"Just her—she got hurt on the trail. Nobody's out there, at least as far as I can tell. Morales is heading in the other direction. I don't expect him to find anyone, either. Not unless whoever did this is stupid."

Morales—wasn't that Ava's last name?

"Well, they were definitely stupid," Brenda says. "You think this has anything to do with the son and....that business last month?"

"Might," he says. "I'll look into it. Haven't ruled out that it was just an accident quite yet. We don't know that it was our boys, either. It could have easily been one of theirs that he pissed off, too. Or maybe even just looking for a rush. You know how they get bored."

Ours...theirs...

"Yeah," she says. "I bet you're right."

But neither of the two seems convinced. I get the feeling they know exactly who did it and why, and that they just don't care to do anything about it unless they absolutely have to.

"Bates!" the officer calls out. "I'm going to take this one home. Found her on the trail. This is Amelia Walker's kid."

"Amelia Walker? No shit," he says, then looks me up and down. "Huh. Spitting image of her."

So I've been told. Small towns are weird. I just smile.

"Almost eerie, isn't it? I'll head right back up here when I'm done."

He opens the back of the police car, I climb in, and he closes the door behind me. We make our way down the mountain with the lights on, but silent, without speaking.

Likely seeing the sirens from inside the house, Emma runs outside just as the officer opens the door to let me out.

"Gene?" she says to him. "What's going on?"

"I'm so sorry, Aunt Emma," I cut him off. "I went up to the falls by myself and rolled my ankle on my way back. I would have called, but my phone was dead."

Come on, Emma. Go along with it.

"Jesus Christ, girl," she says, making her way over to me and throwing her arms around me. "You had me worried sick. I was just about to start calling hospitals."

I feel like I can breathe again when Emma flawlessly leans into the lie and builds on my story.

"I know. I'm sorry. I was getting nervous, too. It got dark so fast," I tell her. I lean onto my injured ankle and even manage some tears. "I was so scared."

That part was true. Scared and...something else, too.

"Let's get you inside. Your mom is going to kill me," she says. "You know, there are so many things that could have happened to you out there alone that are far worse than a sprained ankle."

Sell it.

"I know. I'm so sorry."

"Thanks again, Gene."

"Of course," he says. "You look good, Emma. How have you been doing? Feeling good?"

"I'm fine, Gene. I just want to get her inside. Goodnight."

I throw my arm around her shoulder and limp toward the front door.

"Let me get that for you," he says, rushing ahead of us to open it.

"Thanks," I tell him.

"Take care now," he says before shutting the door behind us.

"Do you want to tell me what that was all about?" she asks.

"Not really. Not right now anyway," I reply.

"You know, I get that answer a lot from you," she says. "I just hope he doesn't come back here."

"Me too," I say, limping over to the couch and removing my boots.

"So the ankle is real, then?"

"The ankle is real," I tell her, propping it up on the coffee table.

"Let me get you some ice," she says. "I take it you didn't go to the movies?"

"No," I tell her. "I didn't go to the movies."

"Ezra?" she asks, sliding a pillow under my foot and setting an ice pack on top.

"He's fine," I tell her. "I think."

She frowns.

But he knows his way around, right? He knows how to get back to the road for sure and could turn his phone on when he got further away from the house and call for help. I power on my own phone. No new messages. I think about texting Ava and asking, but that doesn't seem smart.

He *would* be fine. Right?

"Looks like you're going to have to take a few days off work," she says, walking back toward the kitchen.

Shit.

"Yeah. Hopefully just a couple, but I can't stand on it at all. I'm sorry, Emma."

"Shit happens."

I hear the kitchen cabinet creek open behind me and think of the sound of the cabinets being beaten in at the house earlier, the sound of broken glass crunching beneath my boots. There was no way they'd get inside and rule what happened to be an accident.

"Here," Emma says, extending her hand and offering me a small, white pill. "For the pain."

"Thank you."

"Also for the pain," she says, handing me a glass. I sip the brown liquid, and the distinct taste of whiskey mixed with soda hits my tongue. It's strong, and I wince a little but it becomes soothing after a couple of gulps.

I check my phone again. Still, no new messages. It's after 1:00 AM. How is it possible that three hours have passed?

"I'm going to go to bed, Madison. Do you need help getting upstairs or are you okay sleeping down here?"

"Oh, I have no intention of attempting the staircase," I tell her.

She heads upstairs and comes back with a pillow and blanket as well as a pair of sweats and a tank top. I thank her as she leaves the room, then I change my clothes and lie down on the couch, but even with the pain in my ankle mostly subdued and as exhausted as I am, sleep doesn't come. I stay there in the dark, staring up at the ceiling and ruminating over the past few hours.

I remember how I felt when I swung that club. I remember how I felt when Ezra held me against that tree, his mouth just barely grazing my ear. I wonder if it had made him hard, too—holding me like that—and the same arousal I'd felt then returns.

Wetness pools between my legs and I try to ignore it, tossing and turning, trying and failing to put it out of my head. I squeeze my legs together, hoping it will take the edge off but even just that feels so good. I try to think of anything other than him when I slide my hand inside my underwear and run my fingers over my clit, but it only works for a second. As soon as the pressure builds, it's Ezra again, holding my thigh out to the side and fucking into me against that tree. I finger myself hard and fast, picturing each deep, frantic thrust.

My back arches off the couch and I hold in a moan as best I can, coming hard and surprised by the intensity as it rolls and rolls through me.

Shit. This isn't good.

What does this mean about me?

Nothing, I assure myself. Who hasn't fantasized about a hate fuck, right?

Well, me. I haven't. Not until now, anyway.

And it didn't matter. I could have my fantasy. I was never, ever going to see any of them again—both because I'm sure they were all pissed at me, and because I shouldn't. They almost got me into a shit ton of trouble. *Real* problems. I became a criminal tonight. I lied to the police tonight. I could have died tonight.

I had fun tonight.

Shit. No, I didn't.

My phone buzzes, and I pick it up, finding a text message from an unknown 541 number: You good?

I don't know why I get the distinct feeling that it's Ezra. He didn't have my phone number and wouldn't care what happened to me. I don't ask who it's from. I stare at the message for a couple of minutes before simply replying: Yep.

I watch the text bubble come and go for about a minute, waiting for a reply before it disappears completely, feeling my stomach drop when it does.

I almost convince myself to say something else, to ask if he (or whoever it is) is okay, too. Resisting the urge, I swipe left, delete the message, and let the whiskey, the white pill, and the after-effects of the orgasm lull me to sleep.

SEVEN

EZRA

I can't believe she did that. I can't believe that shit actually fucking worked.

If I wasn't directly benefiting from that ridiculous damsel-in-distress ploy, I'd be pissed off that it did. I still kind of am, to be honest. I watch Madison hobble down the trail leaning on Gene Brady's nasty fucking arm, and shake my head. I bet it's the highlight of that mother fucker's entire week.

Once I can no longer see them and I'm sure I'm alone in the woods, I stick to the treeline and cut through neighborhoods, making my way down to the village. I don't dare turn on my phone or ask Liam to come back and get me because I know where to find him. We had a plan to establish an alibi.

It takes me over an hour to get there, but I do—and undetected at that. I power on my phone before I reach for the handle and pull open the door. I spot my friends sitting in a booth in the back corner and slide in next to Liam and Ryan.

"What have you guys been up to?" I ask. "Everybody having a good night? Anything interesting happen?"

"Jesus fucking Christ, man," Liam says. "What the fuck happened to you?"

"Don't answer that," Ryan cautions. "We'll talk about it later."

"We've actually been here all night, haven't we girls?" Liam says.

"Yeah, they picked us up a little after ten," Ariana says. "And we've been here ever since."

"We were in the back with Kyle and the rest of the guys," Ryan adds, gesturing toward the lead singer of the band on stage. "Just ask him. He'll tell you...or anyone else who wants to know."

Gotcha.

"Ezra, where's Maddie?" Ava asks.

Am I supposed to answer this one?

Everyone stops to look at me, waiting for my reply—even Liam—so I guess so.

"You didn't text her?"

"Figured I shouldn't," she says.

"She's at home. Keeping her mouth shut."

I think. If she knows what's good for her.

"By the way, you're a mother fucker, Ben," I tell him. "Fuck you—for that. I should beat your ass."

"Dude, I—"

"Light *you* on fire and—"

"We're. Not. Talking. About this," Ryan says again.

"You need to relax," Liam says. "You seriously look like you want to kill somebody—more than the usual amount. It's not a good look for you right now. People are noticing."

"Seriously, chill. Go get a drink, man. Go fuck Courtney again; she's been staring at you since you walked in," Ben says.

Yeah, I noticed that. I could still feel it, too. I look up, and—sure enough—she's still doing it. She waves at me with her pinky from the hand holding a strawberry daiquiri.

I nod in her direction and then turn my attention to Ava, whose face is buried in her phone.

"What are you doing?" I ask her.

"Nothing nefarious," she replies. "Don't worry about it."

"Give me your phone," I say.

"Why?"

"Because mine's dead, and I need it."

"No."

"You can use mine," Liam says.

I pluck Ava's phone from her hand. "Nah, it's fine. Ava's gonna let me use hers."

"What the *fuck*, Ezra? Don't look through my shit!"

She tries to take it back from my hand, and I stand up, making the task impossible at her height. I quickly scroll through her contacts, find Madison's name, and send myself the number, deleting the evidence once I'm sure it has gone through.

"Here you go," I say, handing it back. "Was that so hard?"

"What did you do?" she asks. She's likely checking her text messages and browsing history before she lowers her voice and says, "I told you I didn't fucking talk to anyone, Ezra; I'm not fucking stupid."

"Can't be too fucking sure about anyone these days," I tell her. "You're sitting awfully close to Ben, and we don't know if *stupid* is contagious."

I get up before any of them can reply and head to the bar. I'm not twenty-one yet, but that doesn't mean anything here. Not for us, anyway.

"What can I get you, bro?" TJ asks.

"Shot of whiskey," I tell him. "Three, actually. Three shots of whiskey."

He winks and points at me like a fucking douchebag, and I'd tell him as much if I didn't kind of need him. He lines up the shot glasses in front of me and, after he pours, moves on without trying to talk to me.

At least I have that going for me.

I pull out my phone and check my text messages, staring at the one with Maddie's phone number.

Ava will check on her tomorrow. And do I really care what happened to her anyway?

No, I don't. Not beyond what it means for me. I mean, she *did* save my ass. But I wouldn't have been in that situation in the first place if it hadn't been for her temper tantrum and fragile fucking joints.

Fuck it. I down the third shot and click on the number.

Me: You good?

Madison: Yep.

That's it?

I type and delete some version of *'Thanks for saving my ass'* or *'Glad you made it home okay'* about half a dozen times before shoving my phone back in my pocket. I got the answer I needed. I don't need anything else from her, no matter how badly she wants to fuck me.

And she does want to fuck me. That doesn't surprise me. Girls like Madison come up here all the time with a kink for slumming it with the townies, hoping they'll get fucked right for once in their lives before they're forced to go back to their empty, meaningless lives. I don't do that shit anymore.

But the way she looked at me when I held her against the tree with her mouth covered...under different circumstances, I might have made an exception.

"Ezra!" Courtney says from behind me, running her hands up and down my arms. "I didn't know you'd be here tonight."

"Yeah," I tell her. "This is where I've been...all night."

"Really? I feel like I would have noticed if you were."

"You know what, Courtney? I've actually got something to show you in the truck."

"Umm...okay," she says.

I get up from the bar stool and gesture toward the back door. "After you."

She follows me out the door and through the parking lot to the truck. I get in and wait as she climbs in on the passenger side.

"What was it you wanted to show me?" she asks, closing the gap between us and kissing my neck.

I grab her chin and turn her face to the clock on the dash. "See what time it is?"

"Um...yeah. 1:45"

"Nope."

"No?"

"Pretty sure it's around 11...maybe 11:30. If anyone were to ask. Got it?"

"Got it," she says. "No problem."

She unbuttons my pants, and I lift off the seat when she jerks them down, freeing my cock.

"Already so hard for me," she says, stroking me.

'Not for you,' I think. *'For the girl with the big blue eyes I held against a tree earlier tonight.'*

"Good," she adds. "Because I'm already so wet for you."

"Take off that thong," I tell her. I pull a condom out of my wallet and slide it on while she reaches under her skirt and pulls them down the length of her legs, kicking off her heels when she gets to the bottom.

She straddles my lap and sinks down onto my cock, moaning as I fill her up.

"Oh, god. Fuck, that feels so good," she says.

I pull the straps on her dress down, freeing her tits and drawing a nipple into my mouth while she bounces up and down on my dick. It's good; she knows what she's doing, but still, I think of Madison—her much larger tits in my hands and in my mouth, how her face would look when I fuck into her, how I'd make her scream. I'd maybe feel bad about where my mind went if Courtney wasn't enjoying it so much.

My thoughts spur me on, and I flip us so that I'm on top of her, drilling into her pussy, covering her mouth with my hand when she cries out, clenching on my dick. I leave it there, still thinking of Maddie instead—pressed up against a tree with my hand over her mouth, her wide blue eyes rolling back into her head while I bury my dick inside of her—until I come.

EIGHT

MADISON

By Tuesday, my ankle feels okay enough to go back to work at the store.

I don't know what to expect when I see Ava and Chloe. Ava texted me on Sunday to ask if I made it home okay. I told her that I did, and that was it. She said we would talk more when I came back to work. But do I want to talk more? Do I want to have anything to do with any of them after what happened?

If that was their idea of fun, I don't think I want it.

Even if I liked it. Even if I liked it a lot.

It's noon when I get there; I park Emma's car around back and head inside. It'll probably be a while before the shop is within walking distance for me again.

"Oh my god, you're back!" Ava says, crossing the room. She lowers her voice before adding, "I'm so glad you're okay."

"Yeah, just a sprained ankle," I tell her, glancing around at the handful of shoppers perusing the store. "I can get started on stocking."

"No way—sit," she says, gesturing to a stool behind the register. "Emma brought this in for you. You shouldn't be on your feet all day; I can do all of that until you're comfortable again."

"Thanks," I tell her. "I don't want to put you guys out, though. I don't want it to be harder for everyone else because I'm here."

"It's not. It's totally not. You're still helping. And I missed you, girl." She lowers her voice again. "Also, what the hell happened?"

"He...didn't tell you?"

"No. He didn't tell us *anything."*

Nothing? Not about me running out of the house and throwing a tantrum? About the things I said about how they probably started and deserved whatever happened? About it being my fault he got left behind?

Didn't they hate me, and didn't I want nothing to do with them?

I quietly recount a condensed version of events for her.

"Uh, well...I fell while running back to where the truck was parked. He...tried to help me. But by the time we got back there, you guys were already gone."

"Yeah—I'm so sorry. We heard the sirens, and Liam said we had to go—we had the clubs and everything, and they couldn't find us with that stuff in the truck out there."

"It's...it's fine; I'm not worried about that," I tell her. "There was a cop out there, though. And he was going to find us. So...I acted like I was a hiker who got injured on the trail, and he took me back to the house and then drove me home."

"Wow," she says. "Just like that? No questions asked?"

"Well...a few questions asked, but it wasn't that bad."

"I guess Ezra is lucky you were out there then," she says, then laughs. "I bet he *hates* that."

Yeah, really lucky. It was my fault he was out there in the first place. I don't tell her that.

"Is it...over with?" I ask.

She sighs and leans in closer. "Probably not. But my brother—he's a cop—he said they didn't find anything at the house, really. Some muddy footprints outside, but there were so many of them. And there was the fire."

I nod.

"Excuse me," a woman perusing the jewelry says. "Can I get some help with this?"

"I'll be right there," Ava replies. She leaves me with a half-smile.

We don't talk about it for the rest of the shift, which works out great for me; I'd be okay not talking about it again ever. Eventually, Chloe comes in, and before Ava leaves, she pulls her aside. It's clear from her body language she's giving her the same half-assed account I gave her of what happened to Ezra and me after we all got separated that night.

"Hey," she shouts on her way out the door, "we're going to the lake after you get off on Friday. Text me if you need a ride."

What?

"Who's we?" I ask. I swear my heart stops while I wait for the answer. Not him, right?

"You passed your initiation. You're inner circle now," she says before the door closes behind her.

Do I want to be inner circle? I don't think so. I even had this whole speech planned out this morning. I was going to let Ava know that it was nothing personal and that I liked her and liked working with her, but I wasn't going to hang out with her and her friends anymore.

But I don't say no, and I don't say any of that, either. I spend the rest of the afternoon working with Chloe and pretending nothing is wrong.

Once I'm off work, I walk as best I can to the pharmacy around the corner. Emma got someone to call in some pain medication for me, and I have my own prescriptions that I'd transferred up here and need to pick up. I wait uncomfortably in the long line, and after about twenty minutes, I finally have my medications in hand. The ankle that didn't feel so bad this morning was throbbing again now, and I couldn't wait to get back to the house and get off of it. I stop toward the front and peruse the aisles, looking to replace things I didn't think to pack in the five minutes I gave myself to do it—things I'd been borrowing from Emma. I throw in a hairbrush, some toothpaste, sunblock, and a few other toiletries before heading to the front to pay.

Before I can, I feel something jutting into my back.

"Freeze! Police!" a deep voice says from behind me.

I toss the shopping basket, and its contents go flying. Terrified, I raise my hands in the air and try to steady my breath. I can hear my pulse hammering in my ears.

"We know what you did," the voice says.

Wait a minute...

I turn to face the source of the voice behind me, furious.

"Are you fucking kidding me?"

"You shouldn't be so fucking jumpy," Ezra says. "People will be suspicious. You need to get your shit together."

I grit my teeth. I want to kill him.

"That's a weird way to thank me for saving your ass," I tell him.

"I wouldn't have needed you to if you weren't there in the first place," he says.

He bends down and starts picking up the basket and the spilled contents.

"Birth control, huh? You found someone to fuck here already? That was quick. It isn't Ben, is it?"

My eyes go wide. We aren't alone in the aisle—not even close—and he isn't quiet at all.

I snatch it from his hands. "No, I'm not f—" I pause, lowering my voice. "It isn't any of your business. *Leave me alone.*"

"Here's the rest of your shit," he says, dropping the brush and toothpaste into the basket. "You should work on that, though—being so fucking jumpy. It makes you an easy target."

"You're an asshole."

"I'm just trying to help you out, Maddie."

But that wasn't what he was trying to do, and we both know it. He was trying to get under my skin—trying to scare me.

It worked, and I hate it.

"I'm sorry I'm not a better criminal," I sneer. "I guess it just doesn't come naturally to me."

"Yeah, I'm sorry about that, too," he says.

Seething, I turn without saying anything and head to the checkout. On the way to my car, I swear I feel eyes watching me, but I don't dare look back.

I tie on my white bikini and examine myself in the mirror. Normally, I wish my chest wasn't so large and my hips weren't so wide, but not when I'm in a bikini.

Tiny girls look good in clothes. I look good in a bathing suit.

I throw on a crochet cover-up and some sandals, then grab my bag and meet the girls out front. Since Emma took the car to get some supplies and the shuttle stop is a good distance from the house, I end up taking that ride Ava offered me to the beach.

I climb into the back next to Chloe. Ava sits in the front next to her sister, who is driving. And no one says a thing about what happened last Saturday, even though it's all I can think about when I'm alone. No one says a thing about Ezra, either, and neither do I, even though it feels like his name is always at the tip of my tongue.

We park and walk out to the beach, past a couple of rental and excursion booths, a concession stand, and a restaurant where a DJ is currently setting up on the back patio.

"Wow," I tell them. "I don't remember all this being here when I was a kid."

"That's because it wasn't. Most of this just popped up in the last five years or so. Tahoe got too crowded or too commercial or something, and people started coming to Lost Hollow instead. I mean, you've seen the village. It's doubled in size, and then there's all of this and the houses up by the falls...it's brought a lot of good and bad," Ava tells me, and I wonder if she's thinking of Ryan's sister.

We set up a spot on the beach, and—for a moment—I breathe a sigh of relief, thinking it's going to be a girl's day. It's short-lived, however, because the guys pull up just a few minutes later.

"Ladies," Ben says.

"Hey, Ben," Ariana says, her tone bored.

"Maddie—good to see you're alive and in one piece."

"Yeah, thanks," I say.

"We're going to rent some jet skis," he says.

"You mean Gina is working, and she's going to give them to you for free?"

"Yeah, that's exactly what I mean. You want to ride with me, Maddie?" he asks.

"I don't think so," I tell him.

"All right. Well...let me know if you change your mind."

He jogs across the beach to catch up with Liam and Ryan, who are already almost at the rental dock.

"I'm going to go get a smoothie," Ava says. "You guys want to go with me?"

"I will," Ariana replies.

Chloe and I both decline, and they head toward the concessions just as Ezra walks up, drops the cooler in the sand, and sets up a chair next to us. He pulls his shirt over his head and sits down without looking at me or even saying a word.

It irritates me, and I can't explain why. It's as much as I expected—maybe better, even. I think of the things he said to me about not being one of them, of what happened at the store and the mysterious text message, and start to get angry all over again. I think maybe I hate him. I haven't hated anyone in a long time. I also can't tear my eyes away from his body, and that only makes me hate him more. My eyes zero in on his pecks, the left one covered in tattoos—a continuation of the sleeve on his arm—before running down his body, down his abs, and to the deep v that disappears underneath his shorts.

Why can't this asshole be ugly? Surely, with my sunglasses on, he won't be able to tell that I'm looking.

I snap back to reality and manage to look away when I hear Chloe's phone ring. Without saying anything, she answers it and walks out of earshot, leaving me alone...with him.

"You better stop looking at me like that, Maddie. I'm not going to be your stupid fucking story."

"I'm not looking at you," I lie. "And what is with you and this 'story' thing? What story?"

"You know," he says, "the one you rich girls tell your friends at country clubs and spa getaways or whatever you do. About that time you went on vacation and actually got fucked right for the first time in your life—maybe even felt something. The story you'll play in your head to get through sex with your boring husband or when you get your vibrator out after he leaves the room. *That* story."

"*Wow*. You think far too highly of yourself. I'm not here looking for any kind of story, especially not that story. And if I were looking for someone to make me feel something, I wouldn't pick someone like you. I wouldn't want someone who's dead inside."

"You're lying," he says. "But I just wanted to clear the air. Let you know my boundaries."

He pops his earbuds in and settles back in his chair just as Ava and her sister return. Like nothing happened.

"Where's Chloe?" Ava asks.

"Um, her phone rang, and she took off with it," I say.

"Oh, my god. It's *Aiden*."

"Aiden? Is that the guy she wanted to invite over to the bonfire the other night?"

"Yes, shhh. Here she comes," she says. "Oh hey, Chloe. Who were you talking to over there?"

"Shut up," she says.

"Chloe! I thought you were going to break up with him."

"I can't break up with him because we aren't dating."

"Exactly. Because he's a fucking loser who plays video games all night and sleeps all day."

"He eats pussy good, though," she says, shrugging. "And I'm going to need something to do when you guys go back to school in the fall."

"Oh, where are you going to school?" I ask. My tone comes out with a little more shock than I intended.

"Ari, Ryan, and I all go to Southern Oregon University," Ava says. "Ryan will be a freshman like me. What? Are you surprised?"

"No, I'm not surprised. I just...I guess I'm surprised I never thought to ask."

"Chloe is doing EMT training. Ezra and Liam work for their dad's construction company. And Ben...well...we don't really know what he does."

"What about you, Maddie?" Chloe asks.

"I'm starting at UC Berkeley in the fall."

"You have a boyfriend, too, right?"

"Some guy named Ethan," Ava says. I give her a puzzled look. "What? It's right there on your Facebook. Did you think I wasn't going to look?"

"He's not really my boyfriend anymore. It's complicated."

"Why is it complicated?" Ava asks. "Does he *eat pussy good*, too?"

"No," I tell her, feeling my cheeks flush.

"No?" she says. "So...he's not good at it?"

I look over toward Ezra, sitting just four feet away from me with his earbuds in his ears.

"Oh, don't worry about him," Ariana says. "He's not listening. Watch this—hey Ezra! You're an asshole, and I spit in your beer the other night. Also, your tattoos are stupid, and I want to fuck your dad."

The three of us laugh while his expression remains unchanged.

"Well?" Ari presses.

"He won't do it," I tell them quietly.

"He won't what? Go down on you?"

"Nope," I tell them. "He never has. Not once. He says it weirds him out."

"Wow. And you suck his dick, I assume?"

I nod.

"Jesus. How did you put up with that?"

"We started dating when I was fifteen," I tell them. "And I don't know. I asked some of my friends about it. They said that it was okay and that I wasn't missing much—"

"Your friends are morons," Chloe says. "Remind me never to visit Palo Alto."

"So...you're telling us no one has ever—" Ava starts.

"Nope," I say, cutting her off.

"I knew it," Ezra says, plucking out his earbuds. "You *are* looking for that stupid fucking story. I bet he has a small dick, too, doesn't he? Actually, you don't need to answer that. It isn't a question."

I feel all the color drain from my face and turn back toward the girls. "You said he couldn't hear us."

"I miscalculated," Ariana says, shrugging. "What are you gonna do?"

"You'll need something to help you get off when you go back to him...I get it," he adds.

"Fuck you," I tell him.

"I already told you—that's a boundary for me. But you know what? Because I do feel bad for you and because you did kind of help me out that one time, I might be willing to do you a solid and go down on you."

"I don't *want* you to!" I shout, my cheeks now burning with embarrassment. Just then, Ben drives by us on the jet ski. Seeing this as my way out, I flag him down. "Hey, Ben! Ben!"

"And Ari—I swear to god—if you really did spit in my beer...."

"Oh, what? What are you going to do about it?" she challenges.

Noticing me, Ben stops in front of us. "Yeah?"

"I actually do want to go with you now. Wait up," I say, beginning to wade through the cool water to where he's idling.

"I'm not going to tell you what, and I'm not going to tell you when, but I *will* tell you that you aren't going to like it. I'm going to tell my dad what you said, too. He might actually be into it," Ezra continues.

"Cool, let him know. He knows where to find me," Ariana says right before the idling engine drowns her out.

I climb onto the back of the jet ski because I can't climb out of my skin, and we take off, following in Liam and Ryan's wake.

"Have you ever done this before?" Ben yells over his shoulder.

"Yeah," I yell back. "A few times."

"Right. I forgot. Rich kid," he says. "Oh, shit."

"What?" I ask. "What's wrong?"

He points to a large speed boat filled with people around our age a couple of hundred yards away, and I watch Ryan cut his wheel toward the boat, then Liam turns after him.

"Who is that? What's going on?"

"Those are Jonathan's friends," he says as if I should know who that is.

But I think I do.

I think I heard Ezra say that name in the woods. I think he's the one whose house we destroyed last week.

Ben cuts the jet ski and follows after them at a slower speed, and I consider my suspicions confirmed when Ryan grabs the beer can from his cup holder and launches it onto the boat, nailing one of the guys in the shoulder.

It must have been a full one because it knocks him over.

It's only a second before the driver turns the much larger, much faster boat around and starts chasing after the four of us.

Fuck.

Heart pounding, I wrap my arms tighter around Ben's waist. We're quite a bit behind Liam and Ryan, and the boat pulls up alongside us after a matter of seconds. I think for a minute that they're passing us—that they don't really want us, they want Ryan, and that's good because they aren't going to catch him. I exhale the breath I've been holding and chance a look toward the boat, and I swear I see a face I recognize right before the driver decides to settle for us and side-swipes the jet ski, sending us both airborne.

I hit the water, feeling it smack against my back hard enough that it burns before I go under and knocks the wind out of me, and then I keep going under, likely sucked into the boat's wake. I struggle to get up as quickly as possible, fearing that I'll be run over if I don't—either by them or by another boat that doesn't see me.

I finally break the lake's surface, gasping for air and choking as the turbulent waters continuously hit me in the face, threatening to take me under again. I don't see Ben, but I spot the abandoned jet ski a good thirty yards away and figure that's my best bet to at least get afloat and get out of the water. The shallow water closer to the shore was cold, but out here, it's freezing. Even though I'm a good swimmer, it's difficult to move, and I wouldn't dare dive back under the choppy water to make it easier on myself.

I've only covered about half the distance before Liam pulls up, idling beside me and extending his hand. I take it and climb onto the back of the jet ski, and once I do, I see Ryan doing the same with Ben before taking him over to the one we'd been tossed from.

I look nervously over my shoulder for the boat the entire ride back to the dock. When we get there, I'll still shaking both from the adrenaline and the cold, and Ezra and the girls are there waiting.

"I can't believe you'd be that fucking stupid," Ezra says.

"Don't you fucking start shit with him, Ezra, I swear to god—" Liam starts.

"I'm not talking to Ryan! I'm talking to you, fuckface!" he says, pointing to Ben.

"Me? I didn't do anything. I'm not the one who threw a god-damn beer can at those fuckers."

"You went after the boat! And then you stayed after it. Why didn't you cut away? Because you wanted to see how it ended? You just had to be part of the fucking drama, as usual?"

"No, I fucking—"

"You took Maddie out there without a life jacket, and she almost fucking drowned. You almost got her killed because you're a—"

"Enough! Jesus Christ," Ava says. "Maddie, are you okay?"

"Yeah. I just want to go home."

"Come on; I'll take you," Ava says. "Get me the keys, Ari."

"I can take her," Ezra says.

"Why would she want you to take her? She's *terrified* of you." Ari says quietly—but not quietly enough.

We all walk back to the beach area in silence, Ava and I at the front and the rest of them behind us. I pack up my things silently, then head to the car, climb into the passenger seat, and wait for Ava, who is still talking to her sister on the beach.

"Are you okay?"

I turn and see Ezra leaning through the window.

"I don't know. I can't decide if I'm pissed off or if I'm...nothing."

"Interesting," he says, furrowing his brow. "What's *wrong* with you?"

"I'm not sure," I reply.

"You're cold."

It's not a question. I am freezing. I didn't have to look to know I was all goosebumps and hard nipples. My teeth have just barely stopped chattering.

"Is she right?" he asks.

"Is who right about what?"

"Are you afraid of me, Maddie?" He reaches out and brushes his thumb against my cheek. Not expecting it, I flinch. "You are, aren't you?"

"Yes," I tell him. I don't mean to say it, but it comes out anyway. I try to take it back or revise my answer in some way, but nothing comes out. One corner of his mouth turns up, and something changes in his cold eyes again—something carnal that pins me to my seat.

I'd almost say that he liked that answer.

"What scares you more—the kind of person you think I am or that you want to fuck me anyway?"

I swallow hard before I answer. "Both."

"You look good with blue lips," he says. He traces them with his finger, and—without thinking about it—I suck it into my mouth. He lets me, then adds another before pulling them out with a pop right before the driver's side door opens.

Why did I do that?

He leans in further through the window and says right next to my ear, "You know what? Maybe I will fuck you."

"Okay, let's get you home," Ava says. She looks back and forth between Ezra and me. "Everything okay?"

"Yeah, I'm okay," I tell her. "Just ready to get the fuck out of here."

"See you soon, Maddie," he says before backing away from the car.

NINE

MADISON

I'm back in the water.

Somehow, I'm back in the water, and it's night. I can't tell which way is up; everything looks the same. I struggle—kicking and paddling as hard as I can, clawing at nothing—but no matter how hard I fight, something keeps pulling me under.

I open my mouth to scream, but nothing comes out. My lungs are now so painfully empty that I can't fight my natural instinct to fill them any longer. It's a relief at first when I finally give in—when open my mouth to make them full again—but it's only a few seconds before I realize it's a mistake. And the last one I'll ever make.

I'm drowning.

Sinking.

I'm dying.

"Maddie," the thing pulling me under calls out. "Maddie, wake up."

Wake up.

Wake—

I shoot up into a seated position on my bed, hands at my throat and gasping for air. It was just a dream—a nightmare. I'm okay.

"Jesus. What the fuck was that?"

I jump backward and slam my head against the headboard. I'm not alone.

"What are you doing here?! Are you...here?"

"It wouldn't surprise me if this is what you dream about," Ezra says. "But yeah, you're awake now. Get up; let's go. It'll be light out soon."

"Why would I go anywhere with you?"

"Because I think you like to be scared. And you're going to want to find out what these keys go to," he says, holding out a ring with two small silver keys on it. "Get dressed and meet me outside."

Only after he leaves the room do I notice that I'm in just a pink thong and a white cami without a bra. It didn't seem to phase him, though. I don't know why, but I'm disappointed again.

I climb out of bed, pull on a pair of shorts, a bra, a t-shirt, and my boots, then head downstairs, berating myself the entire time for following him into something that would, more likely than not, be nefarious at best. Maybe dangerous, too.

And for how I feel right now—terrified but mostly excited. Intoxicated by the thrill.

I climb into the passenger side of the truck, put my feet up on the dash, and roll down my window. I don't bother asking where we're going. From the corner of my eye, I see him glance over at me, and if I didn't know any better, I'd swear I see a flash of teeth before he turns back toward the front, cranks up the volume, and puts the truck in reverse.

We don't drive for long. We pull off into the woods on a side of the lake I'm unfamiliar with and get out. Ezra waits for me but doesn't say anything, then we cross the street and cut over to some boat docks. We pass about half a dozen before he turns down one, and I think I realize what we came for.

I think I know what those keys go to.

"Is that—"

"The boat that ran you over? Yeah, it is." He climbs over the side and extends his hand to me. I stare at it, hesitant to take it.

"Don't act like you don't want to," he says. "We don't have a lot of time before the sun comes up; we can't really afford to sit here and talk about it."

I take his hand, allowing him to pull me onto the boat, and then sit in the back. He starts the engine and backs away from the dock, keeping the speed slow and the headlights off, likely to keep from attracting too much attention.

"You should be driving," he says. "Come here."

I get up, walk to the driver's seat, and stand beside him. "I don't know how to drive a boat."

He wraps an arm around my waist, pulls me onto his lap, and places my hands on the wheel while keeping his foot even on the gas pedal. "You're going to go straight down here for a while. I'll tell you where to turn."

"What are we going to do with it?" I ask.

"Much less than they deserve," he answers. He brushes some of my hair away from his face and over my left shoulder, and I shiver when his warm fingers brush up against my neck. "On your left, there's going to be an inlet. It'll be hard to see, but I'll go slow."

"Okay," I say, my voice coming out much quieter, much weaker than anticipated.

"Here," he says. And he's right; I barely see it in time. I cut the wheel hard to the left, and even though it's difficult to see what's in front of me, I'm pretty sure we're heading toward land.

"Brace yourself," he says. "It's going to get shallow in about fifty feet."

I tighten my grip on the wheel, and Ezra wraps one arm around my body, pulling me tight against him—tight enough that I can feel him hard against my ass—and grips the boat's windshield with his other hand. Just before the boat hits the lake's bottom, he lays on the gas pedal. We're both launched forward and then back again as the boat hits and the engine digs into the mud, ultimately causing it to come to a stop.

As soon as he releases me, I jump up from his lap and lean against the back seat while I try to catch my breath.

"What now?" I ask. "Is that it?"

"Almost," he says.

He pulls the keys from the ignition, and I watch them sail over my head, hearing a small splash before they're lost in the dark water. I look around and realize we're stuck out here. The only way to get back to shore is to get back into that same dark water that pulled me under earlier—that choked me in my sleep.

"Ezra, I can't—" I start to explain, but when I turn around, he's standing—looming, even—over me. "What are you doing?"

He leans in close enough that our lips just barely don't touch. I close my eyes, and my heart pounds in my chest, fear mixed with desire while I wait for it to happen, but it doesn't. He reaches down, picks me up by my thighs, and sets me down on the back of the boat before pulling off my boots. When he touches me again, it's a hand around my throat, forcing me flat on my back. I look up at the stars and wait, wondering if he's going to try to fuck me or kill me and what I'd do about either one, until the hand around my neck runs down my body, lingering on my chest, exploring and kneading my breasts, before moving down my stomach. Then, he unbuttons my shorts and pulls them down over my hips.

His fingers slide under the sides of my thong, and I instinctively lift my hips to make it easier for him to remove them. I think I hear him laugh; I almost take a moment to feel embarrassed because I know they're fucking soaked. I've been wet since I woke up and found him standing over my bed, uncomfortably swollen since I felt him hard under my ass. Now, he's moving far too slowly, and I'm feeling desperate. If I could form words, I think I might beg. Desperate for any kind of friction, I start to squeeze my legs shut, but he immediately pries them open and spreads me wide. I look up just in time to see him smell my panties before tucking them into his pocket. Then, he lowers his head, and I realize what he's doing.

He's making good on his promise.

"Ah, fuck!" I cry out. His mouth makes contact with my clit, and my hips buck against him. He runs his tongue up and down my pussy. And I'm fucked, because it feels so good that I whimper and squirm and try to dig my nails into the boat—anything to keep me from shamelessly fucking his mouth like I want to.

"You taste so good," he says.

"Please...just..."

Just don't stop what you're doing. I need his mouth back so badly it aches.

"Your boyfriend doesn't know what he's missing."

"He's not my....ahhhhh."

Ezra pushes a finger inside me, then another, and gives me what I want. He sucks my clit into his mouth and circles it with his tongue while he fucks me with his fingers. My friends were wrong—so wrong. I grit my teeth and writhe desperately against his tongue despite my best efforts not to. When it gets to be too much and I think I might explode, I thread a hand into his hair and raise my hips, pulling him further into me. He increases both the pace and the pressure in response, eating me like I'm his last fucking meal, and I don't even know what self-control is anymore.

"Oh my god. Oh my *god*."

He moans against my pussy, the vibrations sending me over the edge. As the orgasm rolls through me, and squeeze my eyes shut and still see stars when I come, trying and failing to keep from crying out in the otherwise impossibly quiet space. And it keeps going. And going.

He doesn't let up until my legs fall limp on each side of him. I feel him standing over me—looking down at me—while I lie there like a pile of jello, staring up at the stars, unable to move or meet his eyes.

"You okay?" he asks.

"...Yep."

"We have to go," he says.

"Okay," I say, still breathless.

I sit up, and he hands me my shorts before climbing down the side of the boat. Once he's in the water, I see it hits him just at the knees, and that makes me feel a little bit better. I look around the back seat and floor of the boat but don't see my underwear. I guess I shouldn't be surprised, and I'm not going to ask for them. I do see cum dripping down the back seat, and it didn't come from me. I fight the urge to run my finger through it and bring it to my mouth and wonder what the fuck is wrong with me. What the hell did he do to me?

"Let's go, Maddie," he says.

I quickly pull on my shorts and boots, then throw my legs over the side of the boat. He reaches up toward me, and when I jump, he lowers me slowly into the cold water. The sky begins to turn pink with the first morning light as we trudge through the muck back to the shore and then head toward the truck.

"Is your ankle okay?" he asks.

"It's not too bad," I reply.

He doesn't say anything else, and I finally ask, "Why did you bring me here?"

"So that you could get revenge," he says. I think that I didn't really need it, then wonder if I'd said it out loud because he adds, "You did need it. You're different than I thought."

"How so?"

"I think you're angry, and you're tired of it. Aren't you tired of it? Of doing nothing about it?"

"I don't know. Maybe."

Yes.

"You need to be careful taking things in stride, or someday you'll wake up and realize you've made such a habit of giving in that you have no fucking clue who you are or how to fight for yourself."

"I think maybe I already have," I tell him.

We climb into the truck. I pull the door closed behind me then he puts it in reverse. "What do you mean you already have?"

"That's why I'm here. Not for a story and not to help Emma. Because I woke up and realized I have no control over my life, and I have no fucking clue what to do about it. The day my grandma died, I went to this party and walked in on my boyfriend with another girl. He said he was at home sick. Everyone knew—our friends knew. And I just...wanted to get away. And so I closed the door, went home, and got in the car with Emma. I didn't even cry. I tried to. I just...didn't care. I don't think I care about anything."

"Maddie, that's fucked up."

I shrug. I can see the wheels turning in his mind; he wants to say something else, but he doesn't. Not until he pulls into the driveway and puts the truck in park.

"You walked in on this guy you've been with for three years fucking someone else, and you just closed the door so they could finish and went home? You didn't scream or yell or hit anyone or anything? You didn't even *cry*?"

"Technically, she was sucking his dick. But...yeah."

"Not ever?"

I shake my head. "Not ever. I keep waiting for it. But...no."

"Jesus. You're *really* fucked up. And you call *me* dead inside. *You're* dead inside. All the way dead if you're not careful."

I open my mouth to defend myself, but nothing comes out. Maybe because he's right and it *is* me—maybe I am dead inside, and it is too late because I already have no fucking idea who I am or how to fight for myself.

At the very least, it'd be nice to have something I actually wanted to fight for.

I open the door of the truck and jump out, slamming it hard behind me. I stomp up to the front door and throw it open and closed just as hard, then watch out the window for a couple of minutes while the truck just sits there.

Why is he just sitting there?

I wonder if he's going to get out. Maybe he's going to come to the door to apologize or comfort me. I don't realize how much I wanted it until a couple of minutes later when he does put the truck in reverse and go.

Once it disappears, I kick off my boots and turn to find Emma standing in the kitchen, staring at me.

"Good morning," she says. I watch her eyes take in my obviously disheveled state and the mud that goes past my knees. I mentally prepare myself for the interrogation that doesn't come. "You want something to eat?"

"Um, yeah," I tell her, realizing I'm starving. "I think...I should shower first."

"I think that's probably a good idea."

"Sorry," I say. "About the mud."

She shrugs. "I'm not worried about it."

I attempt a smile in her direction, then head upstairs and straight into the shower. I scrub and scrub the mud and muck from my legs and finally cry for the first time in a long time, and it's not for Ethan or Ezra or anyone else.

It's for me.

It's for whatever sense of self I had before that's gone now. For the emptiness inside of me that I don't know how to fill. For this hollow shell of a person who doesn't have a fucking clue who she is and who doesn't want anything.

It *is* me. He's right. I *am* dead inside.

TEN

EZRA

"Where the hell have you been?" my dad asks when I walk inside.

I consider my appearance before I come up with a lie. "Fishing."

"Fishing? What'd you catch?"

"Nothing," I say. "Didn't bite."

"You got someone who can corroborate this fishing story? Are you going to need an alibi again?"

"Yes and no."

"I heard Morales came by yesterday," he says.

"Yep."

"Can you speak in full sentences? For fuck's sake, this is serious."

"It's not serious. He just asked where we were last Saturday, and we told him—we were at TJ's Pub. We have *alibis* and people who can *corroborate* the story. And they have nothing."

"You could be a little less flippant about this—both of you. It's not funny, Ezra. You can't fuck with those people. You'll lose...every single time. Trust me."

"I told you we didn't do anything. So you have nothing to worry about," I tell him.

I walk into the kitchen, grab a piece of bacon from the plate on the island, and stuff it in my mouth.

"The fuck do you think you're doing?"

"Eating."

"Get the hell out of my kitchen. Go take a shower. And wake up your brother. We have a job this morning, or did you forget about that when you were out all night *fishing*?"

"I didn't forget. I'm good to go."

"Yeah, looks like it," he says. "And Ezra? If your alibi is that girl they found wandering around the woods behind the house that night, you might want to consider getting a new one."

"That girl?" I say, laughing as I pour myself a cup of coffee. "You know exactly who that girl is."

He narrows his eyes at me, and I stuff a couple more pieces of bacon in my mouth before I do what he says and get the hell out of his kitchen. I head up the stairs, down the hall to my room, and close the door behind me. I take the soiled pink thong out of my pocket and think of Maddie losing control and fucking my face and get hard—again. I wrap the small piece of silky fabric around my cock and stroke it until I cum on it—again.

Then, I shower, wake up my brother, and don't say another word about where I've been or what I've been doing.

It's been over a week since the boat incident, and here I am, still hyper-focused on Maddie.

I wish I could explain it, really I do. Maybe it's just because she's...weird. She's really fucking weird. And I've been bored for a long time.

Or maybe it's that I showed some restraint and didn't fuck her that night, and I feel like I need to remedy that.

It could be both.

I'm done worrying about why, though. It doesn't matter why. I am hyper-focused on Maddie, and I do need to get it out of my system. So when I ran into Ava earlier, and she said they were coming to the pub after work, I made sure we'd be here, too.

"Ezra, what's your problem? What are you doing?" Liam asks, looking over his left shoulder toward the door to the pub. "Why are you watching the door?"

"I'm not watching the door."

"Then what the fuck are you doing? You're spacing out."

"I'm just...thinking."

"I saw Courtney up at the bar," Ben says.

"I'm not really interested in that anymore," I tell him.

As I say it, the door swings open, and Ava walks in, followed by Chloe and Madison.

I lied; I was watching the door.

Liam doesn't really notice, leaning over to show Ryan something on his phone. But Ben, who is sitting next to me, does.

"You're kidding me, right? Maddie?" he asks.

"What do you mean?"

"That's not fucking fair, man. She was supposed to be mine. You knew I wanted her," he says.

"That's not how people work. You can't just call dibs. Maddie's a big girl, she can make her own decisions."

"And what about bro code?"

"Bro code? Based on what? That you almost caught her on fire once and almost drowned her another time? Give me a fucking break. Move."

"You hated her," he says.

"I like how her pussy tastes," I say before I walk away, smiling.

I'd love to see the look on his face right now.

"Hey, TJ. Whiskey and coke and a...." I look over at Maddie. I have no idea what that girl drinks. If I were a girl who was dead inside, what would I want to drink?

"Vodka soda," I decide.

They grab a table by the front door. I'm surprised they haven't seen us yet—we're in our usual spot—but I guess it is packed. Or maybe they did. Maybe sitting separately was intentional.

I guess we have gotten them into a lot of shit lately.

Not my fault.

TJ hands me my drinks and, before I can cross the room, Courtney steps into my path.

"Is that for me?" she asks. "I'm more of a tequila girl, but I'll take it."

"No, it's not," I tell her.

She turns and looks behind her toward the girls.

"Really?" she says. "I mean, she's cute, but she doesn't really seem like your type. She looks so...breakable."

Breakable definitely isn't the right word.

"Looks can be deceiving," I say, walking around her. "Have a good night."

I slide into the booth next to Madison and set the drink down in front of her.

"What's this for?" she asks, eyeing me suspiciously.

"It's for you because I'm seriously worried about your mental health. I mean, who just shuts the door and walks away?"

"Okay, that's not funny. I'm not doing this again," she says.

"What's he talking about, Maddie?" Ava asks.

"Nothing. He needs to mind his own fucking business."

"Oh, come on. I—"

"Madison Ridgeway. *No* fucking way."

"Weston?" she says.

She looks confused, then pissed off. I don't recognize the guy, but I do recognize two of his friends standing behind him as some of the usual summer crew that hangs around with Jonathan. I'd be willing to bet they—and the others they walked in with—were the ones from the boat yesterday. I wonder which one is the lucky owner.

"So, this is where you've been hiding all summer," the guy says. "Does Ethan know? He was fucking *pissed* when he found out you were gone."

"We don't keep in touch," she says coldly.

"Well, hey. You should be hanging out with me and my friends. We're going to grab a few drinks and then go back and party at my place. My parents have a house up by the falls. Your friends can come, too."

"You and *your* friends ran over me with a boat last week," she says.

"Oh, fuck. No way. That was you? That was some crazy shit!" he says and laughs a little. Maddie picks up her drink and downs more than half, white-knuckling the glass and looking at the guy like she wants to tear him in half. I smile because...good. It's better than the usual nothing.

Do something about it, Maddie.

When he finally sees what I see, he backtracks. "Madison, I'm so sorry. I had no idea they were going to do anything like that. I had nothing to do with it. And those guys you were with—they were the ones who started it. I mean, they could have killed someone with that beer can. And I heard they burnt down one of my other friend's houses. How fucked up is that?"

"Your friend is a rapist," she says.

"*That*...is not true. There are two sides to every story."

Now, I intervene. "You should walk away now," I tell him. "While you still can."

He looks at me—really looks at me—for the first time since he came over here. He only considers challenging me for a second before realizing it wouldn't be wise, and self-preservation kicks in.

"Well, you have my number if you ever want to hang out. I'll be here until about the 4th. You'll be home for the 4th, right? At Rockingham?"

She stares at him and takes another sip of her drink. She doesn't respond.

"Right," he says. "See you around, Madison. I'm sorry about the boat."

"Yeah, we're *real* sorry about that boat, too," I tell the guy.

Maddie looks at me and laughs—actually laughs.

"You're terrible. Get me another one of these?" she asks, finishing her drink.

I guess I was right. Girls who are dead inside do like vodka.

"Absolutely," I tell her.

"Um, excuse me," Ava says. "What the hell is going on?"

"I'm just trying to be nice to your new friend," I tell her. "That's what you wanted, right?"

She narrows her eyes at me suspiciously. "Well, I'm not sure now."

I walk back to the bar and order Maddie another drink, this time feeling charitable enough to grab one for the other girls, too, knowing they're probably grilling her for information she won't give them.

Like I said, she's different than I thought.

I give the girls their drinks and leave them alone...for now. I head back to the table with the guys; Ben looks pissed, and I don't care. Liam looks pissy, which is different.

"What are you doing?" he asks.

"Nothing. Did you see who's here?" I ask, changing the subject.

"Yeah, we did. I was just telling Ryan that I think we should leave."

"No," I say. "No way. This is a locals bar. I'm not going to let them run us out of here. Fuck them. Besides, they're not going to do anything."

I watch them try to grab drinks at the bar, but only half walk away successful as they all get carded. They move to the back of the room as a group—all gravity-defying hair, collared shirts, and matching white sneakers—like someone just hit copy and paste on one of them. Probably their personalities, too. My friends talk and laugh and drink, and eventually, the girls do join us, but I'm mostly watching them. I'm pissed off that *they're* laughing and drinking and playing darts and having fun with their friends here, too. I'm pissed that they feel so comfortable here, so close to us after they'd just run over a couple of us with a boat defending a rapist.

I understand why Ryan threw the beer can. I make eye contact with him and see the same look in his eye. He's had a few drinks, and my brother's arm is around his shoulders, and he's still stiff and angry. Seething, even. If he can't be comfortable here, then I don't want them to be comfortable here, either.

Once I see them wrap up their game, I jump over the side of the booth and walk over to the dartboards. "Hey, who's got next? Anyone want to play me?"

"Yeah," one of the guys says. "I'll play. But we play for money. Buy-in is $500 bucks."

A couple of the others laugh. He's fucking with me. He thinks I won't bite because I can't afford it. He's right that I can't, but I'm not too worried about it because I also can't lose.

"Not a problem," I tell him.

The smile falls from his face. He only hesitates for a moment, looking back toward his friends.

"Well?" I challenge. "What's it going to be?"

"All right. Let's do it then."

ELEVEN

Madison

"What is he doing?" Chloe asks. "Did they say $500?"

"They did," Ava says. "Does he have $500?"

"Fuck no," Liam says. "But he's not going to lose, either."

I'm not so sure about that. I don't doubt that Ezra was good, but he also doesn't know this crowd the way I do. Without jobs to worry about or a care in the world, guys from my world had nothing better to do than drink and become proficient at sports that require little to no athleticism or brute strength. Shooting, archery, darts—they were all on that list.

We must not be the only ones who hear the exchange and are invested in the outcome because more people from around the bar start to crowd in close as they get started. The six of us do the same, sitting up on the ledge that runs alongside the booths to get a better vantage point.

As soon as they start, it becomes clear that I was right to worry, and this isn't going to be an easy win for Ezra. They seem to be evenly matched, and I hear Liam expressing concern to Ryan as well.

"What was he thinking?" a girl I don't know asks Ben. "He should have challenged them to arm wrestling or...almost anything else. Everyone knows all of those prep school idiots have nothing to do all day but jack each other off and play darts and shit."

I laugh because...she's not entirely wrong.

"I'm Courtney," she says. "I don't think we've met."

"Madison," I tell her. "Maddie is fine, though."

I realize I've gotten used to the nickname—that I'm happy to be Maddie here. It makes me feel like I could be different.

Maddie doesn't take shit from people and cries in the shower. She doesn't just close the door and go home and feel empty.

When it's finally over, it's a tie.

"Tiebreaker round," the other guy says. "Three darts. Get ready to lose."

"That's boring," Ezra says. "Too easy."

"Oh yeah? Well, what do you suggest? You want to make it one dart? Add another $500?"

"I want to add another person," he says.

"Little late for teams," the guy scoffs. "I understand why you'd want to tap out, but—"

"Not teams. There," Ezra says, pointing at the dartboard. "We each get someone to stand at the other end and then throw those three darts."

"You serious?"

"Dead serious."

"Fine," the other guy says, shrugging. I watch as he approaches his friends, trying to convince one of them to be target practice for him. I hear a girl answer with an emphatic no, saying something along the lines of she likes him, but not that much.

"Maddie, come over here," Ezra says.

My heart plummets into my stomach. I jump down from the ledge and walk over to him. He puts his hands on my shoulders and backs me toward the wall. He looks at me and then up at the dartboard and frowns, unsatisfied with the distance between the top of my 5'5" head and the 5'8" bullseye.

"I can do this," Liam says. "Maddie, you don't have to do it."

"Maddie will do it. She'll be fine," he says.

"She's terrified."

"Maddie likes to be scared. It's better than nothing, isn't it Maddie?"

"What the fuck are you talking about?" Liam asks.

Ezra doesn't answer. He turns and leaves me there, walking toward the front of the pub with Liam on his heels. I can't hear what they're saying, but eventually, Liam relents, shaking his head as he walks back and rejoins the others. Ezra returns with a booster seat and ushers me aside so he can put it in place. I take his hand and climb on top of it and back into the wall again.

"That's much better," he says, reaching out and pushing my hair behind my ears. His eyes fall down to my chest. "Your nipples are hard."

Out of the corner of my eye, I see someone take their place in front of the target next to me. It's Weston, and he looks nervous.

"You picked Madison?" he says to Ezra. "She's going to chicken out. No way she goes through with this."

"You look like you're about to shit your pants, kid. And you're wrong. If you're counting on Maddie to save you, you're going to be disappointed." He grabs my chin and tilts my face upward so that our eyes meet. "You'll be good for me, won't you, Maddie?"

"Yes," I tell him.

He leans in and whispers, "I bet you'll even get wet while you do it," then turns and walks back to the throw line.

"This is stupid," Weston says, laughing nervously. "You're not really going to do this, are you?"

"Ezra's right, Weston. I'm not going to save you."

"I'm not asking you to save me. I'm not scared," he scoffs.

But he is. I watch his eyes move nervously around the room, looking for someone else to save him. His gaze settles on the bartender, who leans against the bar watching casually, just like everyone else. He's thinking someone is going to intervene, but he's wrong.

I look over at the other guy with Ezra, and he looks nervous, too. That doesn't bode well for Weston, either.

"Weston, this isn't Palo Alto. This isn't Rockingham. No one is going to step in and stop them. If you don't want to do this, you don't have to."

"Just shut up, Madison. Shut up."

"Okay," I say, shrugging.

"Why are *you* doing this?" he asks.

I don't know. Maybe because I do like being scared. Maybe because scared feels like so much more than what I've gotten used to, and it's a lot better than dead inside.

Or maybe it was because I wanted to be good for Ezra, and it did make me wet like he said.

"For fun," I tell him.

"You good, Maddie?" Ezra asks.

I nod.

"Don't move," he cautions. "Keep your eyes open. Look at me."

I don't nod this time, but I do what he says. I look at him and not the dart in his hands, and get this feeling in my lower gut...something new. I think about what that police officer said that night—about the rich kids and how they just get bored and how they'll do anything for a rush—and I wonder if that's what this is. Maybe I'm just so used to things being easy that I've gotten bored and it takes something like this for me to feel anything.

Without even knowing he'd released it, I hear the dart thud above my head, and the room erupts in cheers.

"Two more," he says, and it falls silent again.

Thud again. More cheers.

On the last one, I feel the flight end of the dart run through my hair before settling in above my head, inside of the triple ring.

I step back, take a mental tally, and laugh. That would be difficult, if not impossible, to beat.

And I *was* good. It felt good, too. Better than nothing, just like he said.

"Get over here, Maddie," Ava calls out. I join my friends back over on the ledge again, and they're going on and on about it, but I'm hardly listening. I'm looking at him. He's looking at me, too—like he's hungry. And I know what he said before but—

"Okay, everybody! Shut the fuck up! I need to focus," the other guy says. "Ready, Weston?"

He's not, and neither are you.

The guy counts down from three, and that's probably his mistake. The dart leaves his hand on one, and Weston jumps to the side, but he's too late. A collective gasp fills the room as the dart pierces his cheek, then comes the scream.

A couple of his friends rush over, pull the dart from his cheek, and blood gushes from the hole down the side of his face. The guy who threw it just stands there yelling at him. "You shouldn't have moved! Why did you move? You fucked me! God damn it, Weston!"

All I can think is that he's lucky it was just his cheek.

"We need to take him to the hospital!" one of the girls yells.

Okay, *that's* a little dramatic.

I look over at Ezra, who appears unphased by the entire spectacle. He just turns to the other guy, holds out his hand,

and waits until eventually, he pulls on his wallet and pays up. I watch as Ezra counts the bills, then walks over to Ryan and slips him the money. I realize I'm staring when I accidentally meet his eyes and look away.

I turn instead back to Weston in time to see him get up off the floor and watch his friends escort him to the door. I do kind of feel bad for him. I think about texting him, but to say what, really? Your friends are dicks—they ran me over with a boat and threw a dart at your face? Choose better next time?

But I let Ezra throw darts at my face, too, didn't I? And it did make me wet. I'm still wet now thinking about it. Maybe I need to choose better, too.

"That poor fucking idiot," Ava says. "I almost feel bad for the guy."

I almost express a similar sentiment, but stop when I feel hands running up my thighs. I turn to face Ezra standing between my legs.

"That was so fucking hot," he says.

He leans in and kisses me hard. It takes me by surprise; the force of it might have caused me to lose my balance and fall from the ledge if he didn't have such a grip on my thighs. All of the air leaves my lungs, just like the dream I had where I was in the water. Also like the dream, I don't fill them again until it's painful and then wonder if it's a mistake.

I grip his biceps with my hands and kiss him back. His teeth dig into my lower lip hard before he breaks away from me, leaving me confused, with the taste of whiskey mixed with iron on my tongue.

I bring my fingers up to touch my swollen lip and when I pull them away, I see bright red blood.

"What...the hell is going on?" Ava asks me.

"Um, I don't really know," I tell her.

"What?" he says. "We've kissed before."

"We've *kissed* before?"

"I kissed you once," he says. He reaches between my legs and cups my pussy in his hand. "Right here."

"Oh my *god*," Ava says.

I feel my cheeks burn red.

"Come on, Maddie. Let's go."

He doesn't ask and doesn't wait for me to answer, but I do what he says. I hop down from the ledge and follow him out the front door.

"This is your house?" I look around at the expansive open floor plan of the A-frame cabin overlooking the lake just a couple blocks from the village. Floor-to-ceiling windows cover the entirety of the back of the home, running up to the vaulted ceiling with stylish, exposed wooden beams. It's not much different than the houses up by the falls—than the home we destroyed. It's all so...unexpected.

"Why are you so surprised?" he asks.

"I'm not surprised," I lie. "I guess I just assumed all of the houses around here looked like Emma's."

I wonder if it was the wrong thing to say and if he'll be offended.

Fuck, why am I here?

"See where those steps are?" he says, pointing to the middle of the room where there's a slight split in the floor plan.

"Yeah."

"That's where the original house ended. My dad added all of the rest of this like...ten years ago, I guess. Let's go upstairs."

Again, it isn't a question. I follow him up the stairs, down the hallway, and into a room at the end of the hall.

He closes the door behind me, then the space between us, reaching down and pulling my cami over my head, revealing my bare tits.

He cups them with both hands, running his thumbs over my nipples. "Been thinking about this a lot. About your tits...in my mouth," he says, leaning down and sucking one into his mouth. "Covered in my cum."

He backs me into the room until I feel my legs run into the edge of the bed, and I sit down. He pulls his shirt over his head, then unzips his pants and frees his hard cock, stroking it in his hand in front of my face. I knew he'd be big; I know what I felt under my ass the other night, but it still surprises me. I lean forward and give him what we both want—I wrap my lips around the thick shaft, licking and sucking the length of him while I pump him with my hand, tasting his salty precum on my tongue.

It's what I've wanted since I saw it dripping down the seat of the boat that night.

"Mmmm...that's it. That's a good girl," he says, threading his hand through my hair and forcing himself farther down my throat. "You can take in more of me than that. You look so good when your eyes water."

His words have me moaning around his dick. I'm so wet and desperate at this point that before I realize it, I'm rubbing myself against the bed.

"Fuck, that's good," he says. He pulls my head back hard and lays me flat on the bed. His hands move to the button on my shorts. "But I want to fuck your pussy now."

I lift my hips to make it easier for him to off the rest of my clothes. He spreads my legs wide and pushes his fingers in and out of me slowly. It feels so fucking good, but it's also not enough.

"God, you're so wet. I bet you're hurting right now aren't you?"

"Ezra...please."

"Please what?"

"Please fuck me."

"Turn over," he says.

I flip onto my stomach, then he lifts my hips so I'm on my knees. I feel the head of his cock against me and I groan, thinking I might die if I have to wait any longer.

"Please," I say again.

He pushes his cock inside of me, slowly at first, stretching me more than I'm used to, and it hurts. Painful in the very best way.

"Oh, god," I cry out. "Oh, fuck....fuck."

He pulls my hair back as he slams into me over and over again. I fist the covers and push back into him, feeling that tightening in my core building until I'm about to come apart. I don't even bother trying not to scream this time, barely recognizing my own voice when I do.

"Fuck, Maddie. You feel so good squeezing my cock like that. This is what you needed, isn't it? To get fucked hard?"

"Yes," I whimper as he drills into me, harder and faster while the aftershock of the orgasm continues to rip through me and I clench around his dick. I'm nothing but a soaking wet mess of shaky legs and watery eyes, face down on the bed, unable to hold myself up anymore.

He pulls out and flips me onto my back, spreading my legs wide before filling me again.

"I want you to come again," he says as he fucks into me.

"I can't," I force out through my teeth.

Of course, he proves me wrong. He reaches down, massaging my clit with his fingers while his thrusts become both shorter and harder.

"Oh, fuck," I moan, digging my nails into his forearms when I come again.

"That's it," he says. "Feels...so...fucking...good," he groans, thrusting into me a few more times before pulling out and coming all over my tits.

He collapses on the bed next to me, and I realize that he was right about me *again*. I've never been fucked properly—not once in my life. Not until now.

"That's much better," he says. "This is how I like you. Covered in cum, or pressed up against a tree with my hand over your mouth. I thought about that a lot. It made me come, too."

"Yeah, me too," I tell him. I think about all the times I've touched myself thinking about it over the past few weeks. I think about how I'd try not to—and how much I hated him and maybe still do, but it only made it better. Easier, even.

He grabs his shirt off the ground and wipes my chest semi-clean, then reaches into the nightstand, pulls out a bottle of whiskey, and hands it to me. I take a pull from the bottle and hand it back to him, then start to get up to gather my clothes.

"Get back in bed, Maddie," he says. "I'm not done with you."

I do what he says, and he hands the whiskey back to me again. I drink from the bottle, then he takes it and sets it down on the nightstand, and pulls me back onto my back.

He licks and sucks my nipples before moving between my legs. I jerk back when I feel his tongue on my clit, still too sensitive from before.

"Ezra, I can't—"

"Sure you can," he says.

He licks and fucks me again; we drink some more, then I fall asleep with his chest at my back.

TWELVE

Ezra

"What are you doing? I didn't tell you that you could get out of my bed."

I check the time—9:30 AM. It's both too early after the night I had and too late because I'm pretty sure I have to work this morning. Maddie creeps around my room in her underwear and tank top, her eyes settling on my guitar.

"I didn't know you played guitar," she says, then laughs. "I don't know anything about you, actually."

She picks it up from its stand and throws the strap over her shoulder.

"Don't touch it," I say. "I have that exactly how I want it."

But she doesn't listen. She sits down on the stool next to it and surprises me when she flawlessly strums the intro to "Cigarette Daydreams" by Cage the Elephant.

"What...the fuck?"

She laughs and keeps playing. "What?"

"*You* play guitar?"

"Not really," she says. "I've messed around with it a little bit, I mean. It's a string instrument. I play the violin."

A little bit? Yeah, right.

"The violin? Is that a requirement where you're from?"

"No. Or kind of...now, I guess. I used to love it. But then my parents figured out how good I was at it, and it became a job—a means to an end. I sort of forgot what it was like to just play for fun."

"Sing," I tell her.

I'm surprised when she actually does.

"You can drive all night
Lookin' for the answers in the pouring rain..."

"I'm so shook right now."

She continues. *"...peace of mind*
Lookin' for the answer..."

The door flies open. "Ezra?"

My dad looks at me, then Maddie.

"Jesus Christ," he says. "It's like looking at a goddamn ghost."

"Uhh, Dad, that's Maddie. Maddie, that's Ty—my dad."

"Um, hi," she says weakly.

"Hello, Madison," he says. "How's your mother?"

"She's...okay."

"We need to leave in an hour," he tells me, then closes the door.

"Sorry about that," I tell her.

"It's okay. I have a feeling my mom was...an interesting person in her other life."

Wow. She *really* doesn't know, does she?

"What about your mom? Does she live here?" she asks. She places the guitar back on its stand and pulls on her shorts.

"You want to know my family history now?"

She shrugs. "Only if you want to tell me."

"No, she doesn't. My parents lived together until I was twelve and Liam was eleven, but—from what I understand now—they were always just better as friends. I guess one day, they decided they both wanted more, and my mom moved out. She found it a couple of years ago and moved to Bend. Dad's still looking, I guess."

"I'm sorry," she says.

"Why? I'm not. I had a great childhood. My parents are awesome," I tell her. "Hey, don't give me that look."

"I'm not giving you any look."

"You're looking at me like, *'Then what the fuck is wrong with you?'*"

"Well...then what the fuck is wrong with you?"

I shake my head. "Too many mouthy fucking rich girls asking me stupid questions."

I grab her by the arm and pull her back onto the bed and kiss her.

"I'm not scared of you," she says.

"Yeah, you are."

"I need to leave," she says. And I know she's right; I need to leave, too. Even though I'm rock hard and want nothing more than to bury my dick inside of her again.

"Yeah, okay. I can take you," I say. I get out of bed and pull on a pair of sweats.

"That's okay," she says. "I left Emma's car in the village; I have to go get it. Hopefully, she isn't too pissed."

"I'll walk you out," I tell her.

I don't want to risk an unsupervised encounter between Maddie and my dad.

He's sitting in the living room with a plate of biscuits and gravy and is washing it down with a beer. That doesn't bode well for me. He eyes me hard when we walk past him.

"I'm sorry about your grandmother, Madison," he says.

"Oh...thank you. She was...really sick. I didn't know her very well."

"Well, that's a shame," he tells her. "That's a damn shame. She was a hell of a woman."

"Um...it was nice to meet you," she says.

He salutes her with the beer bottle hand like a fucking lunatic.

"See you later, Maddie," I say. She offers me a smile, and I close the door behind her.

"What the fuck is wrong with you?" my dad asks.

"That's the second time someone has asked me that today. Not really unusual for me, I guess, but it is a little early," I tell him.

"I hope you know what you're doing, Ezra."

"I always know what I'm doing," I tell him, grabbing some food for myself from the kitchen as Liam and Ryan come downstairs.

"Do *you* know what your brother has been up to?" he asks Liam.

"...I'm going to need you to be more specific," he says.

I laugh. "He's talking about Maddie."

"Oh...that."

"Yeah, that."

"I'm not his fucking keeper," Liam says.

"Well, maybe you should be."

"He's the older one."

"You're the smarter one," he retorts.

I laugh again.

"Is that why you're doing this? You think it's funny?"

"It's kind of funny," I say. "But...no."

"Then why?"

A lot of reasons. Because I'm fucked up. Because I like that I scared her, and I like that she does whatever I tell her to. I liked the crazy look in her eye when we were tearing that house apart—the same as when I held her against that tree and at the bar with the darts. I like the dark part that maybe she didn't even know about. I wanted to fuck it out of her. Or...maybe not out of her. Maybe more into existence. I think it would help her with the whole lot of nothing she feels.

And maybe it is *just* a little bit because it's twisted on some level. But not to hurt him.

I can't say any of that.

"She's different," I tell him instead. "I like it."

"I can assure you that she isn't," he says.

"She's pretty messed up, Dad," Liam says. "I don't know what they did to her, but I don't think it was good."

"What do you mean?" he asks.

"She let Ezra throw darts at her head."

The look he gives me. I laugh again.

"You need to cut this shit out. Now," he says. "Don't forget that she could link you three to that house fire."

Everyone in this room knows his reaction has nothing to do with the fire.

"We weren't there," I say.

"Finish up and meet me in the truck."

He walks back to the kitchen, throws his plate in the sink, and heads out the back door, slamming it for effect.

"Dude, he's pissed," Liam says.

"I don't see what the big deal is, honestly. He'll get over it. Let's go."

He says goodbye to Ryan and follows me out the back. The ride in the truck is quiet and tense. At least for the next six to eight hours or so, we'll be too busy to talk.

THIRTEEN

MADISON

"Well, look who it is," Emma says when I walk in.

"Hey. I'm sorry about the car. I hope I didn't ruin your day or anything."

"No," she says. "Not at all."

She looks back down at the jewelry she's packing and tries to hide a smile. She's got the TV on—some kind of murder documentary, sipping on coffee and writing down addresses.

"What's that?" I ask. "Online orders or something?"

I grab a cup of coffee for myself and join her on the couch.

"What's that?" she asks. "A hickey?"

"I can help you," I say, not answering the question.

"You can address these envelopes for me," she says. "My hands are a little shaky this morning. Ezra Cross, huh? That's an interesting choice."

I feel my cheeks burning. "It's not serious," I tell her.

"Really? Because those three men are some of the most serious people I've ever met in my life. Just saying."

I don't answer. I guess she's not wrong—they are serious. But Ezra and I...we don't really even like each other. We have nothing in common. And I'm leaving for college in the fall. It's not like I'd try to do a long-distance relationship. Not after what had happened when my boyfriend was on the other side of town.

Not that I'd ever want something like that with someone like him.

"You know, they are the ones that did all of the work inside the house. The kitchen and the floors. And then when your grandma got really sick, they put in the ramp out front and made the bathrooms handicap accessible."

"Yeah, their house is...really nice, too."

"They probably still have a key, actually. I should ask for that back."

Yeah, they definitely still have a key. That explains the 3:00 AM kidnapping.

We're interrupted by a knock on the door. Emma pushes up from the couch, then clutches her stomach and falls back.

"Aunt Emma? Are you okay?"

"Yeah, I'm just not feeling well this morning. Stomach ache. Do you think you could get that for me?"

"Of course. No problem."

When I open the front door, I find myself face-to-face with a police officer. It takes me a minute to recognize him as it had been dark when we met, but it is the same one who drove me home that night.

"Hey there, Madison," he says.

"Gene?" Emma calls. She pushes up from the couch, still clutching her side, but this time is successful. "What are you doing here?"

"Need the clothes Madison was wearing when she went hiking a couple of weeks ago. I've got a warrant."

"Um, they've been washed," I say.

I regret it the minute it comes out of my mouth.

"We figured as much, but it doesn't really matter. The shoes, too."

"I'll just...go get them, then," I say, looking at Emma.

She nods, and I head up the staircase to my room to get the clothing. It doesn't take me long to find the hoodie and shorts. I have no fucking idea what undergarments I wore or if they want them. I debate digging out a random pair, then decide against it but throw in a pair of socks just in case.

When I come out of the room, I overhear Emma talking to him.

"Do you want to tell me what this is all about, Gene?"

"Those people...they're not happy. They want answers about what happened that night. They want someone to pay, and the chief wants to give them that."

"They want someone to pay? That's a little rich, don't you think? After what we all know that boy did to Sienna Williams?"

"Now, you know there's nothing I can do about that."

"Madison had nothing to do with all of that. She went hiking and got hurt and that's it."

"Well, she's got nothing to worry about then," he tells her.

"Here you go," I say. I hold out a pile of clothes. He opens a bag with gloved hands, and I place them inside.

"And the shoes?"

"Right there," I say, pointing to the muddy boots by the front door. "Are you going to keep these for long? They're my only pair."

"I'm sure you can afford new ones," he says. "We'll be in touch."

He shuts the door and leaves.

"What do you think they're going to do with them? What are they looking for?"

"I don't know," she says. "Burn marks? Gasoline, lighter fluid? Something from inside the house on the bottom of your shoes."

"Those shoes have been at the bottom of the lake," I tell her. "I washed those clothes. And I wasn't around the fire."

"And you weren't in that house at all, right?"

Her eyes tell me she knows better, but this is all we will say about it.

"No, I wasn't."

"Now, I appreciate how you're helping me, but you need to take your coffee and go take a shower."

"Right. Sorry."

I go back upstairs and into the bathroom, closing the door behind me. I turn the water on and wait. It takes a long time for it to heat up here; it drove me crazy the first couple of weeks, but I'm used to it now. I strip down and assess myself in the mirror. I see the dark hickey Emma pointed out on my neck—I don't remember him doing it—and a couple more on my breasts. I'm still sore and sticky between my legs, and it feels so good.

I don't know what I've started. Maybe it isn't serious, and it doesn't make sense, but I didn't want to stop, either.

Even if it would drown me.

I spend the next day working with Lisa and waiting for 6:00 PM to roll around—not just because it's when I will get to leave, but because it is when I'd get to talk to Ava in person.

She's early, and she ambushes me the minute she walks into the door, cornering me near the dressing rooms.

"I heard about the clothes," she says.

"I was going to text you. It just didn't seem like a good idea."

"No, it wouldn't have been. At all."

"Well, did your brother say anything? I'm kind of freaking out about it. They have my boots, and you said that thing about the footprints."

My phone buzzes in my pocket.

Ezra: What time do you get off work?

Me: 6:00...why?

"Yeah," she says. "He said they don't really have anything. They're just grasping at straws. That family is desperate to make someone pay. I just—I mean, I don't get it, I guess. They have all the money in the world. They should just have to take this...no offense."

"Why would I be offended? I'm not a—"

"Excuse me, girls." I jump at the voice right over my shoulder. "Can I get a little bit of help over here?"

"Oh, I can help you, ma'am," Lisa says, walking out from behind the counter. "She was just on her way out."

Once she's out of earshot, I continue, "I know what you mean. It's a lenient punishment for what he did—what they helped him get away with. They *should* just take it."

"Okay, now what's going on with you and Ezra? You slept with him." It isn't a question. "So, do you like him now or something?" she asks.

"What? Oh, um. Nothing is going on, really. No."

"Then why is he here?"

"Maddie likes me," he says from behind me. "She sucked my dick and sang me a love song. I'm pretty sure that means she likes me."

He isn't quiet about it, either. There are probably only three customers in the store and Lisa, but they're all staring at me now. Apparently, he likes embarrassing me. This wasn't the first or the second time.

"It wasn't a love song," I mumble.

"You serenaded me."

"You asked me to."

"Can we go now?" he asks.

I think about protesting. Making up something that I have to do instead or pretending I don't want to, maybe acting like I wasn't desperate to feel him inside of me again—desperate to replace the bruises that had already started to fade with new ones.

But I don't.

"Yeah, we can go."

I follow him out the door, and we start to walk the few blocks to his house.

"Hey, Ezra?"

"Yeah?"

"That cop came to my house."

"Yeah," he says. "I know."

"How did you know?"

"Does it matter?" he asks. "Don't fucking worry about it, okay? They have nothing. Nothing is going to happen."

"How can you be so sure?"

He doesn't get a chance to answer. The dark sky has been threatening rain since this morning. I slept with my window open last night and smelled it at soon as I got up. Now, it finally makes good on its threat and comes down cold and heavy with about a block to go.

We make a run for it, but by the time we get inside, we're both completely soaked and freezing anyway.

"You need to relax," he says once the door closes behind us, putting each hand on the side of my face. "They aren't going to do anything to you. Just stop thinking about it."

"Okay."

"Did you stop thinking about it?"

"Only because all I can think about right now is how cold I am."

"I still think you look pretty with blue lips," he says, then kisses me. "Go outside, take off your clothes, and get in the hot tub. I'm going to make you a drink."

"What about your dad and your brother?"

"They won't be back for a few hours," he says. "It's nice out there when it rains—you'll see."

My feet don't move immediately. I think I'm confused by how he's acting and how he's moving. I can't make myself look away.

"Are you going to do what I say, or am I going to have to make you?"

I smile. "I'll do what you say. But I don't think I'd mind if you made me, either."

I walk out the back and hesitate for only a minute before stripping down and sinking into the water, turning on the jets when I do. I'm so cold the water stings at first, but after those first few seconds, it warms me and brings relief. It *is* a nice place to be when it rains. Warm and sheltered, but you can still hear it and see it. You can still smell and even feel it when the wind hits just right. I can still hear the birds chirping in the forest at my back.

After about a minute or so, he comes outside and hands me a drink before stripping down and getting in, too.

"You're right," I tell him. "It is nice out here when it rains."

"I told you that you'd like it."

He's so...casual. Something about it just doesn't fit.

"You keep looking at me like you're trying to figure me out," he says. "You should stop. Just relax...like I told you to. There's nothing there."

"What do you mean?" I ask.

"You think there's something you're missing—like I have this secret dark pain or some kind of hidden scar that needs to be healed, and once you figure it out, I'll make more sense. But you're wasting your time. I don't."

"You don't?"

"Nope," he says, then downs the contents of his drink. "I don't. What you see is what you get."

"So, you're just...normal, then?"

"Completely normal."

I shake my head. "You're abrasive. And angry."

"Maybe. I'm not angry right now. Besides, you're angry, too, and that's more of a problem."

"How is that more of a problem?"

"You hold it all in. You're going to snap one day and end up on the local news. I find a healthy outlet for it and encourage you to do the same."

"Are crimes a healthy outlet?"

"Sure," he says, shrugging. "I was also instilled with a deep-seated sense of justice I feel obligated to act upon. Thus, these so-called crimes."

"They *were* crimes," I say, sipping my drink. "You're bossy, too."

"And you like being told what to do. So, see? Healthy outlet."

I don't reply. I don't like being told what to do. In fact, I was really fucking sick of being told what to do. But I do like it when he does it.

I wonder where that comes from.

"Anything else?"

"I was surprised to see you...at the store."

What do you want from me?

"I liked fucking you. You want to do it again, right? I do. I don't see any reason to play some stupid game and pretend it isn't true. I don't see any reason to make a big deal out of it, either. Do you?"

"I guess not."

"Come over here and sit on my lap, Maddie."

I take the hand extended toward me, and then he pulls me over to his side of the hot tub. I straddle his lap, feeling his hard cock at my entrance when I do.

"Sit down, Maddie," he says again.

I sink down onto it, moaning as it fills me and the toe-curling waves of pleasure roll through me.

"Mmm...good girl," he says, urging me on as I roll my hips and move up and down on his dick. He leans back, causing me to sink down further on him and gasping when I do.

"Does that feel good, Maddie?"

"Yes," I grit out.

"Are you going to come on me?"

"Yes," I force out again.

He reaches down and positions his fingers against my clit while I ride him, quickly forcing me over the edge. I grip the side of the hot tub hard when I come, and he uses a tight grip on my ass to keep me rocking hard and fast against him until he comes, too, then my body, still shaking, falls into him.

I rest my forehead on his shoulder while I try to catch my breath. He runs his hand through my hair and says, "I like it out here when it rains, too."

FOURTEEN

Ezra

I do like it out here when it rains. I always have. I think I'll like it more now.

"What's that?" she asks. "Did you hear that?"

Yeah, I did. And honestly? Probably a bear. It's not uncommon. It's the only thing around here that would sound like that. But that's not what I tell her.

"Yeah. Probably just a wendigo. It doesn't sound hungry, though. I think we're okay."

"A what? What's that? Like a wolf or something?"

"No, not like a wolf. More like...a cannibal."

"Shut up," she says. "You're lying."

"No, really. Did you see its antlers? Were its eyes glowing red? If they were, then it probably *is* hungry."

"Stop," she says. "You just made that up."

"I promise I did not make it up. We probably should go inside before it skins us alive. Or you alive, anyway. I'm a lot faster than you are, and you've got those weak joints. You should take a multivitamin or something."

"A *multivitamin?* You keep a gallon of whiskey in your night-stand."

I stifle a laugh. "It's not a gallon."

Then, I hear the sound of tires on the gravel driveway in front of the house. It's much earlier than I expected them.

"Okay, now we probably should go inside," I tell her. "Let's go."

I grab a towel, toss one to her, and we run into the house. We make it to the top of the staircase before the front door opens, then run down the hall and into my room and close the door.

"My clothes are still out there," she says.

I shrug. "We'll worry about that later. Here," I say, and toss her a t-shirt. She pulls it over her head, then wrings out her hair with the towel. I pull on a pair of sweatpants and lie down on the bed.

"Come here, I want to show you something."

She lies down on the other side of the bed. "What is it?"

"Come all the way over here," I tell her. When she scoots only about a foot closer, I wrap my arm around her and pull her closer so that she's lying at my side with her head on my shoulder.

"This is what I wanted to show you," I say. With my free hand, I search for a picture of a wendigo on my phone. I run the fingertips of the other up and down her lower back. She's tense.

Much too tense. She's quite literally cringing. I'm making her uncomfortable, and I'm not sure why.

I set my phone down, then turn onto my side to face her.

"What's the problem?" I ask.

"What do you mean?"

"You're uncomfortable," I say. "You don't like it when I touch you like this. Why?"

"Um, I don't know. It's not that I don't like it. It's just weird for me."

"So, I can fuck you, but you don't want me to touch you?"

"It's not that I don't want you to..." she says, looking embarrassed.

"I'm not mad. I'm just trying to figure you out. So, what's the problem?"

"I just don't know what to do."

She doesn't know what to do? What does that even mean? You don't have to do anything.

"Did no one ever hold you?" I ask. "Not your boyfriend? Not your parents?"

"He's not my—"

"Stop. You know what I mean."

"Well, he wasn't really a cuddler. I'm not either, I guess. I'm sure my parents did hold me when I was little, just like all other parents do. I just don't remember."

"You have no memory of your parents holding you? Ever?"

"Do you?" she asks.

"Yes," I tell her. "Of course. I slept in my parents' bed until I was ten. I am pretty sure Liam slept in there even longer."

"What? Until you were ten? Both of you?"

I nod.

"And they held you?"

"Yep."

She shakes her head. "No. My parents didn't do that. I wasn't allowed to step foot into their room. So, I guess the answer is no. I don't remember my parents holding me. Ever."

"What about a nanny? Don't you all have nannies?"

"Most of my friends did—yeah. But not me," she says. "My mom would just bring me to the office if she had to. I'd sit there and color."

Jesus. No wonder she is so fucked up. I wonder how many of them are like this. It would explain a lot.

"Okay," I tell her. "I'm going to do you a favor...again. Because I feel bad for you, I'm going to help you. You'll thank me for it."

"What do you mean?"

"Come here," I say.

She closes the six inches between us and props her head up on her hand.

"Lie down," I tell her, then point to my chest. "Right here."

She does what I ask, then I wrap my arms around her and pull one of her legs across the front of my body. As expected, I feel her tense up.

"You'll like it once you get used to it," I tell her, running my fingers through her hair while the other hand rests on her leg. "Just try to relax. What do you like to watch on tv?"

"I don't know," she says.

"You don't—" I pause, shaking my head. This fucking girl—I swear. She doesn't know what she likes to watch? I don't bother asking for an explanation. "How about something scary? You like that, right?"

She nods, still uncomfortable. I scroll through Netflix and settle on a new horror movie I've seen advertised a few times, then press play.

"Just—don't tell anyone."

"About what? That you slept in your parents' bed until you were ten?"

"No, I'm fine with you telling people that my parents love me; that's awesome."

"Well, I'm certainly not going to tell anyone I don't know how to cuddle if that's what you're worried about. I don't really tell people things, anyway."

"Yeah, me neither," I say.

At least we have that in common. She fidgets a little, and I hear her exhale far too deliberately.

"Stop thinking about it, Maddie. Just watch the movie," I tell her. "I already know you're fucked up and don't know what you're doing. That *should* help you relax. That should make it easier."

"I'll try," she says, not bothering to argue with my assessment.

"Do you need to go home tonight? Did you take Emma's car to work?"

"No, I walked."

"You should stay, then. You *can* stay, if you want, I mean. If you relax, I'll touch you somewhere you like better after the movie."

"Because you feel bad for me?" she asks.

"That's exactly why," I tell her. "Maybe I'll even play for you. If you're really good."

"And sing?"

"Mmm...I'll consider it."

"Okay," she says.

I think we're almost an hour into the movie before I notice she does finally relax. And I touch her somewhere she likes better—making her come on my fingers—before it's over.

And because she did good, after we fuck, I play for her and sing just a little bit, too. It's not a love song like she played, and I make her turn and face the other way, but she doesn't complain about either one.

I remember our clothes shortly after she falls asleep, and creep through the dark house and out onto the back deck to retrieve them. But when I get outside, I don't see them.

"I put the clothes in the dryer," a voice says from behind me.

"Jesus, fuck! You can't sneak up on people like that."

"I wasn't sneaking. I was out here first. They're probably dry now," my dad says.

I don't like that he touched Maddie's clothes. I can't quite explain why it bothers me, but it does.

"Kind of weird that you touched her stuff," I tell him.

"Kind of weird that you left it outside," he says. "You're sleeping with my ex's daughter. That's kind of weird, too."

"Well, what do you want? An apology?"

He shrugs his shoulders and takes a drink of his beer. I walk around him and start to open the screen door to go back inside and check the clothes in the dryer, but he stops me before I can.

"Is she really messed up? Like Liam says?" he asks.

"Yeah."

"Well, what's wrong with her?"

"Her parents never hugged her," I say.

He scoffs. "Don't be a smartass."

"I'm not; I'm dead serious. She told me she doesn't remember them hugging her ever. And that she doesn't cry, and she doesn't care about anything."

He looks at me like he's trying to figure out if I'm lying. I see the moment he realizes I'm not. It upsets him; I can see it in his eyes. I don't know why. He doesn't even like her.

"Well, sounds like a dream for you," he says.

Normally, I'd agree. But *that* fucking bothers me, too.

"Yeah, I guess so," I tell him, pulling the door open again. "Don't touch Maddie's stuff anymore."

"Ezra?"

"Yeah?"

"Were you singing?"

"No," I lie. "Must have been the TV or something."

I wait, and when he doesn't say anything, I step inside and cross the first floor to the laundry room. I pull the clothes from the dryer, head back upstairs, and slip into bed next to her, pulling her in close to me.

For practice.

After that, my dad doesn't bother me about Madison again.

FIFTEEN

MADISON

The next couple of weeks went by like that. Hot summer days spent at the store or at the lake with Ezra and our friends followed by nights filled with endless drinking and fucking. I think I've done more of both of those things in the past month than I have in my life.

'Preparing myself for college,' I think, then laugh to myself.

I don't know when exactly it happened, but one morning I woke up and realized everything felt different—not like when I got here and was afraid I'd lost myself in some irreparable way. I didn't feel like everything was fake. I didn't feel empty. I wasn't dead inside. I opened my eyes in the morning and knew that I was alive.

Just like how I can't say when it happened, I can't say exactly what caused the change, either. It was different things at different times. Maybe it was simply the stillness here that brought me peace—the quiet that comes from being outside of the city, the lack of urgency, the absence of rigid schedules.

But it was other things, too. The kindness of strangers. Lisa bringing me food at work just because. Someone playing the guitar and singing songs for me that definitely weren't love songs at all.

On days when I didn't have to work at the store, and Ezra was working, I would binge-watch TV shows or lie on the back porch and read *just for fun*. I've always been so concerned with meaningfully filling my time that I never really did much of either of those things. At first, it was even uncomfortable, like the cuddling. I'd feel panicked—like there was something I should be doing instead that I was forgetting.

Now, I realize how meaningful sitting still can be.

Last week, I messaged my dad and asked if he could send me my violin, and it arrived a couple of days ago. Now, I'm playing for fun again, too.

Sometimes, I think about what it will be like when I have to go home; I wonder if I'll lose this. I try not to worry about it now and convince myself that nothing has to change—that I can still be different at Berkeley. I'll still be on my own. I can choose my friends and choose differently, and I can sit still as much as I want.

I don't *have* to lose anything.

I hear the doorbell from outside, set the violin down on the porch swing, and try to walk—not run—to open it.

Of course, I know that he's a part of my newfound peace, too. It's just not something I want to think about. Not right now, anyway.

"Hey," I say when I open it.

"Hey. Is Emma here?" he asks.

"Yeah," I tell him. "She's in the garage. Let's go upstairs."

I grab his hand and pull him toward the staircase, but before I can make it up the stairs, my phone rings in my pocket.

"Ugh, it's my mom. I'll be there in a minute."

He kisses me again and continues upstairs, and I step out onto the back porch to take the call.

"Hello?"

"Madison, I think it's time for you to come home."

"Um, no. Mom, I'm not coming home yet. I'm going to stay until summer is over. Emma needs my help."

"The 4th of July is in a couple of days. People will expect you at Rockingham. I'm worried about you. Your friends miss you."

"Mom, no, they don't. I don't have any friends there. It's been over a month, and I haven't heard from any of them—not one. Not since a couple of days after I left."

"So, you've made friends there, then?"

"Yeah, I have."

"I've heard some things about what you've been up to. From Weston. He said your friends were psychopaths who vandalized his friend's home and threw a dart through his face."

"That's not true," I tell her. "His own friend threw a dart through his face."

"And that you're being investigated by the police in all of this."

"That's not true, either," I say, even though it kind of is. "I have to go, Mom. I have a friend here. I'll talk to you later."

"What's his name?"

"What?"

"Who is the guy, Madison?" she asks. "Whenever I call Emma in the evening, you're never there. So who is it?"

"His name is Ezra," I tell her. "Ezra Cross."

She's quiet for a minute. "You've got to be fucking kidding me, Madison. Is this a joke?"

"What? What do you mean?"

The line is silent again for a minute or so. I pull the phone away from my ear to make sure she hasn't hung up on me, but the call is still connected.

"Mom, are you still there?"

"So that's why you won't answer my calls, then. And why you won't come home. It's for some guy? Where do you think that's going to go?"

"We're just hanging out, Mom. It's not serious. It's not going anywhere," I say.

"Well, at least there's that—at least you understand that. Because I would hate to see you give up your education and everything you worked so hard for to rot away in Lost Hollow. It might sound romantic, but the reality of that life is that it will be hard and it will become monotonous and Ty will come home drunk every night, and he will never leave that town, and you'll get tired of it all, and when you do, you'll have nothing to fall back on."

"Ezra, Mom."

"What?"

"His name is Ezra. You said Ty."

Again, the line goes silent before she says, "No, I didn't."

But she did...didn't she?

"Madison, don't let that place suck you in. You'll regret it when you can't get back out."

"I don't know, Mom. The people here seem happy. Emma is happy."

"Emma is far from happy. She's *lonely,* and she overcompensates for that by—"

"Whatever, Mom. I have to go."

This time, I'm the one who hangs up the phone. I try to shake off the conversation before I get upstairs. Ezra is standing in the room examining the porcelain dolls on the back shelves.

"God, I hate these things," he says. "They're so creepy. I feel like they're always watching me when I'm here. Especially this one—look at her."

"Yeah, they are pretty creepy," I say, but my voice cracks a little.

"What's wrong with you?"

"Just my mom. She's mad that I won't go home for the 4th," I tell him.

"Hey, you know what might make you feel better?"

"What?"

He pushes one of the dolls, the one he deemed particularly creepy, over with his finger, and it shatters against the hardwood floor.

My jaw drops. I stare at him for a few seconds with wide eyes, and he just laughs.

"I cannot believe you did that!" I laugh.

"Come on," he says, knocking over a second one and letting it break into pieces. "You want to break your mom's creepy dolls?"

"I do," I tell him. I walk over to the shelf. "I want to break my mom's creepy dolls...with you."

"Don't go soft on me now, Dead Inside."

But I'm not dead inside.

I run my arm down the first shelf and let them all crash and break onto the floor. I only feel bad for a minute thinking about how, at one point, they must have been special to her; she must have cared about them, and they must have meant something to her. They didn't now, though. You don't leave things you care about behind to collect dust and never look at them or think about them again. And that's what she did—with this town, this house, and her family. I don't know why, but it certainly wasn't because she fucking cared.

"Feel better?" he asks when they hit the ground.

"Almost," I tell him.

I do the same with the next row and then the last.

"Now, I do. I feel a little bit better."

"You're insane," he says, shaking his head and laughing.

"What? It was *your* idea."

"That's a compliment, Maddie. That's why I like you."

"My first compliment—thank you," I tease.

He picks me up and throws me over his shoulder. I laugh and playfully punch him in the back while he carries me across the room, then throws me down on the bed. He pulls my shirt over my head and climbs on top of me, kissing my mouth, my neck, and then moves down to my chest and—

The door opens.

"Madison, I just talked to your—oh, shit. Sorry," Emma says. She looks away, but her eyes land on the back of the room and the broken dolls. "Now *that* is a *really* weird 'fuck you' to your mom. I'll just, uh, leave the broom outside."

She closes the door and leaves.

"Can I tell you something?" I ask him.

"Sure."

"My mom said something weird on the phone," I say. "I think...she knows your dad or something. Like...I think there might have been something going on."

"Oh...yeah."

"Yeah like...you know something?"

He sighs and turns over on his side to face me. "They were engaged."

"What? Why didn't you tell me that?"

I don't know why it hurts, but it does. I'm not sure if it's because she didn't tell me or because he didn't, or if it's because I can't see her with someone other than my dad. I definitely couldn't see her with someone like Ezra's dad.

Who the hell is she? And what other secrets is she keeping?

He shrugs. "I figured if you found out we were siblings, you'd stop fucking me."

"That's not funny."

"Honestly, I thought you knew," he says. "And then when I realized you didn't, I didn't tell you because...it has nothing to do with us."

"It's kind of fucked up," I say, sitting up in the bed.

He grabs my leg and pulls me back down flat, climbing on top of me. "It has *nothing* to do with us."

"I don't know. It's weird, though. Right?"

"Not for me," he says, then kisses me. I kiss him back, but barely. It *is* weird for me. "Maddie, what's the problem?"

"Well, what happened?" I ask.

He sighs. "I don't know."

"You're lying."

"No, I really don't know," he says. Then, after a few seconds, "I think she ghosted him. Or something. She just mailed the ring back."

"Okay," I tell him. "I should clean this stuff up."

I crawl out from under him, pull on my t-shirt, and grab the broom and dustpan Emma left outside the door.

"Ow, fuck!" I cry out. "Shit. Shit. Shit."

I hop on one foot over to the bed.

"Let me see," he says. He examines my foot. "Yeah, you've got some doll face lodged in there."

He pulls it out and holds up the bloody shard for me to see. He tosses it over to where the majority of the porcelain had landed, then sucks the blood off of his fingers.

"You should be more careful, Maddie. Seems like you're always getting hurt."

Yeah, it does seem that way.

"And you're always around when it happens," I reply.

"You're mad at me," he scoffs. "Why? Because your mom dumped my dad a couple of decades ago? I told you already—that has nothing to do with us."

"What us?" I throw back.

He shakes his head and gets up off the bed. "I'm going to go, Maddie. I don't think you really want to do this right now."

I don't say anything because I don't really think I do, either. I hug my knees to my chest and stare straight ahead, waiting for him to go.

Before he does, he grabs me by my chin and turns my head to face him. He looks furious. I wait for him to say or do something—yell at me, kiss me, fuck me, hurt me—but he doesn't do any of those things.

"I'll see you later, Madison," he forces out through clenched teeth.

Then, he leaves the room. Once I hear the front door slam shut, I release the breath I'd been holding and examine my foot.

It's small. Just a cut. Seemingly insignificant, but there's a lot of blood. It looks like it will bleed for a while.

The next day it rains, and I stay inside.

SIXTEEN

MADISON

"You've been gone a lot," I tell Emma when she walks in. It's the morning of the fourth of July, and it's been two days since I fought with Ezra. I haven't seen him since. It's been two days since Emma left the broom at the door, and I haven't seen her since, either.

"I was with a friend," she says. "I'm surprised you noticed. You haven't spent many nights here lately, either."

"A boyfriend?" I ask.

"A male friend," she smiles.

"Did you know..." I start. "Well, of course, you must have, but..."

"But what?"

"My mom and Ezra's dad were engaged," I say.

"What are you doing today?" she asks, not answering the question.

"I don't know. Maybe nothing."

There was a party at Ezra and Liam's house. I wasn't sure if I still wanted to go. As if on cue, my phone vibrates in my hand.

Ezra: You still coming over tonight?

I read it but don't reply.

"What do you say we go on that hike up to the falls that you never got to go on? You think your ankle is up for it?"

It had been better for a while, so yeah, I would be fine. But...

"I don't have any boots," I tell her. "And what about you? How's your...back or stomach or whatever?"

"It's okay," she says. "I woke up feeling energized today. I think this is a good day for us to do this. We can talk, you know? I'm sure I have some shoes you can wear."

The boots I dig out are old and worn and a little bit big on my feet, but they feel good, and they'll work. We head up to the falls, and I think maybe even park in the same spot where we'd left the truck the last time I was up here. It looks and feels familiar, and it makes me miss him and them. I throw my bag over my shoulder and spot the same familiar trail sign and then, directly to my right, what I know must be the tree—where I thought he might kill me but wished he'd fuck me instead.

What a strange turn of events.

Ezra: You can't avoid me forever, and you won't stay mad at me. You're just wasting our time.

Wasting our time. Our time is limited, and that is a problem in itself. I stuff my phone back into my pocket.

"You coming?" Emma says from the trailhead.

We walk the two-and-a-half miles through the woods in relative silence, taking the time to enjoy nature and the cool, morning air. It is always like this in the morning here. Cold, then climbing sometimes as much as fifty degrees by the after-noon.

"Almost there," she says.

We emerge from the treeline and follow alongside a river, and I hear the rushing water in the distance.

"This is one of my favorite places in the world," she says once it comes into view. "Not that I've been to very many places in the world, but I don't think it would change anything if I had."

And I don't blame her.

"It's...more than I expected," I say.

"It's from the rain yesterday. But the best view..." she says, pointing just over the hill on the other side of the river, "...is right through there. Come on. This is a good place to cross."

I follow her as she wades through the shallower water to the other side of the river, then again up the rocky terrain on the other side. When we reach the top, I find myself staring down at a slope covered in wildflowers of every color.

"They prefer a north-facing slope," she says. She sits down where we stand at the top, and I sit beside her. "They're smart to hide over on this side, though. Since you can't see them from the trail, the tourists don't come over here. They get to stay like this—wild and free to grow roots wherever they please. No one here to trample on them."

"There's this place back home where the poppies grow wild," I tell her. "We went there once when I was little. It was beautiful. People found out about it, though. They started going up there by the hundreds to get a good shot for their social media posts. They'd destroy them in just a few weeks. They don't grow like that anymore. They stopped trying."

"I'm glad you haven't stopped trying," she says. "I'm proud of you, Madison. I'm glad I've gotten to know you like this; I never thought I would. And you look happier and healthier than when you got here. You've got some color in your cheeks and a sense of contentment that I haven't seen in you before. I see you reading or playing your violin outside, and it feels like I'm looking at a different person. You remind me of your mother—of how she used to be, anyway. This place looks good on you, Maddie. So does he."

"Yeah, well. This place is temporary for me," I tell her. "I'm not sure I'll be able to keep being this person when I go back."

"Who's going to stop you?" she asks.

"I don't know if I should keep seeing him either. I can't keep him, it can't be serious. It's getting...uncomfortable."

Or maybe too comfortable is a more accurate description. I definitely don't hate him anymore. I feel *something*, and it never stops.

"It doesn't have to be serious to matter—for it to be what you need. Things don't mean less just because they're temporary.

We leave little pieces of ourselves with every person we meet and in every place we go."

"Leaving behind pieces of yourself doesn't sound like a good thing," I tell her.

"It can be a good thing. It can be the best thing. It's how we stay with them, and they stay with us even after we've gone or moved on."

"What happened to her?" I ask.

"Your mom?"

I nod.

"I don't know, not exactly. I was little. Our dad came and went, and then he went for good when I was still too young to remember who he was, and we struggled. Sometimes, we couldn't pay the bills—we wouldn't have heat or water or the pipes would freeze. Mom would take us to the Cross' until she came back with money. They lived just a few houses down from us. And they would take care of us."

"Ezra's dad's family, you mean?"

"Yep."

"That must have been hard for all of you," I tell her. I've heard some of the stories. About being cold and hungry and not seeing Grandma for days at a time. I never knew what she did, but it sounded like she did whatever it took. And whatever it took must have taken a toll on my mom; maybe that is why she hates this town and everyone in it.

Or maybe it was something else.

"It was harder for Amelia than for anyone else. I think she saw a lot more than I did. I think she knew a lot more. Maybe something happened that I don't know about, I'm not sure. She always felt like she had something to prove—like she had to make up for it somehow. That's why she did the pageants," she says. "It was kind of like gambling, but she won a lot, and we needed the money. She always said she was going to use it to get away, but there was never any left. But, she was smart and charming and got good grades, and she got into USF."

"She just never came back? Why? What happened?"

"That's the part of the story I don't know. What I do know is that shortly before she left, your grandma told us we wouldn't have to worry about money anymore, and Mel was different. I think there are three people who know what happened, but only two of them living, and you're just as likely to get an answer out of either of them as you are the woman we buried a few weeks ago. You can't ask them about any of this, Maddie. But I did wonder when I got older, if maybe someone hurt her, and they literally paid for it."

"And then what?"

"And then, he came with us to drop her off in San Francisco—and that was it. The car ride home was uncomfortable...too quiet. I think he knew she was never coming back."

"She didn't ever come home from college?"

"She did, but only once. See, Madison?" she says, attempting to adjust her somber tone to something more cheerful. "You can be whoever, whatever, wherever you want. Your mom managed it just fine."

I'm not sure how to reply. It doesn't sound like a good thing when she qualifies it like that—not when I can still hear the hurt in her voice.

I pull my phone out of my pocket and send out a text.

Me: Yeah. I'll be there later. Hiking with Emma.

What I don't say, even though maybe I should, is that I'm sorry. And I don't want to waste our time, either.

"Emma?"

"Yeah?"

"Did you never want to get married?"

"I almost did. Once. I couldn't give him what he wanted, though."

"What did he want?"

"Children."

"And you don't? Not even in the future?"

"The future isn't real, Maddie. Here," she says, plucking a dandelion seed head from the ground next to her. "Make a wish. Who do you want to be?"

I close my eyes, lean forward and blow.

Happy.

SEVENTEEN

MADISON

L ater that night, I walk up the hill and past the village to Ezra and Liam's house. I don't think I've ever seen the village this empty or the lake quite so full. It's packed with boats and the beach with people trying to find a good spot to watch the fireworks. Ava says the fourth is the worst time to go down to the lake, and that's why they don't. They started having this party instead.

I walk in the door to the packed house. There are probably a hundred people in here. It isn't what I expected. I guess I was thinking it'd be just the usual group and maybe a handful of other people.

I remember the last time I was at a party like this. It was at Weston's, and it didn't end well for me.

"Maddie! Over here!" Ava calls out from the kitchen.

Or maybe it did.

I walk over to the bar and sit next to Ava, Ari, and Chloe. "Hey, have you guys seen Ezra?"

"I think he's outside," Ariana says. "You have to do a boomerang with us first. Here—take a shot. Hold it up."

I take the photo with my friends, then the tequila shot and chase it with a lime. I think about how I'll miss this and try to stuff it down. I still have over a month left here. And it's okay to leave pieces. I could have this again at school if I wanted. I get to choose.

Afterward, I walk outside to find Ezra. It only takes me a few seconds to spot him sitting next to the fire pit with another girl on his lap. We make eye contact before I turn around and try to walk casually back inside to where my friends are.

We aren't a couple. Not even close. We were fucking on borrowed time, and that was it. Still, it hurts. This small thing hurts the way it should have hurt at the party at Weston's. It ties my stomach in uncomfortable knots, and my breath comes short. I feel my eyes burning, and I tell myself as I approach the kitchen that I'm not upset, that I don't care, and that it isn't even a big deal.

It's hard to swallow, so I chase it with a couple more shots.

"That was quick," Ava says. "Did you find him?"

"No," I lie, hopping onto the barstool beside her. "It's okay, though. I missed you guys."

"Aww," Chloe says. "That's sweet. We missed you, too."

She's sitting across the island next to a guy who leans in and whispers something in her ear. I wonder if that's the one they don't like—the one who just plays video games all day but is apparently good enough with his tongue that she doesn't care. I don't ask.

Ben approaches me and puts his arm around my shoulders. "I missed you, too, Maddie. I still owe you a ride around the lake on the jet ski that doesn't almost kill you."

"Yeah, I guess you do," I tell him. I throw back another shot and bite down on a lime. It's number four, and it's starting to hit me.

"You shouldn't touch things that don't belong to you," Ezra says from behind me.

"What are you talking about?" I ask, turning to face him.

"I'm not talking to you; I'm talking to him."

"Really?" Ben laughs. "That's not how people work. You can't call dibs. Isn't that what you said?"

"What is *he* talking about?"

"I came in it so it's mine," he says.

I scoff. "That's really fucking nice."

"This," he grabs me between my legs, then points to my lips, "and this."

"I'm not yours," I tell him, shrugging him off of me. "And you aren't mine either. And that's fine. That's how I want it to be."

"Really?"

"Yep."

"I need to talk to you. Let's go," he says.

"No, I don't want to. I'm having fun. I'm not going to go with you."

He looks like he wants to scream or break off a piece of the marble countertop he's leaning against in his hand. Since I'm starting to feel the effects of the tequila now, it makes me laugh. It's only a little bit, but it is right in his face.

Maybe I shouldn't have done that.

He grabs my hand and pulls me through the kitchen, the living room, and down the hallway around the corner.

"You're acting like a brat," he says, backing me into the wall. "I didn't do anything."

"It doesn't matter," I say. "I don't care what you did or didn't do."

"Really? You don't care?"

"Nope."

"You're lying," he says, "and you're bad at it."

He leans in and kisses me hard. I feel his teeth against mine before I feel his tongue in my mouth, and as much as I want to keep fighting with him, to be mad about it and put an end to it now before it really does matter, I can't. I fall into him, sliding my hands up his shirt and digging my nails into his back, hoping that it hurts and aching again to have him closer.

His hand moves up my thigh, underneath my dress. Then, his fingers dip down inside my underwear and rub against my clit.

"Oh, fuck," I moan. "I can't...someone is going to see us."

I can barely get the words out, already feeling myself coming apart. He doesn't stop, massaging me faster and holding me back against the wall with his other hand.

"You better come fast then," he says into my ear. "I don't want to have to rip someone's eyes out of their head for seeing you like this."

I do come fast. I dig my nails in harder as the pressure builds, burying my face in his chest in an attempt to muffle the desperate moans it pulls from me when I do.

"Get upstairs, Maddie. Unless you want me to fuck you here, too. Don't waste any more of our time."

"Okay," I tell him.

I follow him back around the corner, then up the stairs and to his room. As soon as the door closes behind him, he pulls his shirt over his head, then my dress over mine. He grabs my hand and leads me over to the bed. I unhook my bra and let it slide from my shoulders, then he climbs on top of me, pulling my soaked panties down over my hips and off my body before tossing them onto the floor.

He licks and sucks on my nipples before his mouth meets mine again. He kisses and bites at me while my hands explore his hard body, and I feel like it's been weeks—years maybe even—since I've been able to touch him instead of just days. I gasp when I feel the head of his cock slot against my pussy. My body arches up in response, begging him to fuck me.

"I love watching you wait for it," he says. "And the look on your face when you finally get what you want."

He grabs my legs underneath my knees and pins them against the bed, then finally gives me what I want, just like he said.

"Oh, god. Yes..." I cry out. He fills me slowly, watching me, before driving into me and fucking me hard into the mattress.

"Does that feel good, Maddie? Are you going to come again on my cock?"

"Yes!"

"Doesn't it feel better to listen to me?"

"Yes! Fuck!"

I come again, and his thrusts become shorter, more frantic before he stiffens with a loud groan, and I feel him pulsing inside me.

"You kept this from me for two fucking days," he says into my shoulder. "Don't do it again."

"Don't tell me what to do," I tease, breathless.

"I feel like we've been over this. You like it when I tell you what to do."

"I think I'd tell you anything you wanted to hear when you're fucking me like that."

"I'm going to remember that," he says.

"I don't like it when other people touch you," I say quietly.

"You don't have to worry about that, Maddie," he says. "No one else touches me."

Just then, there's a loud popping noise. I look out the windows that line the back wall and see fireworks have started exploding over the water.

"Come on," he says.

He tosses me his t-shirt before pulling on a pair of shorts, and I follow him out onto the balcony that runs along the back of the house. He sits down in a chair and pulls me into his lap, and we sit there watching them silently while the party goes on around us outside.

"This is beautiful," I tell him. "It's going to be so fucking hard when I have to leave this place."

"Who says you have to leave?" he asks. "Is someone running you out of town?"

"No," I say. "But I have to. I have to start school next month."

"You don't *have to*," he says. "You don't have to do anything. No one is going to make you. We do what we want. If you want to leave, that's different. But don't say that you have to."

I lean back against him and let it sit there.

"I like it now," I tell him. "Being held. You were right."

"I know you do," he says.

Then, we just watch the fireworks.

I wake up the next morning parched and with a headache. I didn't think I had that much to drink, but maybe I did—or maybe it has something to do with the combo of tequila, little sleep, and a day spent hiking under the sun. I slide out from under Ezra's arm, pull off his t-shirt, and put my own clothes back on before heading downstairs.

I walk into the kitchen, which is empty, but already smells like food. Ezra's dad is an early riser and apparently a big cooker. Every day I've woken up here, there's been food. I don't think anyone in my own home has eaten breakfast in the past six years.

I fill a glass of water, drink the entire thing, and then refill it before heading back to the staircase.

"Liam! Get over here!" I hear his dad call from the back porch.

I look around the first floor but don't see anyone else.

"Sorry," I call back. "Liam's not down here; it's just me."

"Oh...come here, Madison," he says. "I want to show you something."

I hesitate before joining him on the back porch. Granted, he had warmed to me a bit over the past few weeks, but we don't really speak much, and I haven't seen him at all since I learned about him and my mother.

"What is it?" I ask when the door closes behind me.

"See right there? In that clearing under that huge ponderosa?"

"I don't see anything," I tell him.

He leans down so his eye level matches my own. "You're too short," he says. "Here. Get up here."

It catches me off guard when he picks me up and sets me down on the porch railing.

"Do you see them now?" he asks, leaning against the railing next to me.

I follow where he's pointing, and I do see them—two bear cubs wrestling each other under the ponderosa pine while their mother watches.

"Oh, my god. Yeah. I do see them."

"Pretty cool, right? I've caught them on the backyard camera a couple of times, but I've never seen them out here in person."

Amazing. Wait, but...

I think of the hot tub.

"There's a camera in the backyard?" I blurt out the question before I can think better of it.

He frowns. "It's a nature cam. It doesn't face the house."

"Oh."

"Here," he says, handing me a pair of binoculars. "Go ahead and get a better look."

I bring them to my eyes and watch the bear cubs roll around and play, just like any other young mammal would. It's funny to think they'd grow up to be some of the most feared creatures in these mountains when they look like this now. I laugh just a little.

"You know, you're really hard to look at," he says, pushing a stray strand of hair away from my face.

I lower the binoculars from my eyes and turn to face him. I don't know what to say; I decide to apologize, even though I'm not sure what for, really. But before I can get the words out, his warm mouth covers my own. I know I should move, but I'm frozen for those few seconds until I hear the screen door slam, and Liam walks out.

"What the fuck is going on?" he asks.

"Shit," Ty says.

"I didn't..." I start. "That wasn't..."

"I'm sorry, Maddie," he says.

Before I even have to look over and address the sorry, the screen door swings open again, and Ezra walks out onto the porch.

"There you are," he says, wrapping his arms around my waist. "What are you looking at out here?"

"Bears," I tell him.

"Oh, no shit?"

I hand him the binoculars.

"That's awesome."

He sets them down on the railing, then kisses me on the neck.

"Are you still mad at me?" he whispers.

"No."

"What's everyone doing out here?" Ryan asks, stepping outside.

"Finally caught the bears we've been seeing on the camera," Ty says. "Right there under the ponderosa. Come in and eat when you're done. All of you."

After a few minutes, we all go in. I follow Ezra to the kitchen, and he hands me a plate. I follow suit and fill my plate with eggs, potatoes, and sausage with the rest of them, even though I'm not used to eating breakfast like this.

I carry my food and coffee over to the kitchen table and sit down.

"Nope," Ezra says. "We eat in the living room in front of the TV like heathens. Come on."

I look over and see his dad already eating in front of the television, and Liam and Ryan walk into the room and do the same. I pick up my plate again and follow him, then sit down on the couch next to him.

"I think my mom's spirit would leave her body if I ever brought food out of the kitchen like this," I say without thinking about it. Again, I want to kick myself.

"You're kidding, right?" Ty asks.

"Um, no. It's a very serious offense at our house."

"It's crazy how people change," he says, shaking his head and shoving more eggs into his mouth.

That's what I keep hearing.

"Is she still in real estate?" he asks.

"Oh, um. Kind of. She keeps her license active but only really works with friends and acquaintances. She mostly focuses on her philanthropy projects now."

He doesn't say anything, but he's biting back something; I can tell. Maybe something about how it's nice she has such a big heart for people she doesn't know, but not for her own family or her dying mother. It's something that's crossed my own mind before.

We finish eating in relative quiet, and afterward, I help them clean up before leaving.

On the walk home, I stop in front of the pharmacy.

You know, you're really hard to look at.

I step inside and make my way over to the boxed hair dye. I pick up a light brown and try to picture it as my own hair color, but it doesn't quite feel right.

I set it back down on the shelf and, from the corner of my eye, spot a box of pale pink.

I pick it up, head to the self-checkout to pay, then walk home.

EIGHTEEN

MADISON

"I like the hair," Ezra's dad says when I see him the next day. "It helps."

"Thanks."

I try not to look over at Liam when he says it, but I do it anyway. I expect him to be glaring at me, but he's not. He's glaring at his dad instead.

"I'll have to start calling you Cotton Candy instead of Dead Inside," Ezra says from the kitchen where the two of them are packing a cooler for the lake today.

"Thank you; that's an improvement," I tell him.

"Get over here, Cotton Candy," he says.

I roll my eyes, feigning protest, then cross the living room to the kitchen. He pulls me into his body, kisses my neck, and whispers in my ear, "Because you taste *so fucking sweet*."

He runs my earlobe through his teeth before he goes back to what he was doing.

How does he do this shit? How does he get me wet and bothered without even trying? It isn't fair.

"I hope you don't let him bully you or boss you around too much, Madison. I know how he can be."

"I don't," I lie.

"Yeah, Maddie. Don't let me boss you around. I know how you wouldn't like that at all," he teases far too obviously.

I wouldn't dare make eye contact with his dad now, but catch him shaking his head out of the corner of my eye before heading back upstairs.

They finish packing and loading the coolers into the truck, and we head to the lake.

"You'll like this, Maddie," Ezra says when we park.

"Like what? The lake?"

I've seen the lake before.

But not this spot.

We cross the street and move down toward the water. I set my things down and then look up at a cliff about fifteen feet up from the water where Chloe is standing...and she hurls herself forward.

It pulls a gasp from my throat before I see Ava cheering from the top, and I realize it was on purpose. Then, she follows her.

What is this? Cliff diving? He thought I would like this?

"I'm not doing it," I say before anyone asks.

"Oh, come on, Maddie. You're not scared, are you?" Ezra asks.

"Yeah, I am scared. I almost drowned a few weeks ago. I'm not eager to get back in the water *period,* let alone get back in like that."

"You'll do it," Ezra says. He walks away and starts climbing up the rocks. Liam follows, leaving Ryan and me alone on the shore.

"You're not going to do that, are you?" I ask him.

"Yeah, I will," he says. "I just need to warm up first. The water is fucking cold."

Yeah, I know how cold it is.

"He likes you," he tells me.

"Who? Ezra?"

He looks at me like I'm a fucking moron.

"I mean, yeah, I guess he does. But—not like that. It's not serious or anything."

"Are you sure?" he asks.

"Yeah. I'm sure. He said so himself. You can't act like he doesn't...hook up with random girls all the time or whatever. I don't need you to do that. I'm not under any kind of illusions otherwise."

"Oh, no. He does that. What he doesn't do is spend every single day and night with a girl, bring her everywhere he goes, kiss her, and hold her hand in public like he's been doing with you. That's *unusual.*"

I shake my head. "No. It's...if it's different, it's just because I'm leaving. It makes it easier for him or whatever. He doesn't have to worry about me. It's more convenient."

"If you say so," he says, shrugging.

Ava and Ariana climb out of the water and sit beside us. They grab a couple of beers from the cooler, and we all watch Liam and Ezra jump off the cliff at the same time. Ezra knocks him over in mid-air, causing him to land on his back. I hear it smack against the water from all the way over here.

Yeah, I'm not doing that.

But I am enjoying the day. I'm enjoying the sun and laughing with the girls, the slight buzz after a couple of beers. The three guys jump for a while, and we just sit, but somehow, this is so much better than the same day at a real beach with my friends back home ever was. I wonder why.

Eventually, Liam joins us again and starts digging through the bag for food.

"Oh, my god, you guys brought food?" Ava asks. "I want some."

"Don't touch my jalapeno chips, Ava," Ezra says, emerging from the water.

"Seriously? I didn't want them anyway, but that just makes me want to take the whole bag and dump it in the water."

I laugh hard. I love how his friends don't take any shit from him. Maybe I should be taking notes.

"Time to jump, Maddie," he says, pulling me to my feet.

"No," I tell him.

But he doesn't listen. He throws me over his shoulder and carries me to the top of the hill.

"Seriously, Ezra. I'm *scared*. And not in a fun way."

"All the more reason to do it," he says, setting me down. "Go ahead. Go get a good look over the edge. It isn't that high."

But he's lying. It is high. And it only looks higher from the top than it did from the bottom. My palms start to sweat.

"We'll go together, okay?" he says. "One...two..."

"No, don't count yet. I'm not ready—"

But I never hear a three, and he pushes me over the edge. I fall for what feels like a minute, my stomach dropping out while I do, before hitting the water.

It's cold, but it doesn't hurt. I go under but come back up easily, and it isn't a hard fight to stay on the surface like it was the last time I was in the lake. The water is smooth instead of choppy. I feel relief wash over me right before he comes back up.

"Wasn't that fun?"

"You...asshole!" I lunge for him and try to push him under, but he doesn't move.

He effortlessly pushes me off of him. "I can touch here."

"Well, congratulations."

"Did you like it? Are you still scared?" he asks.

And no, I didn't like it. But I realize that I'm not scared anymore either. The water doesn't feel ominous like it has since that day. In fact, as soon as I broke the surface, I stopped thinking about it altogether. I've been treading the calm, clear lake waters for minutes now, not frightened at all.

Like ripping off a Band-Aid, I guess. That's one way to do it.

"No," I admit. "You pushed me off a cliff, though."

"I helped you," he says. "See how I keep helping you? Don't you think it's about time for you to start thanking me?"

"Is that why you did it? To help me?"

"That, and I liked it."

He pulls me back against him so I can feel how much he liked it. I wrap my legs around his waist and his hard dick presses against me through his shorts. I reach down and begin to stroke it in my hands.

"What are you doing, Madison?" he cautions. "You really want me to fuck you out here in front of everyone? Because I'll do it, but they're going to notice."

"No," I tell him. "But they don't have to notice this."

"Fuck, Maddie," he groans. "Just so you know, when we get back home, I'm going to fuck you until you can't walk for this."

"That's not a deterrent," I tell him, picking up the pace, stroking and working his cock. I risk a glance over at our friends, but they all seem sufficiently occupied. No one is watching us, and no one seems to be making any moves to get back into the water.

"How much is this turning you on right now?" he asks. And the answer is a lot, but I hadn't realized I'd started moving against him with my hand, too. "I'm going to cum. I want to finish inside you, Maddie."

He pushes my bottoms to the side and I bite back a moan when he buries his dick inside me. He strokes my swollen clit with two fingers and, when I feel him jerking inside me, I come, too.

"They might have noticed that," I tell him. I don't want to look.

"You started it," he says, shrugging.

If they did, they don't say anything. We get out of the water and return to our friends. Ezra wraps a towel around me and pulls me onto his lap, touching me and kissing me all afternoon.

'Like a boyfriend would,' I think. He holds me and kisses me in front of his friends like a boyfriend. He texts me all day and waits for me to get off work. We do spend every day together, and he always invites me out with his friends, which is more than the guy I was with for three years ever did. He's the only person who holds me. I think he wrecked a boat for me, too.

But Ezra isn't my boyfriend. He couldn't be. This is temporary and I can't keep him, no matter how much I need it.

And this time, when I leave, I know it won't be painless. I can already feel it. Sometimes, I think about leaving, and it hurts in the way Emma described—the way I expected a broken heart to feel and the way I waited to hurt before, but it never came.

I won't be so lucky this time around. There are consequences to waking up, to coming alive.

At the end of the day, we go back to his house, tired and sunburnt, and we fuck again.

And afterward, he says, "It's your turn to play for me."

"No way," I tell him. "I'm too tired."

"You have to," he says. "I've done it like five times for you."

"Fine," I tell him.

I reluctantly roll out of bed, lift the guitar from its stand, and sit on the stool.

"Make it a love song again," he says.

I shake my head. "I'm definitely not making it a love song."

"Maddie, you better."

I roll my eyes and try to think of anything I can pull off. I really *don't* play guitar. And I don't want to sing a love song.

But I do it anyway.

And I sing this person who isn't my boyfriend at all to sleep.

I wake up a few hours later alone. And I can feel that I'm alone. I look around the room, but I don't see Ezra. I'm just about to lie back down and close my eyes when I see him through the back windows. He's sitting on the ground on the balcony, smoke billowing around him.

I open the door and step outside, the strong, distinct scent of weed hitting me when I do.

"I didn't know you smoked," I tell him, sitting beside him.

"I don't...not a lot anyway," he says. "Here."

He holds the joint out toward me. I shake my head. "I don't smoke either. I don't like how it makes me feel."

"How does it make you feel?" he asks.

"Panicked," I say. "I think that's the last thing I need."

I was already panicking, watching the remaining days of summer slip through my fingers. No matter how much I slowed down, no matter how long the days were or how hard I tried to hold on to them—to bathe in them—they were vanishing. The sun would set, late but certainly, and I'd count each one as a loss.

"What are you doing out here?" I ask.

"Thinking," he says.

"What are you thinking about?"

"You."

"Do I want to know?"

"I'm wondering what your life is like at home. I'm wondering what your friends are like. Do you miss them?"

"No," I tell him. "I don't think I have friends at home. Because I don't miss them. I don't think they miss me, either."

"Are you going to miss us?"

"Yes."

"Are you going to miss me?" he asks, turning to face me.

"I already miss you," I tell him quietly.

"Why is it better there? Is it the money?"

"It's not better there. I don't care about the stuff. I wasn't happy there."

"I know I'm not an easy person to be around," he says. "I know I'm difficult. But it's easy for me to be around you. I thought I liked being alone, but I think I was lonely. I was just used to it, so I didn't really notice...if that makes sense."

"Yeah," I tell him. "It makes sense. It's easy to get stuck in a pattern and decide that it's good enough. I did it."

"I haven't had a bad day in a while. I used to have a lot of them. I think it's because of you."

I don't know what to say to any of this. He's high...really high. I take the joint from his hands and level the playing field, inhaling and coughing when it burns the back of my throat.

"Do I make you happy?" he asks. "You said you weren't happy there. You seem happy. But I could try harder. I'd do that for you."

"I am happy. You don't have to do anything else. Just...hold me and play for me and embarrass me in public. And break shit with me when I need to, and that's enough. I'm happy."

"When you go, I'll be lonely again. I think I'll notice this time."

"Yeah," I tell him. "Me too."

"Welcome to my secret dark pain, Madison Ridgeway," he says. "Maybe I have some, after all."

He pushes up from the floor, throws the roach over the balcony, walks back inside, and crawls into bed without saying another word.

NINETEEN

EZRA

"Y ou're *fucked*," my brother says after I shut the door behind Maddie. My dad howls with laughter.

"What do you mean?" I ask.

"You like her," he says.

"It doesn't matter. She's leaving in less than six weeks. That was always the case," I tell him, trying to appear uninterested—in both the conversation and the girl that just left.

"Does she know how much you like her?" Ryan asks.

I don't know. But I also know that it wouldn't matter. She's not staying, and I don't play stupid games or fuck around with long-distance bullshit. It's not an option for me. Not one I would ever even consider.

And Maddie has a life plan that doesn't involve anything like me. All I get to be is a stupid fucking story—exactly what

I didn't want. But I'll get over it. I think it will be easy even, because I know it's coming.

Even if I really like her. And I do. I fucked up, and I got too close. It was too easy not to, so we started spending every day together—because I wanted to and so did she, and what's the point in denying myself something I want?

That's what I told myself, anyway. It was always easy to be with her—I think I told her that. And maybe it wasn't on purpose, but surely she did know how I feel. She'd notice.

I don't say all of that.

"I think so," I reply.

"No," Ryan says. "Not you think so. It's no, then. There's no way she does. Did you tell her? Are you even nice to her? Do you take her on dates?"

"You guys don't go on dates. Do you even like each other?"

"We go on dates all the time, you dumbass," Liam says.

My dad laughs again.

"I think I am pretty fucking nice to her," I tell them. "Probably nicer than most of the people in her life have been."

I try and fail not to make eye contact with my dad after that one slips out.

"But," I add, "like I said—it doesn't matter. Not beyond five or six weeks from now."

"But what if she stays?" Liam asks.

"What do you mean?"

"What if she knew and she stayed?"

"She wouldn't. And I don't think I'd want her to."

"She might," Liam says. "If she knew, she might. I think she might love you."

"That's fucking ridiculous. I've barely known her for more than a month. I have better shit to do than listen to this," I get up from the couch and head toward the staircase.

"You have nothing to do. And it's not ridiculous. As the only person in this fucking family who knows what love looks like, maybe you should listen to me."

"Now, you're just being dramatic, Liam. You are not the only person in this family who knows what love looks like, for god's sake," Dad says.

"What? You gonna get in on this shitshow and run your mouth, too? You don't even like Maddie."

"I don't know about that," Liam says. "From what I've seen, Dad *really* likes Maddie."

"What's that supposed to mean?" I ask.

"Nothing." He narrows his eyes at Liam, then turns back to me. "I like her just fine. And I'm not getting in on anything. The only thing I will say is that no one gets everything they want in life, but we get even fewer of the things we don't even bother asking for."

"How prophetic; thank you," I say sarcastically before turning and continuing up the stairs.

"I'm glad you liked it. I've got one more for you," he says to my back.

"Don't wanna hear it," I shout over my shoulder, continuing down the hallway.

"You'll live to regret the things you don't say a hell of a lot more than the things you do."

I close the door behind me and pretend I didn't hear him. I wasn't going to listen to him. But it stays with me anyway, and I can't help but to wonder if he's speaking from personal experience—if he suffered for the things he never said or asked for. I don't remember exactly what I said last night, but I am pretty sure I all but told her I wanted her to stay.

But I didn't ask.

Fuck it. My dad has his own ghosts, and they are his problem, not mine.

Still, it's Liam's question that stays with me.

What if she did stay? What if I want her to?

The next couple of weeks go by far too fast for comfort. I spend my days working and almost every night with Maddie or with Maddie and our friends. I blame Liam and his shitty fucking commentary for my new uneasiness. I wasn't thinking about whether she would stay or even consider staying until he put that shit in my head.

Now, I think about it all the time.

What if she stayed?

She said she wasn't even happy there, right? So, why wouldn't she stay?

I think she might love you.

Did I want her to love me? I'm not sure. If she does love me, then she's seriously fucking deranged.

But that doesn't bring me much comfort because I already know that she *is* seriously fucking deranged.

She walks past me in another tiny ass pair of shorts and a crop top and slides into the booth next to Ava. Pink hair, pink lipstick, and freckles on her sunburnt cheeks and shoulders.

"What?" she asks from across from me. "Why are you looking at me like that?"

"This isn't how we're doing this," I tell her.

"What do you mean?"

"Come here."

"I am here."

"Get up and walk over here."

She smiles, gets up, and walks over to my side of the table, and I pull her onto my lap. "That's more like it."

She relaxes, not like before, then wraps her arms around my neck and kisses me.

"You know, you're kind of turning into one of those gross couples people don't want to be around," Ava says.

"We're not—" Maddie starts before letting it fall off. She shakes her head and takes a swig of her beer.

A couple. That's what she was going to say. We're not a couple. And we aren't. I'd tell anyone else the same thing if they asked.

It doesn't mean I like hearing her say it.

Does she know how much you like her? Did you tell her?

Ugh, fuck them.

I wrap my arms around her waist and hold her tight against me.

"You know, you make me really happy," I tell her quietly in her ear.

She eyes me suspiciously. "Is this what you look like happy?"

"You know what I look like when I'm not."

"Don't go soft on me now, Dead Inside," she says.

I shake my head. She's not taking me seriously. "When do you get off work next Saturday?"

"Saturday? Um, I don't know. I think I close...why?"

"I want to take you somewhere. Will you go with me?"

"Where are we going?"

"It's a surprise; I can't tell you."

"Most of your surprises have been crimes," she says. "Is this going to be another crime?"

"It might be a small crime. Not one that anyone is going to notice, though. We won't get into any trouble. I promise."

"What's the crime?" she asks.

"Trespassing," I tell her. "Maybe squatting. Indecent exposure, if I'm lucky. You'll like it."

I pick her up at her house after she closes the store on Saturday night, and we head northwest, further into Deschutes National Forest. The drive is less than an hour. She asks for hints on the way there, and I don't give her much to go on.

"So that's it, then? Just we aren't leaving Oregon, and we aren't invited?"

"Yep. And you'll like it—I told you. So don't worry about it."

"I'm always worried when I'm with you," she says.

"Liar."

"Are we going to your mom's house?"

"Do you want me to take you to meet my mother?" I ask.

"No," she says.

She's lying again. Interesting.

"Just sit back and enjoy the scenery, Maddie. We're almost there."

She takes off her seatbelt, slides across the bench seat until she's up against me, and rests her head on my shoulder for the rest of the drive.

Eventually, we turn off the highway and onto a side road, then I slow down, looking for a newer dirt road that would be easy to miss in the dark, even though I have been here a few times myself over the past month. I just barely manage to turn in time.

"You're finally going to kill me," she says. "That's the surprise, isn't it?"

"No, it wouldn't make sense to kill you. Not for a couple more weeks, anyway," I tell her.

Eventually, we pull up next to the structure, and I put the truck in park. We both get out of the driver's side door, and I close it behind her.

"What is it?" she asks. "A treehouse?"

"It is...one of those super fancy glamping treehouses with a bathroom and electricity that you rich people love so much. In progress, anyway. We've been working on it for a while now. He wants to throw a whole collection of them back here—whoever the guy is. Probably another one of your friends. Someone you know."

"Yeah, probably a friend," she smiles. "This is really cool. You're right. We—*the rich people*—do love these."

"After you," I say, gesturing towards the ladder.

"How polite," she says and starts to climb.

"Not really. I just wanted to stare at your ass on the way up."

She laughs, and I follow her up, staring at her ass the entire way.

"Now, like I said—it's not finished," I tell her as I push open the door. "And we will have to leave early. Like, really early and take all this stuff with us. But I think—"

"Wait. Did you do all of this?"

"Yeah," I say, shrugging.

The woman looks at me like I have two fucking heads.

It really isn't much. The treehouse is just over five hundred square feet. In the front of the room, you can still tell it's a construction site. There are cabinets and light fixtures against the walls and on the floors. Wood stains and various tools. On the backside, there's a makeshift bed on pallets that should be comfortable enough to do only a little bit of sleeping, string lights, and a bottle of wine.

"Why?" she asks.

I shake my head. "Do you want to see something? Come here."

I walk to the back of the room and through another door that leads out to a deck.

"This is some kind of suped-up telescope—I guess the dude is super into astronomy—and this is a dark sky spot, so you can see a lot. The thing must have run him like ten grand."

"Oh, yeah. It definitely did," she says. I have no idea how to use it, really. But apparently, she does. It doesn't surprise me. She walks up to the telescope, removes the cover, and starts to focus on something.

"This is amazing," she says. "Thank you. You're right—this is a good surprise. I've never seen a telescope like this; I've never seen the sky like this. Come here—look."

I step toward her and look through the eyepiece.

"That's Venus," she says.

"Are you studying astronomy or something?" I ask.

"No," she says. "I just like it."

"Well, what are you going to study? I never asked. Do you even know?"

"Um, yeah. Philanthropy and Performing Arts."

I laugh.

"What? Why are you laughing? Don't laugh."

"I'm sorry," I say, still laughing. "I'm so sorry. You probably don't realize this, but giving away money and playing the violin are not viable career options for most of us."

"Cool. Make fun of me some more. Thank you, and I hate you," she says. But she laughs, too.

"You make it too easy," I tell her.

"*You're* too easy."

"Is that supposed to be an insult?"

She rolls her eyes before she walks back inside. She picks the wine bottle up off the floor and uncorks it, then takes a hard pull from the bottle and lies back on the makeshift bed.

"You know, you're going to have to stop being nice to me like this. Or I'm not going to want to leave."

That's the idea.

"I'm always nice to you," I tell her. "Take your clothes off."

"Make me," she says.

I lunge toward the bed, and she screams; she tries to scurry away but doesn't make it very far. I grab her by the ankle and pull her back, then climb on top of her and pin her arms to the bed.

"You had to know how this was going to go," I tell her.

"So what if I did?" she laughs.

I pull her shorts and her thong down over her hips and bury my face in her pussy.

"Ah, fuck...that's not going to help either," she says.

Again, that's the idea.

I lick and suck her clit and fuck her with my fingers until she's shamelessly bucking her hips against my face, then squeezing my head between her thighs when she comes on me. It doesn't take long—by now, I've figured out exactly what she likes.

Once her legs relax at her sides, I pull her toward me, burying myself inside of her in one hard thrust while she's still recovering from her orgasm.

Just how I like her. A wet, sticky, shaking mess.

"Ezra...oh, god...."

"Fuck. So wet and tight," I say, rolling my hips into her. "So good."

I spread her legs open wide with my hands and bury myself hard and deep inside of her, watching her tits bounce and her eyes roll back in her head with each relentless thrust.

"Oh, god. That feels so good. Harder," she pants. "Hurt me."

"Be good," I tell her. "Say please."

"Please, Ezra."

It's all I can do to keep from coming when she begs me like that, but somehow I do. I give her what she wants and lean forward and bite her chest hard; she screams, body arching up toward me, begging for more.

I wrap my fingers around her throat and squeeze hard enough to quiet her while I fuck her and don't let go until I feel her pussy pulsing around my cock.

"Ah, fuck," I groan, coming hard inside her. "Shit...that was so good. Are you okay, Maddie?"

"Yeah," she says, still out of breath. "Yeah, I'm great."

"Fuck. You sure you want to leave?" I ask her.

"I don't know," she says. "I'm trying not to think about it. I'm trying to be like Emma, but it's hard."

"Emma? What do you mean?"

"Emma says that the future isn't real and we shouldn't waste time worrying about it. She says it's okay for good things to be temporary and to just enjoy them for what they are."

"Emma is a hippie," I tell her.

She laughs. "Yeah, maybe. It sounds right, though, doesn't it? I love it here, and if I think too much about the fact that I'm going to have to leave soon, then I love it a little less. I can't enjoy it like I want to. So, I don't. I don't think about it. And I tell myself that just because I have to leave doesn't mean that it has to be like it was before."

"What do you mean like before?"

Was she talking about that guy? Was she seriously talking about going home and getting back together with him?

"I don't want to be dead inside. I don't want to be the person who just closes the door and leaves and doesn't even cry. Fuck," she says and wipes her eyes with her fingers. "I'm fucking sorry. Let's talk about anything else. Or just stop talking. That'd probably be best."

"Maddie, you don't *have* to go," I say.

"Yeah, I know, but...I really do."

"No, what I mean is...I don't want you to. I want you to stay here with me. I didn't go to college, and I don't have a lot of money, but I could take care of you. I could do a good job, I think."

"Ezra, I don't—"

"I'm not telling you that you have to decide now. I just want you to know—in case it matters—that I want you to stay. And that if you did stay, I would want to be with you."

It's quiet—deathly quiet for a very long minute—before she says, "Yeah. If I stayed, I would want that, too."

TWENTY

EZRA

We pack up and leave early the next morning, getting back to Maddie's at an earlier time than we'd typically even be out of bed.

"Do you want to come in? Go back to sleep?" she asks when we pull into the driveway.

"Yeah," I tell her. "I do."

We get out of the truck and walk to the front door, but when Maddie turns the knob, it doesn't move.

"Shit," she says. "I forgot my keys."

I grab my keys from my back pocket and flip through to the one I know will open the door. She glares at me when it turns in the padlock, and I push open the door.

"You should give that back."

"I will...when you leave."

She shakes her head and walks inside. I follow her up the staircase.

"I'm going to go check and see if Emma is here," she says. "I'll be right back."

"Hey, Maddie? There's something I need to tell you," I say. I'd agreed to keep it a secret, but that was before we were like this. I remember how upset she had been when she found out that I knew about our parents. I don't want this to be the same thing. "It's about Emma."

"Just a sec," she says. She pushes open Emma's bedroom door and steps inside.

"Emma?" she says. "EMMA?"

There's something wrong with her voice—something that makes the hair on my neck stand on end.

And then, there's the scream.

Inside the room, everything looks quiet—normal and in its place. Except for the hysterical girl leaning over her aunt, screaming.

I grab her by her shoulders and pull her back. "Go call 911, Maddie."

"I can't," she sobs.

"You *have* to! Get out of here, Madison. Call 911."

She pulls her phone out of her pocket with shaky hands—far too shaky to dial. I grab it from her, hit the three numbers, and press send.

She brings the phone to her ear, and I start CPR. It doesn't take long for me to realize it is pointless. Emma is cold...too cold. She's been like this for a long time.

"Leave the room, Madison!" I shout as she recites the address to the operator. Once she does what I say, I close the door behind her and lock it. I sink down onto the floor and pull my own phone out of my pocket. He answers on the second ring.

"Dad...I need help," I choke out. "Emma is dead."

I leave the room when I hear the ambulance arrive and help Madison down the stairs and onto the couch.

"I need to be in there," she says. "I don't want her to be alone. I want to go with her. Was she breathing? Did it work?"

"Just let them do their job, Madison," I tell her, even though I already know how this is going to end.

The stretcher rolls out of the room a few minutes later with no sense of urgency. Maddie sees it, and I see the panic in her eyes.

"No!" she yells. "NO! Is she in there? Is she in that bag? What's going on? You're supposed to help her!"

"I'm so, so sorry, honey," an EMT says to her. "There was nothing we could do."

"What do you mean?" she sobs. "She was young. She was fine! She can't just die. She can't be dead."

She gets out of my grip and lunges at the EMT, hitting him hard with both of her fists before I can grab her from behind. Sometime during the chaos, my dad must have walked in because he steps in front of her now and places both hands on her shoulders.

"Sweetheart, I am so sorry. So, so sorry. You need to sit down."

"I *can't!* I need to go with her," she says as the last one leaves and closes the door.

"You can't go with her. They aren't going to let you go. She's gone, Madison."

"What?"

She hears the click, and her eyes dart to the door and then back again in panic.

"No!"

"Baby, sit," he says again.

"Ezra, is she dead?"

"I'm sorry, Madison."

"Is she dead?" she asks me again.

"Yeah, Maddie. She's dead."

She hangs her head in her hands and weeps.

"Sweetheart," my dad says, "Emma was sick. She's been sick for a while now. She was terminal."

"No, she was fine," she says. "She was fine. I was with her almost every day, and she was *fine*. She just...got migraines. And stomach aches sometimes, but that's fine."

"She had ovarian cancer," he tells her. "It was very aggressive, and treatment wasn't helping."

"I'm so sorry, Maddie. She didn't want to tell you. She didn't want you to worry, and she asked me not to say anything. I was going to tell you, but—"

"So you lied to me? Again? And now my aunt is dead?"

"No," I say. "No. I did what she asked me to because it was what she wanted. She said she wanted to get to know you as a person, not a sick person. I didn't think—"

"You didn't think what!?"

I don't know how to answer. I wasn't the only one who knew this secret—a lot of people knew. Ava knew. I didn't think that I would ever give a shit about Madison when I agreed to it. I also didn't know how close it was to the end because Maddie was right, and most of the time, she really didn't seem sick.

I didn't think she'd drop dead while she was here or that Madison would find her body. *That's* what I didn't think would happen.

Now, she *really* wouldn't stay. The realization hits me like a punch to the gut.

"Maddie, I need to call your mother," my dad says. "Can I borrow your phone?"

She points at the coffee table without saying a word. I grab it, unlock it, hand it to my dad, and he walks out onto the back porch.

"I was going to tell you," I say again. "I was about to tell you."

"It doesn't matter now."

We sit next to each other in silence until my dad comes back inside.

"Let's go home," he says, wiping his own tears and closing the back door behind him.

"Come on, Maddie."

I take her hand, and she gets up off the couch and follows me out the door and into the truck without saying a word.

"Maddie?"

She looks at me.

I'm not sure what I want to say. She hasn't spoken since we left the house. It's on the tip of my tongue to ask her if she's okay, but that's a stupid fucking question. You're not okay after you find a dead body. Especially not when that body belonged to someone you loved.

"What do you want? Do you want something to eat?"

"I want to take a shower," she says, looking down at her hands. "Can I?"

"Yeah. Yeah, of course. Come on."

She follows me up the staircase and down the hall to the bathroom. I close the door behind us and turn on the shower. Maddie, still in her clothes from last night and my flannel, sits down on top of the toilet. She hangs her head again and cries behind a curtain of pink-blonde hair.

"Hey." I kneel down in front of her and cup her face in my hands. "What can I do?"

"Nothing," she says. "I'm fine."

She's not fine, but okay.

"Coffee?"

"Sure," she says sadly. "Ezra?"

"Yeah?"

"I think you're my best friend."

"You're my best friend, too, Maddie."

I help her undress and climb into the shower, and then I head downstairs. I smell coffee brewing before I get there, so I sit on a barstool and wait.

"I'm so sorry, son," my dad says.

I shake my head. Why was he sorry for me? Emma wasn't my aunt. She wasn't my family.

But I'd touched a dead body today. Put my mouth on a dead body. And that dead body had belonged to someone who was close enough to a friend. And she was something else to him, too.

"Are you okay?" I ask him.

He takes one bite of his food, then scrapes it all into the trash and throws the plate in the sink.

"Emma was like a little sister to me. I knew how bad it was. I knew she didn't have much time left. But it doesn't make it much better."

"Is her mom coming?"

"Yeah," he says. "It's about a seven-hour drive. She'll probably be here in six now."

"How'd that go?" I ask.

He just shakes his head.

I hear the three distinct beeps that indicate the coffee has finished brewing, then I go to the cabinet and grab a couple of mugs.

"She's going to leave now," I tell him.

It isn't a question, but he answers anyway.

"Yeah."

I walk upstairs with the coffee and knock a couple of times before pushing open the bathroom door. Maddie is sitting down under the shower water, leaning against the edge of the tub.

"Here's your coffee." I kneel next to the tub and set it down next to her, then wipe some of the wet hair away from her face.

She picks up the mug like maybe she will take a drink, then sets it back down. She stares at it for a minute and then turns to me with mascara-streaked cheeks, her wide, sad blue eyes meeting mine.

"I love you," she says.

I lean down and kiss her forehead.

"I'm going to go get you something to wear," I tell her, then leave the bathroom.

TWENTY-ONE

EMMA-TWO DAYS AGO

"What was it that you needed that was such an emergency that it had to happen at 10:00 PM?" Lisa asks when I open the door.

"I need your assistance," I tell her. "As my best friend and as a notary. I've made some changes to my Last Will and Testament."

"Where's Maddie?" she says, looking around. "Does she know now?"

"She's not here," I tell her. "She's with Ezra. I doubt she'll be back tonight. Sit."

She pulls out a chair, sits at the table, and looks at me—waiting.

"It's going to be soon, Lis. I can feel it."

"Don't say that," she says. "Don't talk like that. You've been doing so well. You even went hiking a few weeks ago."

"Yeah, I felt great a few weeks ago. That happened to Mom, too—before she went. It's bad, Lisa. The last few days have been hard. I can't eat. I haven't eaten, and I don't want to. And it hurts all the time."

"Well, that's just—" she starts, then stops. We've known this day was coming for a while. I've accepted my fate; I made plans. When it became apparent that the treatment wasn't going to do anything except maybe kill me a little bit slower, I decided to stop and just live while I could instead. I was watching my mother suffer and die slowly at the time, and as soon as I made the decision, I knew it was the right thing to do. It felt right—like a weight lifted from my shoulders or, maybe more accurately, from crushing my insides. It felt better to stop fighting forces out of my control and just give in. Breathe deeper, move slower. Make art while I still can and leave tiny pieces of myself and my soul behind in it and with the people and places I've grown to love.

That's how we make it count. It doesn't matter if it doesn't seem fair. There is no fair.

"They said six months. It's been five," I tell her.

"People take six months and turn it into years all the time," she says. But as much as she wants it to be true, even she doesn't believe it. I can hear it in her voice.

"This is it," I say simply.

"What about Maddie?" she asks.

"This is about Maddie."

Getting to know Maddie over the past couple of months was the dying wish I'd never bothered to make—something the universe decided to reward me with in my final hour, and I hadn't anticipated it. And I got to know her as a person, not a sick person. It was a gift, and probably my last one.

But I couldn't have asked for a better one.

Well, maybe just one more.

If my insides didn't already hurt like they do, they'd hurt a little bit more now. My sister's face flashes in my mind. The one who bathed me and tucked me in at night, the one who made sure I got something to eat every day even if it meant that she didn't. And then she left.

"That poor girl..." she starts, choking back a sob.

"Don't start crying on me now. We have business to attend to." I set the papers in front of her. "Only small changes. Maybe that's not right; what I mean is only a couple of big changes. The business and the rights to all my designs still go to you. The house and all of my personal belongings—those are going to go to Maddie instead of Mel."

She stares at me.

I get out my pen. "Ready?"

"Are you sure?"

"It's the right thing to do. It belongs with her. She's supposed to be here—I can feel it. This house has been home to a Walker woman for the better part of a century. It's what it wants. You know Mel would rather sell it than look at it."

And I understood—to an extent. She'd been through a lot of pain here. But there was a lot of love, too. A lot of good. I loved her. Lisa loved her. A lot of other people loved her, too.

"She won't be happy," Lisa says.

"Mel? About the house?"

"About any of this. How am I supposed to tell her about you? That you were sick and...?"

"She wouldn't understand," I tell her. "She would have wanted to take over. We would have fought about it, and she would have made it worse."

"Still, you should call her. You should say something."

"I'll see her when she comes to get Maddie in a couple of weeks," I tell her.

Unless she decides to stay. With him.

"I'll say something then—something that will count as goodbye. I'll make sure that it's good. I'll make sure she knows that I love her, and I'll make sure I leave it in a way that will bring her peace."

Unless I don't make it that long.

I don't think I've asked for too much up until now. I know I'm long past the bargaining stage, and the die has been cast. I asked to outlive my mother—for her not to have to watch her daughter die. Now, I just wanted a couple more weeks. Just until Maddie goes home.

And then, if it gets worse, I'll take care of it myself. I'll have a nice dinner and drinks with my friends, and afterward, I'll come home, put on my comfiest pajamas and my favorite movie, then I'll go to bed, and I won't wake up.

We sign the necessary changes, and I rack the papers and set them aside.

"See? Hardly painful at all."

But her eyes tell me that's not true.

"Do you want a drink?" I ask, pouring two glasses of gin before she can answer.

"Do you think you should be drinking?" she asks.

"I don't think any of that matters at this point."

I set the glass down in front of her, and she sobs.

"Don't," I tell her. "Please don't do that."

"What am I supposed to do when you're gone? What am I going to do without my best friend?"

"You're going to keep doing what you always do. You're going to keep being an amazing mother and friend. You're going to take care of the store and all of the beautiful things we made together. And you'll remember me when it's important. And I want it to make you happy, not sad."

"It's hard. It's hard to think of the end. Most of the time, I look at you and see the amazing woman you've become. Sometimes, I still see the little girl sitting in the corner of the gym, waiting for Mel and me to be done with cheer practice. I feel like there's something else I should have done. What do I say to her?"

"There is nothing else you could have done. You did everything. We thought of everything," I tell her.

But I understood the sentiment. I just buried my mother, and even though I knew it was better for her now than it was in the end and that there was nothing I could do, some days, it still hurts. And even though I wanted to outlive her, some days when I hurt and when I think of dying and feel scared, I cry for my mom and wish she were here to make it better.

"So that's what you tell her. You tell her you did everything. That you took care of me and you were my best friend. Remind her that, for a long time, you were her best friend also. And that, when she's ready, you'll take care of her, too."

TWENTY-TWO

MADISON

I sit in the bottom of the shower, coffee cup in my hands.

I told him that I loved him.

What the fuck was I thinking?

I take a drink, force it down. I take another, force it down. I pour the brown liquid into the tub and watch the water from the shower wash it down the drain.

The door opens, and Ezra sets some clothes on the bathroom counter next to the sink and then closes it.

It's been on the tip of my tongue for a while now, but I managed to hold it in because it didn't make any sense. Has it been long enough to love someone? Is there a time requirement, and does it matter?

I remember when Ethan told me that he loved me. We had been dating for five or six months, so it seemed like the right amount of time for him to say it and for me to say it back. I don't really know if I felt it. It wasn't anything like how I love Ezra.

I did a good job keeping it to myself, though. Living in the moment and letting it just be what it was instead of worrying about what it wasn't. What the fuck happened?

But I knew what happened.

He asked me to stay. I found my aunt's dead body.

On my worst day, I told him I loved him, and he walked away and closed the door.

Everything hurts in a completely new and paralyzing way.

Before this summer, I had never seen a dead body. When I saw my grandma in her casket, it was...different. It was like it wasn't her. She was so much smaller than I remembered, so frail looking. She had too much makeup on, and between that, the embalming, and her sunken cheeks, I almost didn't even believe it was her. It made it easier.

It wasn't like that when I saw Emma.

Eventually, I turn off the shower and get dressed in the sweats and t-shirt Ezra left for me. I leave the bathroom and walk into his empty bedroom, close the door behind me, and crawl under the covers alone.

If I could cry any more, I would. But I can't. I wish I could just be dead inside. Again.

I don't know how long I'm in there alone before he comes in. He climbs into bed behind me, wraps his arms around me, and kisses the back of my head.

"Hey, Maddie?"

"Please don't talk to me," I say. "I don't want to talk right now."

So, we don't talk. I don't know if I sleep; if I do, it's dreamless and just barely. I come in and out of some sort of almost-sleep haze, each time needing to remind myself that what happened this morning was real. I didn't imagine it. Everything that felt good is gone.

I won't be able to be the same.

I don't know how long it goes on like that, but eventually, I'm brought out of one of those almost-sleep patterns by a knock on the door.

"Hey," Liam says. "Someone just pulled up. I think maybe Maddie's mom is here."

That gets my attention. I drag my impossibly heavy body out of bed, out the door, and down the staircase.

And there she is in all her glory: jeans and a t-shirt, dark sunglasses, shoulder-length blonde hair left down, arms crossed across her chest. It's more casual than I almost ever see her out of the house, and it trips me up for a minute.

"Jesus Christ, Madison," she says, shaking her head when she sees me. "What the hell did you do to your hair?!"

Do I look like shit? Probably. Yes, I do.

How can she care about that right now?

"Don't do that to her," Ty says. "Don't you dare pick on her right now."

"Don't tell me how to treat my own fucking kid, Ty," she says back. I can't see her eyes, but I recognize the pursed lips and strained look of her jaw. She's pissed. Of all the things she could be feeling right now, why pissed?

"Let's go, Madison," she says.

"I can't. I can't find my—"

"It doesn't matter!"

"Jesus, Mel—"

And then, for the first time in as long as I can remember, the woman lets out a sob. "My sister is dead. My *baby* sister. Do you know what that feels like? She was sick, and she didn't even tell me. *No one* told me. *Do you not understand what I have just been through?!*"

"Mel, why don't you just come in? Sit down for a minute."

"No," my mom says. "I'm not going to do that."

"I found your bag, Maddie," Ezra says, coming downstairs now and handing it to me. "I put your phone in it."

"Where's your husband?" Ty asks my mom, looking over her shoulder toward her SUV. "You didn't drive up here yourself, did you?"

"That's none of your business."

"At least let me drive you back to the house. You shouldn't be driving like this."

"I can drive myself. I don't need your help," she says, "and *someone* should have told me."

"I *know* you're not talking about me," he says.

"Now, Madison," she says.

I realize I've just been watching them for the past few minutes and start moving toward the door.

"Maddie," Ezra says, grabbing my arm. "You don't have to leave if you don't want to. Or I could go with you...if you want."

"No," I tell him. "No, I don't want that."

I walk through my mom and Ty, and then she follows me to the car. When we drive through the village, almost everything looks normal. People are out like any other Sunday, the trendiest restaurants have lines out to the sidewalk. There's a car line waiting at the boat launch, and the main beach is packed.

But the boutique on the corner has a sign in the window, written in big red letters: CLOSED. FAMILY EMERGENCY.

Family emergency.

"Mom, where *is* Dad?" I ask.

"He was busy," she says. "Work has been crazy for him lately. You'd know that if you were home."

And you would have known that your sister was sick if you ever came home—if you were better.

We pull into the driveway of the house that, for weeks, felt so much like home but now feels ominous. She puts the car in park, but neither of us moves for our door.

"Mom?"

I wait for her to answer, but she doesn't.

"Mommy?" I choke out.

Maybe it's the tone of my voice, or maybe it's because it's been so long since she's heard the name, but this time, she does turn to me.

"I saw her body. I *found* her body. I...I touched her," I say. "It hurts so much."

"I'm so sorry," she says. Then she drops her head and sobs against the steering wheel.

"Will you hold me? Please?" I ask.

Wordlessly, she sits up and wraps her arms around me.

"I loved her," she says. "I did. Things were complicated, but it wasn't ever because of anything *she* did. It wasn't her fault, and I *loved* her. I would have taken care of her. She didn't have to do this. She didn't have to be alone."

"She wasn't alone," I tell her.

'We're alone,' I don't say.

"God, you smell like him," she says.

I assume she means Ezra. I am wearing his clothes. I was in his bed all day. But...maybe he smells like his dad. They live in the same house and probably share laundry, and maybe they smell the same.

After more than twenty years, would she really know?

I let it hang there.

We stay like that for a few minutes until a car pulls into the driveway behind us. She shoots me a puzzled look, but I recognize the old 4-Runner.

"It's just Lisa," I tell her.

"Lisa?" she says. "How do you know Lisa?"

I must look at her like she's crazy. She really doesn't know anything, does she? I mean, I knew that she was disconnected from this place, but I've been working at the store all summer. Didn't she know that Lisa worked there with Emma?

Lisa approaches the car with red puffy eyes and knocks on the window. My mom rolls it down and stares at her, not speaking.

"We need to talk."

We sit down at the table inside and talk. Lisa tells us some things we already know and a lot of stuff we don't. Emma had late-stage ovarian cancer. She found out too late, and it had spread to her other organs. She did a round of chemo and radiation, but it was pretty obvious that it wasn't going to save her life. It wouldn't even buy her years. She was dealing in far smaller increments of time.

So she stopped and decided to live instead. She made plans. She arranged to be cremated and made her own urn. They wouldn't have her ashes ready for a few days. She left the store to Lisa and—apparently—everything else...to me.

They argue for a while, and I sit. They argue about Emma and about how she can't just leave me a house. They argue about how someone should have told her she was sick. Lisa says that my mom should have known, and wasn't that the real problem? They yell and cry, and I quietly leave the room. I curl up on the couch and turn on the TV, but I still can't drown it out.

Eventually, my mom storms out onto the porch, almost knocking the old screen door off its hinges and letting it slam behind her.

Lisa walks over to the couch and sits down next to me. "Are you okay, Sweetie?"

"No," I tell her.

"About the house, Maddie—before you leave, you need to go to the county recorder's office and transfer the deed, or they can take it. Okay? It's yours; she wanted you to have it. She already signed it over to you, so you just have to sign it and give them this. And whatever you decide to do with it—she said she was fine with that, too."

I nod.

"This is for you, too," she says, handing me an envelope with my name on the front. I recognize the handwriting easily as Emma's. "There's one for your mom on the table. I'm here for you—whatever you need. Her, too. When she's ready."

She pats me on my leg, leans down and kisses the top of my head, then heads toward the front door.

"Wait," I say. "I'm sorry, Lisa. For you. I didn't tell you that. I'm sorry for your loss, too. She was your best friend. I...I didn't even really—"

"You knew her," she says, cutting me off. "Of course, you knew her. But thank you. It's been a heavy, heavy day. Call me, Maddie. Anytime."

I stare at the envelope in my hand. I can't open it—not right now. I hear the back door swing open again and instead, fold it and stuff it into the pocket of Ezra's sweatpants.

"Did Lisa leave?" she asks.

"Yeah," I tell her. "I'm going to bed, Mom."

She grabs a bottle from the liquor cabinet. "Me too."

I walk up the stairs with her close behind me, then turn down the hallway, and we both stop in front of the same door.

"This is my room," I tell her.

"Bullshit. It's my room."

"No, it's *my* room. I'm sleeping here. You can sleep somewhere else."

"Someone I loved died *in both of the other rooms*, Madison."

"Yeah, well. Me, too."

We both stand at the door's threshold, neither of us wanting to move.

"Goodnight, Mom," I say forcefully. "Lisa left something for you on the table downstairs." She looks over the railing, likely spotting the white envelope on the kitchen table. While she's distracted, I step inside and close the door.

I flip on the light and move toward the bed, catching my reflection in the mirror as I pass. I do look like shit. My pink hair had dried wet on the pillow, and my eyes are so swollen I'm barely recognizable.

I don't want to take off Ezra's clothes.

I dig my phone out of my bag for the first time since returning to the house.

Ezra: Do you need anything?

Ezra: Are you going to leave?

Ezra: Please don't leave without talking to me.

Me: I do need something. Do you know where the county recorder's office is?

Ezra: Yeah

Me: Can you take me there tomorrow?

Ezra: Yes. What time?

Me: Preferably early. Whenever they open.

Ezra: I can come and get you around 9. I miss you so much, Maddie. I'm so sorry.

I lock the screen, turn off the light, and climb into bed. In *my* room. I wonder if it will be the last time I ever sleep here.

"Madison," a woman's voice says as she shakes me. "Madison, wake up."

It takes me a minute to reorient myself. I know where I am—at the house in Lost Hollow. I think for a moment that the woman kneeling next to my bed on the floor is Emma, then I remember. Again.

And it hurts. Again.

How many times am I going to go through this? How many times will I have to remember before it sticks?

"Mom?"

She falls back on her ass and hits her head on the nightstand. "Oh, shit."

"Are you okay?" I ask.

She settles into a seated position on the floor, a bottle of dark liquor and a crumpled-up piece of paper in one hand. She's drunk. I've seen it before a few times—after a party or a fundraiser. She'd get emotional and speak in riddles I never really paid much attention to. I wish I'd paid more attention now.

"What's he like?" she asks.

"Who? Ezra?"

"No," she says.

What?

Oh.

"Oh...you mean Ty?"

She doesn't answer.

"Oh, umm...he's nice," I tell her. "And talented. I mean, you saw the house, right? He did all of that. And he did the kitchen and stuff in here, too. Emma said he put in the ramp and the handrails in the bathrooms and stuff for free. He wouldn't let her pay him."

"That sounds like him," she says quietly.

"And um, he cooks a lot. And he's actually good at it. He has a nature cam in the backyard. And I think he's a good dad. He spends a lot of time with Ezra and Liam. Ezra said they slept in his bed until they were ten. He's home a lot. But...I think he's kind of sad, too."

"Okay...thanks."

She sets down the bottle and the paper and wipes away the tears running down her face.

"Are you okay?" I ask.

"Yeah. I'm fine."

"You can sleep with me if you want."

She wordlessly gets up off the floor and climbs into the bed next to me.

"No one died in Grandma's room, though," I tell her. "They had a hospital bed set up downstairs. It was still there when I got here. That's where she died. Emma told me."

"Okay," she chokes out. "Thanks for telling me."

It's quiet for a couple of minutes before she says, "I can't believe they're both just gone. I can't believe...how did this happen? What are we going to do?"

"I don't know."

"Does he love you?" she asks.

I swallow hard before answering. "No."

"Don't leave me, Madison," she says before her sobs quiet, and she falls asleep.

TWENTY-THREE

MADISON

I wake up before my alarm the next morning and creep out of bed. I leave my mom, still passed out in a t-shirt and her underwear from however much she had to drink, where she is, and grab everything I need before heading to the bathroom. I take the time to wash and dry my hair, put on a little bit of makeup, and some of my own clothes. After a couple of cups of coffee, I almost look like a normal human being, aside from the puffy eyes. When Ezra texts me that he's on his way, I sit out on the front porch and wait for him so he doesn't wake up my mom.

He pulls up a couple of minutes later. I climb into the truck, close the door, and buckle my seatbelt.

"Hey," he says. I turn to face him, and he leans over and kisses me. "Are you..." he trails off.

Am I okay? No, not really. Not in any way.

He shakes his head, turns toward the front, and puts the truck in reverse.

"I missed you, Maddie. I don't remember the last time I went to sleep without you. I guess it was probably before the 4th of July. When you got mad at me."

I blink back tears. "Yeah, I guess so."

"Are you mad at me right now? It kind of feels like it."

Can he really not know? I start to wonder if I imagined the whole thing and maybe I didn't ever say it out loud. It was a fucked up morning. It wasn't outside the realm of possibility.

But no. There was no way. I said it, and he closed the door and pretended like it didn't happen. I feel stupid. This is good sex. A stupid fucking story. Anyone else would have known better, but I—with my very limited experience with things and people who aren't faking *everything*—did not.

When I think of it that way, I can't really blame either of us.

"I'm not mad. I'm sad," I tell him.

It isn't a lie.

"Why do you need to go here? What is all of that?" he asks.

"Emma left me the house."

"Really?"

"I don't know what I'm going to do with it. But yeah."

I'm not staying here with you.

He doesn't say anything. The drive down from the mountains to the biggest small town that is the county seat isn't exactly short, and it's tense. Right before we pull into the parking lot, I risk glancing over at him and see that he's white-knuckling the wheel, the muscles in his jaw tense.

He's mad. Good.

I must still be tired, or maybe just emotionally wrecked, because then, I start laughing. And not a little bit, either. I laugh hard. I don't stop when he pulls into the parking lot and turns off the engine. I risk a second look and catch an angry scowl that only makes me laugh harder.

"Did I miss something funny?" he deadpans.

"Oh, god, I'm an *idiot*," I laugh.

"Care to elaborate?"

"Not really," I say, attempting to gather myself. "Okay. Um, thank you. I'm sorry. Thanks. For getting up early and bringing me. You don't have to come in with me if you don't want to."

I unbuckle my seatbelt and get out of the truck, the last of my hysterics seeming to dissipate when I do. I start walking toward the building and hear the other door slam shut, then feel rather than see him follow me inside.

The building is a lot emptier than I'd expected, and the process a lot less complicated. I think I was expecting something more like a visit to the California DMV. This is nothing like that. We pass maybe two other people in the hallway, and five more are waiting inside the office. Ezra and I don't speak, but I can still feel how mad he is, and for what?

I don't look at him because I don't want to start laughing again.

Once it's done and the office door closes behind us, he does speak.

"Do you want to tell me what the fuck is going on with you right now?"

"Umm...my aunt just fucking died," I say.

"Nope," he says, grabbing my arm and turning me to face him. "Try again."

"I'm not mad at you."

He narrows his eyes, waiting for a better answer.

"I'm not," I insist again, shaking my head.

"Really? Prove it then."

"How do I—"

Ezra grabs my hand and pulls me down the hallway and into a bathroom, closing and locking the door behind us. Then, he leans against the wall with both hands on either side of my head, brings his mouth to mine, and kisses me. But when he does, my arms stay stiff at my sides. My lips don't part when I feel his mouth against me.

He pulls back and shakes his head. "See? I fucking knew it."

But because I do still want him—love him, even—I wrap my arms around his neck, lift onto my toes, and kiss him hard, tasting him, breathing him in even if it's the last time and even if it is just a stupid fucking story.

It's complicated.

He reaches behind me, picking me up by the back of my thighs, and sets me down on the edge of the sink. He slides my underwear to the side and pushes his thick cock into me. I cry out at the sudden intrusion, then lean back, gripping each side of the sink with my hands and spreading my legs further, and he fucks into me deeper, hitting all the right spots.

Fuck, I feel like I'm going to rip this sink off the goddamn wall.

I scream his name when I come on him, my legs fall heavy as the orgasm rips through me, and he doesn't let up. He grips my shaky legs beneath my knees and takes me harder while my pussy throbs on his dick.

"Good girl," he says. "That's better. You're mine, aren't you? This is mine. Say it."

"Yes. Oh fuck."

"Say you're mine."

"I'm yours," I whimper.

He pounds into me hard, over and over again. The sound of skin smacking skin and my own desperate moans echoes throughout the space until he finally buries himself inside me, pulling my hair while he fills me with his cum.

He breathes heavily into my shoulder for a minute, then kisses my collarbone before he pulls out of me. I slide my underwear back into place and head for the bathroom stall, but he stops me.

"No."

"No, what?"

"I don't know why you were acting like that this morning, but I don't like it," he says. "I don't want you to clean yourself up. I want you to feel my cum dripping out of you for the rest of the day."

"But...I'm wearing a dress. And a thong," I argue.

"Or we can talk about why you're really mad if you want. Then..." he gestures toward the stall.

"This is fine, actually," I tell him, then leave the bathroom.

But when we get into the truck, I slide over next to him—sticky thighs and all. It isn't his fault that I did this. It isn't his fault that I read it wrong or that no one ever even held me, so I didn't know.

This was always going to be temporary. I knew that in the beginning; I just forgot. And it's okay.

Because it was what I needed. And I think maybe I'm glad he knows that I love him. I'm glad I know that he doesn't love me back. Because if I didn't, I would have stayed.

"Isn't that your dad's truck?" I ask when we pull into the driveway.

"Um, yeah," he says.

We both get out and walk to the front door, a sense of trepidation overwhelming me when I turn the knob. I don't know what I expect to find, but it isn't this.

The two of them are sitting on the couch laughing. It seems innocent enough, but also...not quite right. Not after last night.

"Stop. You have to stop....talking," she laughs. "I can't—oh, hey, guys," she says, trying to stifle her laughter and wiping the resulting tears from under her eyes.

"Hey," I say.

"Um, Ty brought food if you guys are hungry."

I look over at the kitchen. There isn't an inch of countertop visible with all the various food containers. I look at her with furrowed brows, perplexed. They both start laughing again.

"Okay. Not all of that. Ty and everyone else in town," she laughs, "brought food."

"Well, I'm hungry," Ezra says. "Worked up an appetite this morning."

I shake my head as he walks past me and smiles.

"Let me help you with the plates," my mom says, getting up from the couch. I watch Ty watch her as she walks to the kitchen, and she turns back and smiles at him over her shoulder. Again, it seems innocent enough, but it feels like something else entirely. There's something about that look on both ends—something intimate that makes me feel like I shouldn't be watching. "Luckily, everything is still in the same place it was twenty years ago, even if the cabinets aren't the same."

She stands on her toes, pulls down a plate, and hands it to Ezra. "Forks and spoons are here," she says, opening the drawer before returning to the couch.

"Thanks," he tells her. He fills up his plate with food and carries it back to the table. And just eats. Like this is normal. They go back to whatever it was they were talking about, laughing and barely not touching like that's all normal, too.

I watch them for a couple of minutes, then grab a beer from the fridge and twist off the cap, making sure my mom sees me when I do. I wait for the lecture that doesn't come, then walk over to the table and down next to Ezra.

"It's weird, right?" I ask, gesturing toward our parents.

He shrugs. "I don't know. Not really. Did you like it better when they were fighting on my front porch?"

No.

Maybe.

"Do you want a beer, Ty?" my mom asks, walking over to the fridge.

"It's a little early on a Monday for a beer, don't you think?" he asks. "Well, maybe not for *you*."

What.

"Madison is setting the tone, I guess," she says, shrugging.

She grabs two and brings them back to the couch.

I fidget in the wooden kitchen chair, not just uncomfortable with the scene before me but physically uncomfortable with my still-sticky thighs and the wet mess of my thong, and it isn't getting any better. Ezra notices and smiles.

I frown in return, then get up from my chair and sit down on his lap. He laughs hard, then wraps his arm around my waist, leans in, and kisses me.

"Hey, how long are you staying, Mel?" Ty asks.

We both turn toward them, invested in the answer as well. I watch my mom's entire demeanor change as if a switch was flipped. Even her posture stiffens, making her look less like the woman I saw when I walked in and more like the one I know. I hadn't even realized how drastic the difference was until now.

"Hopefully tomorrow," she says. "They put a rush on Emma's ashes since we're from out of town, and then I just have one more thing to take care of later today. Shouldn't take long."

I guess it ends tomorrow, then.

"We should do something, Maddie," Ezra says.

"Like what?" I ask.

"I don't know," he says. "Whatever you want. Go boating. Play darts."

He kisses my neck.

"More crimes?"

"If you want."

"I want to change my clothes," I tell him and head upstairs.

TWENTY-FOUR

MADISON

W hat I want to do is have one last normal day. I want to pretend it isn't so heavy. I don't want to think about what I have already lost or what I was about to lose; I don't want to worry about what my life will look like when I wake up tomorrow.

None of this means any less to me just because it's temporary.

And so that's what we do.

It's easy enough to convince the girls to meet us at the lake. Lisa kept the store closed again today, so neither Chloe nor Ava had to work. Ty had obviously taken the day off, too, so Ezra and Liam didn't work either.

We went to the lake and laid in the sun, and I tried to feel normal. And for the most part, it worked. It worked as the afternoon rolled seamlessly into the evening, and we strolled into TJ's pub. It isn't until the summer sun finally sets—late like it does this time of year—that I start to feel it. That feeling of impending doom, a tightening in my chest when I laugh with Chloe and Ava or when Ariana yells at Ezra, trying to figure out whether or not he really did spit in her beer while she was in the bathroom.

"I'm not saying that I did or didn't," he tells her, shrugging. "I'm saying that I might have. I told you before that I won't tell you how or when I'm going to get you back. So...drink it or don't. I make no promises."

"There's no way all of these assholes would sit here and watch you do that and not tell me," she says while we all laugh.

"You sure about that?"

"Ava, seriously. Tell me that truth."

"He didn't touch it," she says.

"Fuck you," she tells him. "Fuck you, Ezra. You're not fucking funny." She picks up her beer and gulps down half of it. "I don't know how you can stand him, Maddie."

"I guess because I don't have to for long," I reply. I mean for it to come out as a joke, but it comes out sad, and everyone hears it. He squeezes my leg under the table.

"Do you want to leave?" he whispers in my ear.

I shake my head no.

He wraps his arms around me and kisses the side of my head. "Come on, Maddie. Let's go."

"Go ahead and go with him," Ava says. "We get it. Besides, I know it's not goodbye forever. I know you won't be able to stay away. I'll miss you, though."

"I'll miss you, too," I tell her. "I'll miss all of you guys."

"Don't start crying on us," Chloe says. And I don't, but just barely. I say my goodbyes to all of them and walk out into the cool August night air. And I try to just be grateful. I try to be quiet and still and just take it all in and enjoy it for what it is while we walk hand in hand one last time through a place that has come to mean so much to me and step into the dark, empty house.

Before we do, I don't fail to notice that his dad's truck still isn't in the driveway.

We pass through the living room, and I start toward the stairs when he stops me. "Madison, can we talk for a minute?"

I shake my head and kiss him instead. "No," I tell him. I reach down and unzip his pants, taking his cock in my hand and stroking it. "I don't want to talk."

"Just for a second," he groans.

"Don't waste our time, Ezra," I tell him. I drop to my knees and take him in my mouth.

"Mmm, fuck, that feels good," he says, grabbing a fist full of my hair and pushing me forward until the head hits the back of my throat. I'm used to it now. My eyes water, but I work with it. Feeling and hearing him lose control when my mouth is around his cock always gets me so turned on, so wet that it becomes unbearable, and all I can think about is making it good for him so he'll tell me how good I am again and he'll give me what I want. It's a welcome distraction for my mind and body and shuts him up, too. It's even better when he finally does give me what I want. He pulls me up, bends me over the table, and fucks me from behind, wrapping his hand around my throat and squeezing much harder than usual when he comes.

I think maybe it'll leave a mark this time. I hope it does. I'm suddenly aware that this was the last time I'd ever feel him inside of me. I'm painfully empty.

"Maddie—"

"Can I go to the bathroom this time?" I ask.

He gives me a 'go ahead' gesture. "I'll be waiting."

I get what he's saying. We're going to have to talk. For that reason, I take my sweet fucking time in the bathroom.

When I walk out, he's still there, sitting on the couch. I sit down next to him just before the front door flies open, and Ty walks in, slamming it hard behind him.

He kicks over a side table, sending a lamp soaring and crashing before he notices us. I gasp and jump back in response.

"Oh...sorry," he says. "I didn't see you guys there. I didn't mean to scare you, Maddie. I—" he pauses. "I'll leave you two alone."

Neither of us says anything. We watch him walk up the stairs and down the hall until we hear the slam of a bedroom door.

I don't know what happened, but I get the feeling it has something to do with my mom.

"Hey...look at me," Ezra says. I turn to face him again, meeting his eyes in the dark room. He places his palms on the sides of my face. "Maddie, I love you."

"You don't have to say that," I tell him, shaking my head. "I was just...it was the worst day. I shouldn't have done that to you. You don't have to say that because my aunt died and because I'm leaving. I don't think it will make either of us feel better."

"No, I do. I do have to say it; I mean it, Maddie. I'm in love with you. I'm so sorry I didn't tell you the other day. I should have. But I've never said that to anyone else before, and I didn't know."

I don't know what to say. It's what I wanted. It doesn't, though—make me feel better, I mean.

"Maddie, say something."

"You know how I feel about you," I tell him.

"Then don't leave," he says. "I don't want to be like them."

"What do you mean?" I ask.

"You know what I mean," he says. His eyes settle on a spot over my shoulder. I follow them, my gaze landing on the knocked-over table and destroyed lamp lying on the floor.

Yeah. I know what he means.

"I don't think it gets better than this, Maddie."

"I can't stay, Ezra. I have to go home. I can't just walk out on my entire life. I have to go to school and get a job and—"

"You already did walk out on that stuff, though, Maddie. And you *have* a life here. You have a home. And a job. And friends. And you have me."

"For now," I say.

"You don't even like it there. You hated it; you were miserable."

"I don't have to be."

"What makes you happy right now?"

"You do," I tell him. "Being here with you makes me happy but—"

"The future isn't real. That's what you said, right? Are you really going to leave just because six years from now, you *might* end up being glad that you did?"

"You can't tell me not to go to college," I tell him. "That's...that's not fair."

"I'm not saying don't go. Just don't go right now. Don't go to Berkeley, and don't go right now."

"Maybe this is just bad timing," I say, maybe more to myself than to him.

"That doesn't matter, Maddie. There's nothing we can do about it now. There's not going to be another time. This isn't some stupid fucking movie where, when you're ready, we'll walk into the same bar at the same time, or we'll meet in the middle of a fucking bridge five years from today. That's not how real life works. And if you do leave—if you come back next summer or whatever—I won't do this again. I *won't*."

"But—"

"I don't want to be a stupid story. All or nothing, Maddie."

"Okay," I tell him. I almost choke on that one word. I swear I can hear my heart hammering nervously in my chest.

"Okay? Really?"

"Yeah..." I say. "Yeah, I don't want to be like them either. I love you, so I'll stay."

"Okay," he says, audibly exhaling before kissing me on the mouth. "Thank you. I feel a lot better now. Do you?"

"Kind of. I'm kind of freaking out."

"It'll be okay. It'll be fine. I promise."

"Are you sure?" I ask.

"Yeah, of course. Why wouldn't it be?"

"Well, you hated me the first time you saw me," I say.

"No, not the first time I saw you."

"Um, yeah. You did."

"Oh, you mean at the festival? Sure. But that wasn't the first time I saw you."

"What do you mean?"

"The first time I saw you," he says, pausing to kiss me. "You had your hair pulled up and a big red bow on your head. You were standing in front of Emma's—or your grandma's house—kicking a ball against the garage. Like...kicking the shit out of it. You looked pissed. And I was walking by, and the ball bounced off the garage and went over your head and hit me in the fucking face. Do you know what you said?"

I smile. "I said, 'I'm so sorry about that. Can you please pass me the ball?'"

"Nope. Do you want to try again?"

"Yeah," I say because I do remember. And I know exactly what I said. "Are you just going to stand there and stare at me like an idiot all day, or are you going to give me my ball back?"

"That was it."

"I remember that day. I *was* pissed. I wanted to go to the lake like everyone else. I could see the shuttle stop down the hill from the driveway and watched all the kids my age pile on, but my mom wouldn't let me go. We never went to the lake. We never even left the house. You did give the ball back, though."

"Probably would have rather stood there and stared all day if you hadn't called me out like that. I was a creep then, too." He kisses me again and adds, "So see? If it makes you feel better, I didn't hate you the first time I saw you. Everything is going to be fine, Maddie."

"Okay. I think I should go home...or back to Emma's...my house, I mean. I think I have to tell my mom."

TWENTY-FIVE

MADISON

"Do you want me to go in with you? I can if you want," Ezra says when we pull into the driveway.

"No, that's okay. You don't have to; I'll be fine."

"Really?"

"She's going to be upset," I tell him. "But it'll be okay. She'll get over it. She'll get it."

I think. Won't she?

"Text me after you talk to her, okay?"

"I will."

I kiss him before getting out of the car, my intent to make it short and sweet, but it isn't. He pulls me onto his lap, and I straddle him, kissing him deeper, tasting his mouth and dragging his lower lip through my teeth. I rock my hips against the hard ridge beneath me before breaking away.

"Okay, I have to get out of the car now," I laugh.

"All right, fine." He kisses me again quickly. "I'll see you to-morrow, Maddie."

"See you tomorrow," I tell him. I bite back a smile and get out through the driver's side door.

When I get inside, my mom is on the couch watching television in the dark. I walk over to where she is sitting and find her in her pajamas, eyes puffy, with a glass of liquor in her hands. It isn't necessarily unusual or unexpected considering the circumstances and what we've been through over the past few days—considering what she's lost.

"Hey, Mom. I need to talk to you about something."

She doesn't answer.

"Mom? Are you okay?"

And then, she starts to sob. "No," she chokes out. "No, I'm not okay. I did something...wrong, I think."

"Well, what? What did you do?" I ask.

Did she mean she did something...with Ty? Did I want to know?

She must see what I'm thinking in my eyes because she answers the unspoken question. "Oh, no. Nothing like that. I just...I don't know who I am, Madison. And I miss them. And I miss..."

"Him?"

She doesn't answer. She doesn't have to.

I don't want to be like them.

"Mom, I have to tell you something." Her eyes meet mine, and I continue. "I'm not going to go back tomorrow. Or at all.

I want to stay here. I want to live in this house, and I want to work in the store. And I want to stay with Ezra."

"What?" she asks, her eyes hardening. "You what?"

"I love him, Mom. And I love it here. I'm happy here. I need—"

"You need your education, Madison. That's what you need. I'm not going to let you do this. No."

"I'm not asking," I tell her. "And I'm not saying that I'll never go to college. I just don't want to go right now. I'm happy, Mom; I wasn't happy before. And I didn't even realize how bad it was...."

"My god, Madison," she says, shaking her head.

"What?"

"You could not have possibly picked a worse way to hurt me than this," she laughs through her tears. "Not even if you tried."

"Mom, this has nothing to do with you. I'm not *trying* to hurt you."

"Don't you get it?! I..." she trails off, burying her face in her hands and then running them through her hair. "I left here so that things would be better. So that I could be better and so that when I had a daughter of my own, she could have the things I never got to have and choices that I didn't have, and she wouldn't know what it was like to struggle the way we did, to *suffer* like we did...in ways you couldn't even *begin* to understand."

"Well, then, help me understand! Because you're right, Mom. I don't fucking get it. I know you have bad memories from your childhood and from this house. I just don't under-stand what that has to do with me."

"I gave you everything! Everything I ever did was for you before you even existed. And yeah, I have bad memories of this house. A lot of them. And it makes it hard to be here, and I don't like it. And it was better when I moved away because no one there knew any of that stuff about me anymore. They didn't know who I was or what happened to me."

"I get that, Mom—"

"But do you want to know the real reason why I never come back here? It's because I can't risk looking at his face."

"So this is about Ty?"

She doesn't answer.

"Mom, what about my dad? You don't love him?" I ask through tears.

"Of course I love him," she says. "I love him very much. He is a wonderful man and a wonderful father."

"Just...not as much as you loved Ty, right?"

"I loved him differently."

"How? How was it different?"

"I don't know. It was a long time ago, Madison. I'm not that person anymore. And I don't like to think about it."

"So, you regret it? You regret it, and now, you want me to do the same thing?"

"*No*," she says harshly. "Not at all. Don't compare...." she pauses, changing course. "When I met your dad, he showed me an entirely different world. He blew me away. And we built a life together, and I don't regret it. Not for a minute."

I look away, lean back against the couch and stare up at the ceiling.

"I don't want a different world. What if this is as good as it gets?"

I don't think it gets better than this, Maddie.

"I get why you feel that way. And I believe you—that you love him—I do. But Madison, there will be other loves. There will be something else that will be a little bit easier. Something that makes more sense and fits better with every side of you. And you won't have to make any sacrifices because it will just be easy."

"This *is* easy."

"And what will you do if this doesn't work out?" she continues. "You can't survive on a minimum wage job, and you can't count on him to take care of you forever."

"Maybe it will work out, and maybe it won't." And I know, based on odds alone, it is more likely that it won't. "But I still want to try. And it's not just him, Mom. I'm happy here. It just...fits."

"You can't do this to me," she says, her demeanor shifting back from concerned mother to a scorned one. "You can't leave me now, and especially not for this place. I have lost *everything*."

"What about what I'll lose?"

"I can't support this," she says. "I won't. You need to leave with me tomorrow or...that's it, Madison."

"Or what? I'll just be de..." I stop to adjust my word choice. "You'll just be done with me like Emma and Grandma?"

She doesn't answer.

"You can't be serious," I tell her.

But she is. I can see it in her eyes. I see her pain, too, and I wonder how long it's been there. I wonder how often it still hurts—if it's always like this or if most days, she's able to bury it and doesn't notice it at all. Maybe that's why she stays busy like she does; maybe it's why she's never quiet or still and doesn't rest.

And maybe if I stayed, she wouldn't be able to handle it. Maybe these things and the choices she's given me are all that have held her together up to this point. But could I give it up for a hypothetical future that might be better? For more, like she did, even though I already know those things don't fill the void? For her, so she doesn't have to feel like her sacrifice was wasted?

Do I owe her that?

"Don't be that girl, Madison. You're better than that."

"Maybe I'm not better."

"You've already let one guy make a fool out of you."

My jaw drops. So, I guess she found out what happened with Ethan.

"You know what, Mom? I'm not going to miss this at all."

"Wait—wait a second, Madison. I'm sorry. I didn't mean that. I'm just...drunk and angry, and everything hurts so bad. You can't imagine how bad it hurts."

"It hurts me, too!"

"No. Not like this. Emma was my baby sister. I *raised* her. I loved her, and I took care of her. And now, she's dead. She suffered, and they're *burning* her, and I never got to say sorry. I made it bad because I couldn't deal with my own shit. So, she didn't even tell me. She didn't even trust me. She didn't *want* me. And I have to live with that every day now."

"I'm sorry, Mom," I sob. "But Emma didn't hold grudges; she wasn't like that. She loved you the whole time."

"That doesn't make it better," she cries. "Madison, please. You can't leave me—not right now. It will *break* me."

"I'm going to bed."

"I love you more than anyone, Madison. You know that I'm right—about school and everything else."

"I love you, too, Mom."

"I'll see you in the morning," she says. "I told your dad we'd leave early—as soon as we can get the ashes—and be home by the afternoon."

I wipe the tears away from my cheeks and nod. Then, I walk up the stairs to my room, close the door, and pull out my phone.

Me: I can't stay. I love you. I'm sorry.

I sink down the door onto the floor and weep.

I wake up to my phone ringing. I'm not sure how long after—I must have fallen asleep on the floor at some point. I reach for it, seeing his name across the screen, and it feels like a punch in the gut.

I accept the call and bring the phone to my ear.

"What do you mean you can't stay?" he says before I can even get a word out.

"I can't leave her, Ezra. She's been through too much, and she's too sad. I can't do that to her right now."

"You're not responsible for her happiness, Maddie. That's her own fault."

I know he's right. On some level, I do. "It's bad timing. Emma just died. I'm supposed to start school in a couple of weeks, and it's too late to get in anywhere else."

"Can I come over? Can I just come over, and we can talk in person? I don't want to do this on the phone."

"I can't see you right now. It'll make it too hard to leave, and I can't stay."

"Jesus, Maddie. They fucked you up worse than I thought," he says.

"Ezra, this...this doesn't have to be goodbye forever. It doesn't have to be all or nothing," I plead.

"Yeah, it does. I told you that. I won't do this again. I won't sit around and wait for you to change your mind, either. God, you're just like her. And I got exactly what I deserved, I guess, for fucking with you when I knew I shouldn't have."

"You're just like her," I tell him. "You both deal in these fucking absolutes, throwing ultimatums and threats at me if I don't do what you want."

"Well, maybe that's your fault. Maybe if you knew how to make a fucking decision on your own, you wouldn't have people telling you what to do all the time. At least when I do it, you get something you want."

Fuck.

"Come on, Maddie—be a good girl. Let me come over. I'll tell you what to do, and we'll both get what we want."

"I can't."

"Don't get in that car tomorrow. You'll regret it. And you'll have to live with it, too."

"I love you, Ezra," I say, my voice cracking when I do.

His own softens in response. "I love you, too, baby. I'll see you later, okay? I'll see you tomorrow. It's supposed to rain. We can watch it in the hot tub."

"Yeah, that sounds nice," I tell him. "I do like that."

"Don't cry, Maddie. It's going to be okay, I promise," he says. "I'll come over early. Before work. Don't leave before I do."

"Okay."

"I love you so much."

"I love you, too," I tell him, then hang up the phone. But I do cry because it's not going to be okay, and I won't see him tomorrow.

And I'll have to live with it. Every fucking day.

TWENTY-SIX

MADISON

When I was a little girl, all I wanted was to be just like my mom. She was always so beautiful, so confident. She commanded attention in any room she was in. And I heard so many times from so many other women how impressive and how inspiring she was. I could tell that they wanted to be more like her, too.

She was their leader. And she came from nothing.

So, when I got to the age when I should have been fighting for more freedom—when we should have been struggling for control, and I should have been trying to figure out who I was and what I wanted outside of what my mom wanted for me—I just...didn't. I let her win, and I did what she wanted. Because she had it all, right? I wanted to have it all, too. She was so proud of me.

But it didn't make me happy. So why am I doing it again?

"This is for the best, Madison. You'll see. I know you're upset with me, but ten years from now—probably less—you'll thank me for it."

I look at her, and she shoots me a smile that doesn't reach her eyes. It doesn't make me feel any better.

Surely, she's right, though. It is logical. Surely, I'll get more chances. I'll find something that will be easier like she said. And this will be fine. A memory, a story. Something I needed at the time, but just a season in the course of a lifetime.

Just a cut.

But for something so small, so seemingly insignificant, it feels like it will bleed a lot.

I toss the last of my things into the trunk and climb into the front seat, watching the raindrops roll down the window.

She gets in after I do, then puts an address into the car's GPS and backs out of the driveway.

"God, I hate the weather here," she says. "I hate the rain and the cold. I bet you won't miss that, will you? I bet you missed the California sun."

She reaches over and squeezes my hand when she says it. I shrug and turn back toward the window. I would miss all of it. Even the rain.

Especially the rain.

"We'll have to get the house up for sale soon," she says. "You'll lose money if you wait too long. I have a friend who is licensed in Oregon, too. She can help us. And you can keep the money, Maddie. It's your house, after all."

"I'm not ready for that," I say quietly.

"But—"

"I can't sell the house, Mom. Not right now. I don't want to talk about it."

"We're going to be okay, Madison."

I pop in my earbuds but don't bother to turn on any music. I just don't want to talk anymore.

We pull into the funeral home about an hour later, and my mom parks the car and shuts off the engine. She runs her hand through her hair, exhaling heavily, before turning to me.

"Do you want to go in with me?" she asks. "I'd like it if you did."

"No," I tell her.

She stares at me for a minute, looking as if she might argue, but ultimately gets out of the car alone. I understand why she might need me for something like this, but it's hard for me, too, and she's asked a lot of me lately. I won't feel bad about it.

I check my phone and the time. Nothing. But if Ezra did come to the house this morning before work, he'd be there now, and he'd find it empty. I wonder how it would make him feel.

I wonder if he will hate me. It hurts so fucking much.

It takes longer than I expect, but eventually, she comes out carrying an urn in her hand. It looks heavy, covered in mosaic glass tiles put together in a way that looks a lot like wildflowers growing on a mountain slope.

She opens the back door and sets the urn into a box on the floor. She stuffs a blanket around it to keep it secure before closing the door and getting back in the front seat.

"I feel like we should do something with them," I tell her as we pull out onto the highway. "You know that hill on the other side of the falls, Mom? The one with all the wildflowers?"

"Yeah," she laughs. "I do. I used to take her there all the time."

"She brought me there. She said it was one of her favorite places. Maybe we should bring her there, too."

"That's a good idea, Madison. Maybe next summer. We can come up here and spread some of her ashes. I think she'd like that." She smiles at me and wipes a tear from under her eye.

But something about her tone tells me that we won't. She'll never come back.

I turn around in my chair to better examine the urn. I run my fingers along the colored glass tiles and think of the time it must have taken...the amount of care she must have put into it. I wonder where her head was when she created the thing that she knew would soon hold what was left of her when she was gone.

"She was so talented," I say.

"Yeah, she was."

Before I turn around, my eyes catch something behind my mom's seat. Two plastic bags. Are those...?

"Mom, are those my boots?" I ask. But I know that they are. I can see the red letter 'S' on the front of the black hoodie in the other bag—my clothes that the police had taken. "How did you get those?"

"I worked out a deal. Got your stuff back, and that family is going to leave you—and your friends—alone."

"What kind of a..." I start, but I know the answer. "You paid them, didn't you? You gave them money."

"I cleaned up your mess."

"Mom, there was no mess. They had nothing on me. And they deserved it. Do you have any idea what their kid did? What they did?"

"It doesn't matter. They know who did it, Madison. They would have found something. And even if what they found wasn't good enough, it wouldn't have mattered. You're just lucky that when the police found you that night, they didn't know who your friends were yet. It was pretty obvious once they started seeing you around town with them that you were involved. Gene said you put on a five-star performance, though. He said it would have even put my younger self to shame," she says, shaking her head. "So congrats on that."

"Great, Mom. That's really fucking great. Now, they win. You get that, right?"

"They were *always* going to win, Madison. What part of that don't you understand? They were always going to win, and people like us..." she stops and corrects herself, "...people like them are always going to lose. I did you and your friends a favor."

"It's not right, though. Don't you care?"

She slams on the brakes. "Of course, I care. You cannot *begin* to fathom how much I care. I've just spent enough time on the other side to know just how much it doesn't matter."

I did something...wrong, I think.

"This is the thing, isn't it? This is the thing you did last night that you knew was wrong, and you did it anyway."

She looks over at me and doesn't answer. She doesn't have to.

I relent, sinking back into my seat as she pulls back onto the road. I watch the last stretch of Oregon highway disappear in the side-view mirror as the 'Welcome to California' sign comes into view. I think about Emma. I think about how she said we leave pieces of ourselves with every person we meet and in every place we go, and that it can be a good thing—the best thing—and I think she's probably right. Sometimes, it's a small piece like a memory or a lie, or something we can afford to spare. Maybe it's even a piece we need to get rid of like whatever it was I left with Ethan.

But sometimes, it's something else. Sometimes, they're pieces we can't afford to lose, like an arm or a heart, and then you have whole-looking people walking around with missing limbs and gaping holes in their chests, and no one is ever the wiser. I think when my mom left Lost Hollow, she left something more like that. I think maybe she's been walking around without something she really needed for a long time. Maybe she even got used to it. But I don't want to.

"It gets easier," she says after we cross the border, as if she can hear my inner monologue. "I know it hurts now, but one day, you'll wake up, and you'll just be okay. It'll happen sooner than you think."

I think I fall asleep not long after that because the next thing I know, we're pulling into the garage. I guess we hit traffic, too, because it's already early evening. And I'm still tired. So tired.

My dad meets me at the door with an embrace and condolences for my loss; I thank him and tell him it's good to see him, then head up the staircase toward my room.

"Dinner will be in an hour, Madison," my mom says to my back.

"I'm not hungry."

"That doesn't matter," she says.

"Did you take care of it?" I hear my dad ask when I turn the corner.

"I did," my mom replies.

An hour later, I'm sitting with my parents at the dining room table, pushing food around my plate.

Dinner is quiet like it always is—everything is like it always is except for the mosaic urn on the mantle. I stare at it through the dining room entryway, just over my dad's head.

He stares at his phone in one hand while he eats, just like he always does. Not because he's disconnected but because he's busy, important. At least, that's how I've always viewed it. I've never given it a second thought. I realize that I've never really paid any type of attention to their behavior or their mannerisms when they don't directly concern me. I've never wondered whether or not they were happy—together or separately.

But I do now.

I think about how weird it felt and how uncomfortable I was watching her with Ezra's dad the other day. I've never seen her like that. I've never seen my parents laugh like that. But I guess that didn't mean that they never did, right? And they saw each other every day and have for more than twenty years, so maybe it's just different like she said. And that's not bad.

I watch them not talk now. My dad looks up occasionally to ask me some generic questions about my summer, and I give him some generic answers. When my mom gets up to refill her glass of wine and asks my dad if he needs anything, no lingering looks or smiles pass between them. He doesn't even look up. She doesn't look back, either.

And afterward, he goes up to his office and shuts the door. That's where he'll be all night, as usual, because he's busy and important. But often, I'll walk by in the evenings, and he's watching tv or has fallen asleep on his couch.

She's cleaning up; there's never anything out of place in our home. I think we're the only family among my friends that doesn't have a regular housekeeper, but she likes to do it herself. Once she's done, she'll go to her room, too. Or maybe she'll take her laptop and work by the pool since it's nice outside.

She says that I'll get another chance. That I'll find something that will be better and easier, something that will fit.

And I want to believe it.

"Do you need any help, Mom?" I ask.

"No, I've got it. Thanks for asking, though, Madison."

I head upstairs to my room, turn off the lights, and crawl into bed. When I do sleep, I dream of cold, dark water. I don't even bother fighting anymore.

TWENTY-SEVEN

EZRA

I wake to a pounding on my bedroom door and a pounding in my head. I didn't sleep much. I think I drank a lot. I reach over and feel the cold, empty space next to me and jerk awake, settling back into reality.

Shit.

"Get up," my dad says through the door. "We have to go soon."

Fuck.

I pull on some sweats and a t-shirt, then run down the stairs toward the front door.

"Hey!" he shouts, trying to stop me. "Where the hell are you going? We have to leave in thirty minutes."

"I know," I tell him. "I know, I'll be back in thirty minutes."

"Where are you going?"

"I have something I need to do; I'll be back in thirty minutes, or I'll meet you there, okay?"

I get into the truck and race through the village, then down the hill to Maddie's.

And when I get there, I pull into the empty driveway. It's like a punch in the gut.

"Maddie...you better not have gotten into that fucking car," I say to myself while turning my key in the locked door.

Maybe she didn't. Maybe she's still here.

But she isn't. And I know that. I can tell when I get into the house and find it empty and lifeless. All of the blinds have been pulled shut. No shoes by the front door, no dishes in the sink. The house is quiet and spotless. Everything looks like it's been put away. Like really, really put away—the way that you would leave it if you weren't planning on coming back for a long time.

Still, I hold onto a sliver of hope and take the stairs two at a time, stopping at the first bedroom on the left.

It's just as empty—just as dead inside. I walk over to the dresser, open the top drawer, and—of course—find it empty, too. I pull it harder, letting it fly across the room, then do the same with the next three.

I'm a fucking idiot. I really thought she'd pick me. I really thought she'd stay.

And I guess I should have known better. She's one of them, and the summer people always leave. We're nothing to them.

I'm nothing, too.

Well, that's not true. I'm angry and abrasive like she said. I'm completely normal, and I don't have any secret dark pain—just like I told her—but I have a questionable relationship with alcohol. And if she came back right now, I'm not sure if I'd want to kiss her or choke her. Or tie her to the bed so that she couldn't leave again. Or all three.

That doesn't exactly scream normal.

I think of the look on her face when she told me she loved me, and I didn't say it back.

No wonder she didn't stay. I wouldn't fucking stay either.

Dad: You're down to ten minutes.

I run my hands over my face and through my hair. I want to rip it all out, but I don't. I go back downstairs, get back in the truck, and head home so I can get ready for work. Because what else am I going to do? I'm not going to call her and beg. I'm not going to fucking cry. She made her choice. And I learned my fucking lesson, didn't I?

What was it my dad said? Oh, right. *You can't fuck with those people. You'll lose...every single time.*

I get home with five minutes to spare and slam the front door behind me.

"What's wrong?" my dad asks. "What happened?"

"Nothing," I tell him. "I'm fine. Let me go change, and we can go."

I go upstairs, quickly pull on something work appropriate, and almost leave the room. *Almost.* Before I can close the door, I catch a glimpse of my guitar out of the corner of my eye.

Make it a love song.

She told me she loved me. I didn't ask for that. Maybe Liam is right, and I don't know what love looks like, but I'm pretty fucking sure it doesn't look like this. It's not an empty house; it's not telling someone you'll see them tomorrow and disappearing without another word.

I'm not going to fucking cry or call her and fucking beg. But I'm not the kind of person who can just close the door and leave, either. Without fucking saying anything.

I'm not like her.

I pick it up off the stand, turn it over in my hands, then lift it over my head and smash it against the hardwood floors. Unfortunately, twice is all it takes before there isn't anything left to destroy, and I don't feel much better. I toss the fretboard over my shoulder, then turn and find my dad standing in the doorway, watching me.

"Nothing's wrong, huh? Is she gone?" he asks.

I swallow the lump in my throat. "I thought she'd stay."

"I did, too," he says. "I'm sorry."

I shrug. "Well, we should go, I guess."

"You don't have to—"

"No, I'm fine. I just need some coffee. We should go."

Then, I close the door and leave.

TWENTY-EIGHT

MADISON

"**M**adison?"

"Madison, you need to get up. It's one o'clock."

"I don't want to," I tell my mom.

"It's been days, Madison. You can't keep doing this. I have a surprise for you," she says, sitting down on the side of my bed.

"What is it?"

"Harper is here."

Harper. Great. Did I want Harper to be here? Not really. A few months ago, I would have told you she was my best friend. I don't think she even noticed I was gone. I think she texted me once or twice, asking about Ethan, but that was it.

I've gotten several texts from Ava and Chloe since I've been back. Even Ryan. When I text them, I try to pretend like I'm okay or like I'm trying to be okay, even though I'm not. Then, I go back to bed.

I don't hear from Liam. I'm sure he's as mad at me as Ezra is. I miss him and don't hear from him, either.

She leans down and kisses me on top of my head. "Have you washed your hair lately?"

"Yes," I lie.

She purses her lips. "Hmm. I'm going to send her up, okay?"

I don't reply, and she walks out the door, leaving it open. A few minutes later, I hear a couple of knocks, then her voice.

"Hey, Madison," Harper says.

I sit up in the bed. "Hi."

She sits down next to me and wraps her arms around me. "It's so good to see you; I missed you. I'm so sorry about your aunt. I didn't realize you two were so close."

"Thanks," I tell her.

"A bunch of us are going to go to the beach. I thought I'd come by and see if you wanted to go. I texted you yesterday, but you never replied."

She did? I guess maybe I remember that. I've just been so tired. Maybe it would be good to get out of the house and try instead of just waiting for that magical day when I wake up happy. Maybe I should do it.

"Yeah, I'll go," I tell her. "I just need to change really quick. I'll be down in a minute."

Her eyes run up and down my body, taking in my appearance and not looking entirely pleased with what she finds. "Oh, okay. Great! I'll wait for you downstairs, then."

Once she leaves the room, I crawl out of bed, open the top drawer of my dresser, and pull out a yellow halter bikini. I undress and, once I put it on, realize I need to retie the sides and straps—it's practically falling off my body. I examine myself in the mirror for the first time in a while, and yeah, I've lost some weight. My eyes look heavy. My hair is a fucking mess. The pink has grown out and faded, and despite what I told my mother, I haven't washed it in days. I run a brush through it and pull it up into a bun before covering myself in bronzer and applying a little bit of mascara and lipstick. I throw on a white coverup and some sandals and head downstairs.

"Ready," I tell her, grabbing my bag.

I get into her car, and we drive down to the beach. Harper falls into our usual conversation easily, like no time has passed and nothing has changed, and I do my best to follow suit. She tells me what she's been up to this summer and about how tomorrow she is going to meet up with the girl who will be her roommate at USC. I can't seem to make myself interested, but I play along. It does feel good not to be alone. It feels good to feel the sun again.

"Are you still upset about Ethan?" she asks once we park.

"Is he going to be here?"

"No!" she says. "No way. I wouldn't spring that on you like this."

"No, not at all. I don't think I was ever upset about Ethan, as weird as that must sound."

"You left town because of it. No one heard from you for months."

"I was angry," I tell her. "Not sad. I needed a break."

"I get that...I'm sorry it ended the way it did," she says, offering me a genuine smile.

"Me too," I tell her as we exit the vehicle.

"I bet you're glad you didn't get into Stanford now."

Uh, no. Not at all.

"I didn't apply to Stanford to be with him. I don't need to avoid it now to stay away from him. I have moved *so far* on, Harper. Just..." I pause. I've fallen in love with someone else and found out what a real broken heart feels like since the last time I saw her. I've come alive and died again since I last saw her. How do you begin to explain something like that? I can't, so I don't. "I'm really excited to start at Berkeley."

"When do you move in?"

"Tuesday," I tell her.

We make our way down to the beach, meeting up with four other people who graduated in our class. I sit next to Harper in one of the chairs she brought and try not to think about sitting at the lake with Ava instead.

"Oh my god, is that you, Madison?" Erica asks after we've been sitting there for a couple of minutes. "I didn't even recognize you, you know—with the hair and you've lost so much weight! You look amazing."

"Seriously, you do look really good," Harper says.

"Thanks," I tell them but do so bitterly. My weight has always been a bit of a touchy subject for me. I don't want to hear about it—good or bad.

"How'd you do it?" Erica asks.

"Depression," I tell them.

Everyone laughs, and I offer them a shitty ass smile in return.

"Oh my god, I saw Bailey Burke at a pool party last week. You guys remember her? She graduated last year; she was on the volleyball team. Anyway, so fat now. She's probably gained at least twenty pounds."

"Ugh, gross. No wonder Alex broke up with her," Harper says.

Oh, right. This is how it always was. I feel like I'm going to scream. This is why I left. This is why I didn't care when they didn't call. This is why I couldn't get that fucking word out of my head.

Fake.

"I heard she is hooking up with Ryder Thompson now."

"That makes sense," Brenden, Erica's boyfriend, says. "He dated Kaitlyn Wright, remember? Maybe he's just into fatties."

"Oh my god, can you all just...shut up...please? Can we talk about anything else other than what other people are doing with their bodies and with spare time that does not concern us at all?"

"Why are you acting like such a bitch, Madison?" Erica asks.

"I don't think I am. I think I'm trying to lower the level of bitchiness overall—for all of our sakes."

"So, what? You...dyed your hair a shitty shade of pink and lost some weight, and now you think you're better than us or something?" she asks.

"She's just having a hard time right now," Harper says. "You know she lost her aunt and her grandma this summer, and she and Ethan broke up. Give her a break."

"I don't give a shit about Ethan," I say. "And this has nothing to do with what kind of time I'm having—I just want to talk about anything else."

"No, you know what? Sure," Brenden says. "We can talk about you instead. I've heard a lot about what you've been doing this summer, Madison. From Weston."

I shrug.

"What do you mean?" Harper asks, then turns to me. "What is he talking about?"

"I heard Madison was up in Lost Hollow running around with a bunch of the locals acting like a criminal all summer."

"I know you can't see my eyes right now, Brenden, but I'm rolling them at you."

"No, really. I heard they broke into this house and trashed it; Madison even got arrested. I heard some guy threw a dart through Weston's face—tried to kill him. I heard you were fucking that guy, too."

I laugh hard. There is so much wrong with that recount of events.

"No," I tell them, still laughing. "No one tried to kill Weston, and I definitely wasn't fucking the guy who threw the dart through his face. That was his own friend. Oh, god—I needed the laugh, though. It's been a while."

"Is it true that you found the body?" he asks.

And now, I stop laughing.

"Yes."

"What was it like?"

"Cold. And terrible."

"Okay, you know what? Madison, can I talk to you?" Harper asks. She gets up from her chair and walks a good fifteen feet away from them, and I follow.

"Maybe this wasn't a good idea. Maybe you're just not ready for something like this yet. And that's okay, you know? Why don't we just go back to your house and we can hang out by the pool for a while, all right? Baby steps."

"You're right," I tell her. "This wasn't a good idea, but not for the reasons you think. You can stay. I'll get an uber home. I don't want to be here."

I storm off, pick my bag up from the sand, and head back to the parking lot to call a ride.

"Oh hey, Madison," my mom says when I walk in the door. She's in the kitchen in her own bikini, making a smoothie. "You're back early. Did you have fun with your friends?"

No, I didn't. And those aren't my friends. But I don't say that because it's the last thing she wants to hear.

"Sure."

She frowns. "Well, you look good. You look great, actually. I don't think I've seen you in anything other than pajamas since we got home."

"Thanks."

"How much weight have you lost?"

I grit my teeth. "I don't know, Mom."

"I know it's hard, Madison. This is hard for me, too. You're not the only one who lost someone."

Her eyes dart to the urn on the mantle. I know I'm not. And I know that it's complicated by the air that was never cleared between them and so many other things that I don't know about. It's the only reason why I continue to cut her some slack. It's the only reason why I'm even here.

"I know that."

"Will you come sit with me? Outside for a bit?"

"I think I've had enough socializing for today. I'll take one of those, though," I tell her, pointing at the blender. "But I'm gonna put vodka in mine."

"Fine. So am I," she says, shrugging.

She adds more fruit to her concoction, then reaches into the liquor cabinet and pulls out a bottle of vodka, going heavy on the pour. I wait while she blends and then evenly distributes the liquid into two cups. She hands one to me wordlessly, then takes her own with her out to the pool, passing my dad in the living room on her way out.

In what I've come to notice is his usual fashion, he doesn't even look up.

"You're a good dad," I tell him before going up the stairs. "I love you."

"Thanks, Madison," he says. "I love you, too."

TWENTY-NINE

MADISON

Time passed a little slower than I was used to, but it passed all the same. All of a sudden, it's the day before I'm supposed to move into my dorm. My mom has been asking me to start packing for days, and now I'm finally doing it. It feels good in a way—or at least better. Maybe a change of scenery will help like it did before.

It's weird to think that days ago, I wasn't going to go at all.

Now, as I start to fill suitcases and boxes, it hits me that I never bothered unpacking after I came back from Oregon. I guess I shouldn't be surprised—it makes sense. Like my mom said, I have only been wearing pajamas.

I dig through the bags, unpacking just to repack things like makeup, shoes, and hair styling tools. I start to pick through the clothes and sort them by what needs to be washed and what doesn't, but everything's been packed for so long, it's probably best to just wash it all at this point. I reach into the bag and scoop up as much of the laundry as I can, hearing something crumple as I do. I'm not sure what it could be, but I'm sure it's something I don't want to put through the wash. I set it all down on the bed to try to determine the source, and when I do, it all but crushes me. I pull out Ezra's gray sweatpants—the pair he had given me to wear the morning we found Emma—then reach into the pocket and pull out an envelope with my name on the front in her handwriting. I completely forgot about it. I put it away for a time when I was ready, and I don't think I'm ready now, either.

Still, with shaky hands, I run my thumb through the seal of the envelope and pull out the letter.

Dear Madison,

If you're reading this letter, it means I'm no longer with you.

This is the second letter I've started with that sentence. It doesn't sound right, though. It's supposed to sound softer—to be more palatable than just saying I'm dead. But it just sounds wrong, so let me start over.

If you're reading this, it means I'm dead.

But it doesn't mean I'm not still with you. I'm just there in a different, less physical way. Remember what I told you about the pieces we leave behind? I'm with you like that still—in memories, in the house and the lake. In the wildflowers. In your mom, too.

I want you to know that I'm glad you got in the car. I also want you to know that I lied when I said I would have left after seven minutes—you actually took eight. Getting to know you has been a gift. I hope throughout your life, you find yourself surrounded by

*people who feel the same way, and if you ever find that you aren't, I
hope you look for more.*

*I think a lot about what you said about the wild poppies. I hope
you always remember how strong you are. I hope you never stop
trying to grow.*

*I also want you to know that I'm okay with whatever you decide
to do with the house—whether you want to live in it, sell it, rent it
out, or burn it to the ground and build something new. It belongs to
you. It's supposed to go to you. So whatever you decide is the right
thing.*

*And if you're reading this and you're at home, or you've just
started school and you're still worried about how to keep being the
girl with the pink hair who plays the violin outside on a sunny day,
the one who takes the time to stand still and stand up for herself when
she needs to, then I hope you remember that it's simply a choice. No
one can make it but you.*

I love you.

Love,

Emma

I fold the letter, put it back in the envelope, and stuff it into
the top drawer of my dresser. I give myself only a couple of
minutes to cry since I've been doing far too much of that lately.
Then, I grab my keys and get in the car.

"Madison?" my mom calls, knocking on my door an hour later.
"Can I come in?"

"Um—" I start, but the knob is already turning.

She pushes open my bedroom door and finds me sitting in front of my mirror with a towel around my shoulders, painting thick pink hair color into my hair.

She sighs and approaches me. I wait for her snide comment, but instead, she holds out her hand. "Here," she says. "If you feel like you need to do it, then we should at least do it right."

I hand her the brush, and she takes over coating it onto my hair.

"You hate it like this," I say.

"I hated it because it was patchy before," she says. "This time, we'll do better."

"You are such a liar," I tell her, and we both laugh.

"God," she says. "I haven't laughed since we've been home. It feels so weird. Have you?"

"Laughed? Um, once. But not because something was funny—because it was *stupid*."

She laughs again. This time I catch the hint of vodka on her breath. At first, it makes me jealous, but then sad.

An hour later, we've washed and dried my pink hair, and I have to admit, it does look a lot better than when I did it myself. I feel better, too. More like myself somehow.

"Are you ready for tomorrow?" she asks.

"Honestly? Yeah, I am. I have to do something. You know what I mean?"

"Well, you look great, at least," she says. "Even if you don't feel it."

"Can I ask you something? Actually, no. Tell you something—this is non-negotiable."

"Um, sure."

"I don't want to hear any more comments about my body ever again. Not my weight, not my hips. Nothing about how much of it is showing or the way it looks in clothes. Good or bad, it feels bad every time. I don't want to hear it."

"I'm sorry. I try my best, Madison. I'm kind of figuring out that I messed up a lot with you, though. I think maybe I...overcorrected."

"Yeah, you did."

"Thanks for not kicking me when I'm down or anything," she says.

"Well, what? It's true. And you know what *I'm* kind of figuring out? That I don't know you at all."

And I don't think that's my fault. I don't know my mom. I don't even think of her as a normal person. Up until recently, I'd rarely seen her act like one. She didn't forget how to dance and sing or scream and feel, but she did stop doing it—at least in front of other people. I have no idea what is hidden beneath her flawless facade, and I'm not so sure I'll like it if I find out.

"That's fair. Maybe we could change that now, though. Maybe we could be different."

"How?" I ask.

"Maybe we could be friends."

"Friends?"

She shrugs.

"Yeah, okay. I guess we could try."

"Have a safe trip, sweetie," my dad says. "Call me later this week once you're settled in, and let me know how classes are going. I'm really proud of you."

"Oh, I thought you were coming, too."

"I wanted to; I planned on it but work got away from me this week. I'll come up there as soon as I can, though. We can go shopping and grab lunch."

"Yeah, that sounds good," I tell him. He hugs me and helps me load the last of my things into my car, and then I back out of the garage. My mom follows me in her SUV down the driveway, through the gate, and up to the East Bay. It isn't far from home, but the drive is long, and traffic is terrible. I spend far too much time sitting still and have too much time to think.

I think about him and how different everything was just days ago. I think about how I could just keep driving north and be "home" in six hours. I'd have a house, friends, and a job. I could go to school if I wanted. But I wouldn't have him. He wouldn't do this again—that's what he said.

And then, the universe decides to fuck with me, and "Cigarette Daydreams" blares through my speakers, filling the airwaves around me.

"It's not a fucking love song," I mutter, hitting the next button on my steering wheel several times. When the track still doesn't change, I turn the volume all the way down and resign to finish the drive in silence.

After I park, my mom meets me at my car and helps me drag my things inside. My roommate is already there and—from the looks of it—mostly unpacked, sitting cross-legged on her bed, looking through the welcome packet they were handing out at the door.

"Oh, hey!" she says when she sees me walk in. "You must be Maddie! I love your hair. I'm Jenelle."

"Madison, actually," my mom says, correcting her.

"Um, no. Actually, it's not," I say. "Maddie is fine. I prefer it."

"Oh...okay." She looks back and forth between the two of us. "Well, great. Nice to meet you, Maddie."

"You, too."

THIRTY

MADISON

It's been over two months since I started college. Over two months since Emma died, and I left Lost Hollow for good. Sometimes, it feels like a century ago—like another lifetime. Sometimes, it feels like it was just a dream. It was the most unexpected, most intense summer of my life. It left a mark on me. It changed me at a basic level. I left pieces of myself there that I needed to get rid of.

But I lost some that I really needed, too. And it left me with a void that I've been unable to fill.

It's not like I haven't tried. I'm doing more than just going through the motions. I still feel things; I want things. It's not like before.

It's just that thing I really want is something I'll never have again.

Some days are easier than others. I'll get to the end of the day, realize I didn't spend any time being sad, and congratulate myself on that feat before drifting off to sleep. Some days are harder. It's usually something small that triggers me. A cool, foggy morning that bleeds into a perfectly sunny day, wildflowers growing somewhere they shouldn't. The other day, there was a little blonde girl wearing two different shoes playing in the quad, and she jumped into a fountain to try and catch a bird. When her mother started scolding her, I learned her name was Emma.

I skipped the rest of my classes that day. I do that a lot.

Sometimes, I'm angry. I'm mad at him because he said he loved me, and he didn't try, either. He's not here, either. And why should it all fall on me? Angry days are easy days, too.

But I know why he's not here. I left him. I made that choice. I fit there. I'm trying to fit here, too. But what would he do?

I try my best to stay off social media. I keep in touch with the girls, but yesterday, Ava posted a picture with Ezra in it, and that ended up being a bad day, too. He looked good. And it hurt.

It's been hard not to text. I'll take out my phone and my fingers will hover above the keyboard, itching to say something, anything.

I'm sorry.

I miss you.

Do you ever think of me?

But he said never. And I understand.

When I woke up this morning, it felt bad again.

I've found a few ways to partially fill the void, but only temporarily. Parties, alcohol. Drugs. A random fuck. It does help, but it wears off. Even then, it doesn't feel any worse, so I don't stop. I rinse and repeat. I wake up in the morning and cure the hangover with another pill, chase it with a screwdriver, then try to do more than go through the motions and hope no one notices.

Today is Halloween, and it's no different. Rinse and repeat.

"You know, I actually wore something like this to school for most of my life," I say, adjusting the tied-off top on my sexy schoolgirl costume. "Same colors. A lot more boring, though."

I was probably a lot more boring then, too. I was bored, at the least. My college friends know nothing about the girl I used to be—the overscheduled, buttoned-up blonde who'd only ever slept with one guy and was a living, breathing ball of repressed anger. They didn't know anything about the one who spent her summer breaking things and getting that anger fucked out of her, either—the one who figured out that she does like being told what to do, but only when certain people do it.

They only know Maddie the Party Girl. That is all I have to offer right now. But they don't seem to mind.

"Your boobs look so good it makes me want to stay home," Jenelle says. "Don't stand next to me tonight, seriously. Unless it's like...super dark and there's a fog machine or something, I don't want to be seen next to you."

"Yeah, right. You look amazing," I tell her. It isn't a lie. We were looking for different things, anyway. I wasn't competition for her.

"You were having night terrors again last night," she says. "What was it? The same thing? The drowning thing?"

"Oh...yeah, sorry."

It was always the drowning thing. It was a little different each time, though. Sometimes, I'd see Emma's body floating in the water. Sometimes, the boat caught me, and it did run me over. Sometimes when it caught me, it was filled with all of the people I knew from home, and they'd all just watch me go under. And sometimes, when I went under, I'd see my mom.

But it always ended the same. I'd wake up after I opened my mouth and let the water in.

"It's okay; I just worry about you," she says. "You're probably just doing too much, you know. You should take fewer classes next semester. Try to sleep more—at night, I mean."

"Yeah," I tell her. "Yeah, I'm going to do that. Thanks."

Shay and Natalie from across the hall feign a knock on the door and step inside. "Knock, knock. Let us in, bitches. We come bearing tequila."

They sit on my bed, and we start passing around the bottle, chasing it with diet soda. It isn't the best combination, but I've had worse. I think I have a stomach of steel at this point.

"Oh, I almost forgot—do either of you have black lipstick?" Natalie asks.

Jenelle answers that she does, and they walk over to her desk and start sifting through her makeup bag. I take a long pull on the tequila and wince before chasing it with the soda again, then take advantage of the distraction.

"This is great," I tell Shay, "but do you have anything stronger?"

"You're out already?" she asks.

I shrug.

She shakes her head. "Sorry. No pills tonight. It'll probably be a while. I'll get some more when I go home for Thanksgiving...unless you know someone here."

Shit. No, I didn't know anyone. I tell her as much. "Guess I'll have to feel my feelings tonight," I add.

She laughs, but she has no idea. Like I said, it hurt when I woke up this morning.

After Natalie gets the lipstick she wanted and everyone is happy enough with the selfies we took, we walk to a frat we've been to a couple of times before. And there is a fog machine.

I was drunk when we left. An hour, another beer, and a keg stand later, I'm wasted. Jenelle is sitting on the couch talking to some guy. I'm not sure where Natalie is, but we ran into a bunch of people she said she knew as soon as we walked in. Shay and I are dancing together, looking for different things.

It isn't that hard to find.

A decent-looking guy with dark curly hair and a nice body comes up and starts dancing behind me, running his hands over me. I lean into it, and after a while, he asks me if I want to go upstairs.

I nod, then wrap my hand around the back of his neck and pull his face to mine and kiss him, running my tongue over his over-eager one, tasting whiskey and feeling my heart stop for just a second. It's a little thing, but it brings me back, hurting me even in my inebriated state.

When I pull back, he takes me by the hand and upstairs to his room. He closes and locks the door behind us, and I untie and remove my top, then toss it on the floor.

"Not wasting any time—I like it," he says, removing his own shirt.

Don't waste our time, Maddie.

God. Fucking. Damn it.

"Leave the skirt and the socks on," he says.

Okay. That's more like it.

He unbuttons his pants and takes his hard cock in his hands, stroking it before pulling a condom out of his pocket.

I kick off my heels, then reach under my skirt and pull off my underwear, then push him back on his back on the bed. I climb on top of him and sink my wet pussy down onto his dick and fuck him hard.

You never know what you're going to get around here. Sometimes, if you want things done right, it's better to do them yourself. At least he gave me something to work with.

"Ah, shit," he says. "That feels so...good."

It does feel good. Good enough to forget the things that feel bad for a while, at least. I lean back, shifting my weight from my knees to my heels, and that's even better. I'm close, but so is he—I can tell by the way his abs and his grip on my thighs tighten while I ride him. He takes one of the hands, licks his fingers, then uses them to put pressure on my clit. It's enough to push me over the edge. When I sit down hard and come on him, he looks relieved. He pushes up into me, and I feel him throbbing inside of me, too.

Then comes the awkward part. The leaving part.

"That was fun," I tell him, "but I should go find my friends. I'm sure they're looking for me."

I get up from the bed and pull my underwear back on, then pick my shirt up off the floor.

"All right," he says. "See you later, Maddie."

"Hmm," I say. "Pretty sure I didn't tell you my name."

The guy looks at me like I'm insane. "You're kidding, right? We have a class together, Maddie. We talk. We've...done this before."

"Oh...right."

Shit.

"You don't remember?"

"No, I do. You're..."

I have no fucking idea. And I don't know why I bothered starting the sentence.

"Preston," he says. " Wait. Shit. You...you really don't remember? *Nothing?*"

"No, I do. I...oh! *No.* You didn't do anything wrong. This is me. It's my fault. I'm the one with the...problems."

"What the *fuck*, Maddie?"

"Um, I'm sorry...Preston. I'll see you in..."

"*History.*"

"History, right. Sorry."

I close the door behind me and lean back against it, letting the humiliation wash over me and sober me up. I stay there just a few seconds too long, though. It opens behind me, and I almost fall back into the room.

"Oh, good. You're still here," he says sarcastically.

"I'm sorry," I say again. "Can I ask you something?"

"I really don't want to talk to you right now," he says, then sighs. "But, okay. Fine. Sure. Make it quick."

"Okay. Have you ever seen a dead body before?"

"*What?* You mean like at a funeral?"

I shake my head. "No. Not like that. I found my aunt's body a couple of months ago—in her bed. And then my boyfriend broke up with me because I wouldn't drop out of school and stay with him. And I have this house in Oregon that's completely mine, but my mom's whole family died in it, and she wants me to sell it, but I can't. I can't go back, either. And so I drink too much, and I take pills, and I keep having that dream again—the one where I'm drowning, because that almost happened, too—and nothing fucking fixes it."

"Jesus. Um...I'm sorry?" he offers, confused.

"It's fine. No one here knows about that, though. Kind of nice to say it, I guess. Anyway...see ya."

Fuck, I'm stupid.

I turn and head down the hallway, searching for a bathroom and holding my breath the entire way, knowing that when I let it go, the tears will go with it. I close the door behind me and sink down onto the floor, releasing them both.

When I was twelve, I got my first violin solo. My parents were so excited; they told everyone they knew. I remember sitting there playing along with my peers, my heart pounding in my chest, my hands so sweaty I was afraid I was going to drop the bow. I saw my mom beaming at me, holding her phone up in the air, recording. Then, when my moment came, I froze. I just sat there. And after what felt like the longest sixteen seconds of my life, the group was conducted to carry on without me. I missed it. I missed my chance, and she was devastated. I saw it on her face, and it ripped me apart.

For the rest of the song, I sat with my violin in my lap and cried.

When I met my parents afterward, they said nothing. They didn't congratulate me or tell me it was okay; they didn't tell me they were still proud of me. When we got into the car, I heard my mom mutter the words, *'so disappointing,'* under her breath.

But loud enough. And that was it.

So disappointing.

We didn't talk about it at dinner, either.

Afterward, I lingered in the kitchen and accidentally brushed the fingertips of my left hand against a still-hot burner. And it hurt.

Then, I laid my entire hand on top of it and left it there until I couldn't take it anymore. That *really* hurt.

But it didn't hurt as much as when I went to violin practice the next day and played through the strings digging into and ripping through my burnt, raw skin. I didn't complain, and I didn't tell anyone. I just thought...this is what I get. I deserve this pain. I'll know better next time, and I won't do it again.

I didn't, either.

So, I understand why he said never. I've told myself never a thousand times. Pain is an excellent teacher. I've learned more from pain than I have ever learned in any classroom.

It's also the very best deterrent.

Still, I dig my phone out of my knee highs, scroll down to Ezra's name, and hit send.

THIRTY-ONE

EZRA

I'm drunk at a house party, surrounded by people, and I'm bored as fuck.

It's a shitty combination.

"Hey, you actually came!" Ariana says, then frowns. "And...you're not wearing a costume. That's boring."

"This whole thing is fucking boring," I scoff.

"Ugh, whatever. Get a beer. And get in a better mood. You're scaring people more than usual."

"It's Halloween," I say. "I'm being festive."

She rolls her eyes and walks away. I only take some of her advice—I get a beer, and I don't get in a better mood. I sit on the sofa, take out my phone, and start scrolling Instagram. I stop on a photo of a girl with long pale pink hair smiling with her friends with a shot glass in her hands. They're all wearing the same stupid slutty Halloween costumes as the girls surrounding me here now.

"Way to be fucking original, Maddie," I mumble to myself as if that's what I'm really mad about and not how good she looks. She does look good, though, and it doesn't help with my shitty mood. The tattoo is new. I can't quite tell what it is; it looks like flowers, but most of it dips down under the waistline of the skirt she's wearing.

I click on her name and start going through her photos—just because I want to see if there's another picture of the tattoo. No other reason.

She hasn't posted much since she's been home or at school or whatever, and I don't find one.

"Oh, my god—Maddie, Ezra? Seriously?" Ava says from behind me.

I lock my phone and toss it down on the couch.

"I was just scrolling," I tell her. "I'm bored."

"Why don't you just talk to her? Have you talked to her?"

I shake my head. "No."

"Ezra..." she says. And I hate how she says it. Her voice is filled with pity. Or sympathy. Either one sucks.

"No," I say again.

"You should talk to her."

"I don't want to talk to her."

"I bet she misses you, too."

"I don't miss her. Stop trying to psychoanalyze me. I'm not the first person in the world to fucking...look up an ex on social media on a shitty day," I tell her.

"Yeah, but...it seems like most of your days have been shitty since she left."

"I'm *fine*."

"She hasn't sold the house," she says. "She'll probably be back."

"I don't want her to come back. I hope she doesn't."

"You don't mean that."

"She left me just like she left that fucking guy, Ava. She didn't even say anything. So yeah, I do mean that. I told her if she left, that was it; she made her choice."

And it's true, too. It still feels shitty, and I would not, under any circumstances, be doing it again. Not with her. Not with anyone else, either. Not on purpose, and I'd make sure it didn't happen by accident. It wasn't what I wanted before, anyway.

"Yeah, I heard all about the shitty ultimatum you gave her at the very worst time," Ava says. "I just really don't care."

I told her I loved her and asked her to stay with me. I asked her to do what *she* wanted to do anyway. Was that really that shitty? I don't think so. So, fuck Maddie.

But I really thought she'd stay. After everything, I still wasn't good enough. I think of how I felt when I found the house empty—when she left without saying anything at all. Maybe she didn't even spend any time thinking about it. I do hope she stays gone.

"I don't really care what you think, either, Ava. Cute costume, though."

"Gee, thanks, Ezra. I wish I could say the same for you, but your grumpy asshole costume is a bit overplayed."

I laugh as she shakes her head and walks off. That was actually a good one. I can't even be mad about it.

My mood doesn't improve much as the night wears on, but eventually, I do get up off the couch and socialize with friends. And when a cute brunette I've hooked up with a couple of times before makes it obvious that she wants to go home with me, it's not like I'm going to say no. While we walk back to my place, my phone buzzes in my pocket with an incoming call. I assume it's probably spam or, at best, a shitty drunk dial from Liam, so obviously, I'm not going to answer it. I never answer it.

"Um, is there a bathroom?" she asks when we get inside.

No, dumbass. My house doesn't have a bathroom.

"Just past the stairs," I say, pointing. "Same place it was last time."

She kisses me before disappearing down the hallway. I pull my phone out of my pocket and sit back on the couch.

1 New Voicemail from Madison Ridgeway.

My heart drops into my stomach. No fucking way.

I should delete it. That's what I should do. At the very least, I shouldn't listen to it right now, but I do anyway.

Probably just a butt dial.

"Hey, Ezra..."

Not a butt dial.

"If this was a standoff, then I lose, I guess. Not that I think that's what it is...or was. I know you said never. Never again, never come back, never call. And I don't expect anything from you—I know you. I don't even expect you to listen to this. I expect you to be fine. But

me...I'm not fine. I'm trying—really hard. My best, I guess. But my best is pretty shitty, and I just keep fucking up..."

Around this point, Brittany—the girl I brought home—comes back from the bathroom. She sits down next to me, then leans over, and pulls my earlobe through her teeth while sliding her hand into the waistband of my pants. I jump up from the couch, holding up a finger to signal that I just need a second, and listen to the rest of the message.

"I just want you to know—in case it matters and even if it doesn't—that I regret getting in the car. That I miss you and the house and the lake, and I really miss being there with you. Some days, I think maybe it's getting better, but I think it's more that some days I'm better at being distracted. I can't be quiet and still anymore. I don't ever play music just for fun.

Anyway, I don't want you to feel bad for me. I'll do better. I'm going to try harder. I'll be okay, I just—"

Then, the line cuts off.

"Fuck!" I yell, then throw my phone across the room.

I sit in the chair across from the sofa instead of next to the girl on the couch. I lean back, run my hands through my hair, and stare up at the ceiling.

"Um...are you okay?" she asks.

"I want you to leave."

"Are you sure? Whatever it is, I bet I can make it better." She gets up from the couch and starts toward me.

"No," I tell her. "I don't want to fuck you. I want you to get out of my house."

"But—"

"Bye." I stand up, walk around her, and then start making my way up the staircase.

"You're a fucking asshole, Ezra," she shouts at my back.

And yeah, she's probably not wrong. But it doesn't change anything. Neither does the message, except that I check my phone religiously for the next couple of weeks, waiting for a follow-up call or a text that says she didn't mean any of that—she was just drunk. Or maybe I'm waiting for the rest of the message or for her to actually come back. But even if she did, I'd probably do just as much about it as I do the voicemail.

Which is nothing.

And the regret would probably eat away at me just like it does now.

Shortly after Thanksgiving, a 'For Sale' sign goes up in the yard.

'Her choice,' I tell myself. *'It has nothing to do with me.'*

THIRTY-TWO

MADISON

I spend the rest of the weekend sober. I'm surprised how hard it is. It's so hard, in fact, that I have to get into my mini fridge and dump whatever leftover alcohol I do have into the toilet and flush it.

I guess my mom isn't the only one who over-corrected.

I think about Emma and her letter. I don't think that what I've been doing is helping me grow in any way. I think about Ezra and that fucking voicemail. I don't regret it, and I didn't really expect him to call, but it hurts just the same. It makes me uncomfortable and makes it impossible to be still. Thus, the vodka down the toilet.

Then, I spend my Sunday doing something I haven't done since I first moved in—I get out my books and try to figure out what the fuck I'm supposed to be doing in my classes.

When I walk into history on Monday, I spot Preston immediately. I sure as hell won't forget his name or face now. I bet he wouldn't forget mine either, no matter how much he probably wants to. We make eye contact when I walk by his row in the lecture hall, and I give him a pathetic wave. He nods in response and looks just about as uncomfortable as I feel.

I sit toward the front and don't fall asleep.

After the lecture, I gather my things and prepare the head to my next class, but the professor calls my name.

"Madison...Walker-Ridgeway? If you're here, please see me before you leave."

I walk up to the podium. "Hi, I'm Madison Ridgeway."

"So, you decided to stick it out for the rest of the semester, I guess? You're past the drop date now."

"What do you mean?" I ask.

"I emailed you a couple of weeks ago and suggested you drop the class and try again next semester," she says. "You did get it, didn't you? You're failing, Madison. This is a core class. You have to pass it to graduate."

I'm...what? I mean, I guess I knew my grades probably weren't as good as I was used to, but school has always been easy for me. I've never had to try that hard. I guess I assumed it would stay that way.

But I guess I've *really* been not trying hard lately. Like I told Ezra, my best has been shitty, and I just keep fucking up.

"So, I can't drop it now?" I ask.

"No," she says. "It's too late now."

"Is there any way I can still pass the class?"

"That's what I wanted to talk to you about. I want to offer you some extra credit. If you complete that and do well—really well—on your remaining assignments and your final exam, you should be able to pass."

"I'll do it," I tell her. "I can do that."

"Here you go," she says, handing me a paper.

"Thank you."

"And Madison?"

"Yeah?"

"If you need to talk to someone, we have resources for that here on campus. Let me know if you need help."

Shit. Is it that bad? Do I look like someone who needs help?

'You do need help,' the voice in my head replies.

"Thanks," I say over my shoulder as I leave.

I spend the next few weeks buckling down. I turn nineteen on a Tuesday alone in my room, and I don't mention the day to anyone. I do go out and drink a couple of times, but I keep my shit together and, for the most part, stay in. I try to remember how to be the girl with the pink hair who plays the violin outside on a sunny day—the one who takes the time to stand still and stand up for herself when she needs to—like Emma said. I go back and forth on how exactly to do that, but I do know that I'm not doing it now. And something has to change.

I sleep, and I eat, and that's a start. I put back on some of the weight I've lost. I still have the nightmares. I figure out quickly that history isn't the only class I am close to blowing it in, and I shouldn't be surprised.

And when the time comes to sign up for classes for my next semester, I change my major to 'undeclared' and register only for core classes offered online.

Thanksgiving rolls around, and I stay on campus and continue playing catch-up. My parents will be at some spectacle of a dinner with their closest friends, and it isn't something I really want to be dragged to, anyway. There will be some people there who I've pissed off, and I didn't want to have to deal with that. They aren't on my list of regrets and I can't fake it anymore.

I call my parents to wish them a happy Thanksgiving, and they update me on what's been going on in their lives and ask what's been going on with me. I tell them I've mostly just been studying and staying in, but yes, I have made quite a few friends, and I am happy.

Only the last part is a lie.

"Madison?" my mom says just as I'm about to hang up the phone.

"Yeah?"

"We really do need to do something about the house."

"I don't know..." I start.

"If you aren't going to sell it right now, I'm going to have to have someone go up there to winterize it and drain the pipes. What do you want to do right now?"

I think about Ezra. About the voicemail and how he hasn't called or texted at all. I think about how I'm trying to move on, and I'm doing such a bad job of it, and how maybe it would be easier if I would really and truly close the door.

I miss the lake, and I miss my friends. I miss that life. But am I really going to go back up there during summer break? Am I going to be able to see him or sit across the table from him with them?

I'd like to think that it would be easier by then—we're talking about half a year from now. But it hasn't gotten much easier yet. And if getting easier continues to move at this abysmal pace, I don't think I'll be able to do it.

Do you want to know the real reason why I never come back here? It's because I can't risk looking at his face.

"We should sell it, Mom."

"Are you sure?"

"Yeah, I'm sure. Call your friend with the Oregon license. We should sell it."

"I think so, too," she says. "You're doing the right thing, Madison."

Yeah," I tell her. "I know I am."

"We have three decent offers," my mom says when I get home on Christmas Eve. The house has been officially on the market for about a week now. My mother hired someone to clean it up and put all of Emma and Grandma's personal items in storage. She donated the clothes. I told her I wanted to keep some of Emma's art, and she said we could go up to the storage facility she rented in Klamath Falls once it gets warmer, and I could have whatever I wanted.

"That was fast," I say.

I don't know what I expected—I know Lost Hollow is in demand now. The new Tahoe. She sits down in front of me with the offers in hand.

"One of them is over asking price, but this one—the one I think we should go with—they're willing to purchase the property as-is and forgo an inspection. An inspection of that property is going to find some things. And they won't be small things. They'll be things we don't want to have to deal with or pay for."

"Are any of them local?" I ask.

She shakes her head. "No. But they are all-cash offers."

"That doesn't mean anything to me."

"It should. It means it'll be easier. It means they won't fall through, and you won't have to do this again. You can be done, Madison."

"What are they going to do with the house?" I ask.

"I have no idea," she says. "Whatever they want, once it's theirs."

"Well, can you ask her? Your friend? It matters to me."

"I could ask, but they don't owe you an answer. They don't have to keep the promise. They don't even have to know what they're going to do with it right now. They'll probably live in it part-time and rent it out for the rest of the year. Fix it up."

"The neighbors won't like that," I say.

"No, probably not. But the area is changing. It's going to keep changing whether you're a part of that or not."

"I don't want to do the one without the inspection," I tell her.

"What? Why not?"

"Because I'm afraid they're going to knock it down. While I was there, someone did that to a house a couple of blocks over. I don't want them to knock it down. It will feel bad."

"Might feel good for me, though," she says, then relents. "You know what? I will text Rita and tell her that we're a little bit busy with family stuff and will let her know what we decide after Christmas. That's fair, right?"

"Maybe I'll get a new offer if I wait. Maybe someone local?"

"Probably not, Madison. And you can't really wait with things like this. They have an expiration date."

"You got something in the mail from Berkeley," my dad says, entering the room. He hands me the envelope and sits at the table across from me.

"Dinner is almost ready," my mom tells him. "About ten more minutes."

"I'm glad we stayed in tonight. I'm glad it's just us," I tell them, then correct myself. "I mean, it would be better if...."

"I know," she says. "What's in the envelope? Is it your grades?"

"What? No. They don't send out grades like this."

"Dean's List?" my dad asks.

I laugh. "No. I definitely did not make the Dean's List."

"Are you sure? Open it."

Oh, I'm sure. I open the envelope. I guess I should have seen this one coming, too.

"Dear Madison Walker-Ridgeway," I read. "Based on the Academic Policies and Procedures of the University of California, Berkeley, your academic performance has been deemed...."

Oh, shit.

"What?" my mom presses.

"...unsatisfactory. Your status has been changed from 'Good Standing' to 'Academic Probation' for the Spring 2023 semester. See? No Dean's List."

"Oh my god! *Madison*," my mom says, "what happened?"

"You know what happened, Mom."

"I'm really disappointed in you, Madison," my dad adds. "What have you been doing up there for four months? Obviously, not studying."

Getting fucked up, mostly.

"I don't know if either of you noticed, but I've been having a hard fucking time."

"Don't talk to us like that, Madison," Dad says.

"I'm doing better now," I tell them. "It still isn't easy. It's still hard."

"Well, get it together! You're better than this," my mom adds.

"You keep saying that," I laugh. "But am I? Based on *what?*"

A timer goes off, and my mom gets out of her seat to pull the roast out of the oven.

"Help me set the table," she says calmly.

I do, and we eat in relative silence, my dad scrolling his phone next to his plate like he always does. I wonder what it's like here in the house now that I'm gone. It was always too big, too quiet. Don't they feel it, too? Does it not make them want to fucking scream?

We finish our meal, then my mom serves cheesecake, which my dad declines, retiring to his office instead.

"Maybe I shouldn't have made you go," my mom says once he's out of earshot.

"What?"

"Maybe I shouldn't have made you go. To school, I mean. Maybe you should have taken the semester off or something. You weren't ready for it."

"What did you just say to me?"

"Madison..."

"Because when I told you I wasn't ready...that I didn't want to go and that I wanted to stay in Oregon, you said no. You said I would ruin my life. You said I couldn't wait and you would be *done* with me. I was *vulnerable*, Mom."

"That was before I knew you would just...mess it up anyway."

I scoff. "I thought we were friends now."

"I'm trying, Madison, I really am. Do you think I like that you're hurting like this?"

"I don't know. I'm just going to go upstairs."

"Do you want to talk about it? What's been going on at school or any of it? I won't judge you; I promise. I want to help you."

"No, I don't. Because I can't change anything now, even if I want to. I did leave, and I did put the house up for sale. And I'm just barely not kicked out of school, and I can't do anything about that either. I just have to hope that, someday, I wake up, and I'm glad I did all of this—that I don't regret any of it. Like you, right, Mom?"

"Honey, I have no doubt that it will happen."

"You don't have any regrets, right? You're completely happy?"

"I have one big one. It sits on my mantle, and I think about her every day. But you're right; there is nothing either of us can do about any of that. So yeah, Madison. I am happy. I *choose* to be—because what's the alternative?"

"Cool. Thanks. That was totally convincing."

"He's not here, either," she says to my back as I start to leave the room. "Has he tried to see you? Has he even called?"

I squeeze my eyes shut. I don't turn around when I reply. "I'll see you in the morning."

I go upstairs, close my door, and lie in the dark, but I don't fall asleep.

THIRTY-THREE

MADISON

She shouldn't have made me go. I shouldn't have gone. I shouldn't have had to make a decision like that right then.

But there's no point. I know that. I did go. And now the house is up for sale. And that'll be done soon, too.

The past is over and done with. The future isn't real.

I need to let it go. I want to, even. I scream it in my head over and over again, but I still can't seem to do it. When the house is dark and quiet, I grab my purse and my keys and get in the car.

It's after 4:00 AM when I pull into the driveway of the house in Lost Hollow. There's a light dusting of snow in the front yard.

I got lucky, and the roads were clear on the way up, but it's starting to come down now.

There's a white wooden post with a 'For Sale' sign hanging from it in the yard in front of the house. It's got a picture of the realtor on it—a redheaded woman probably in her fifties with her arms crossed in front of her blue blazer. I don't know why, but it pisses me off. I told myself I'd come up here to say goodbye—so that I could let it go, and that was it.

But I can't look at the woman on that fucking sign.

Before I can think about it, I buckle my seatbelt again, put the car in reverse, and back out of the driveway. Then, I throw it back into drive and lay on the gas, running the Mercedes sedan straight through the yard and right over the sign.

It hits a lot harder than I expected. It's enough to deploy my airbags and bring the car to a stop. The skin on my face stings from the impact of the airbag. I get out of the car, fearing that I haven't even accomplished my goal, but I am pleased to find the sign itself successfully demolished. I'll worry about the car later.

I leave it like it is, walk up to the front porch, and turn my key in the lock. I step into the cold, dark house and close the door behind me. And it is cold. I immediately head to the thermostat, which is set at fifty-five degrees, and turn it up to seventy, knowing it will take a long time to get there. Despite the temperature and the bare walls which have been covered in a fresh coat of white paint instead of the dark blue I was used to, the house still feels warm. It still feels good. On the way up, I'd convinced myself that it wouldn't—that I'd step inside and the house would feel like nothing, just like I used to, and then it'd be easy for me to move on. I'd realize that I didn't belong here, and I'd been faking it the entire time.

Instead, it feels like coming home. And I'm tired. I feel like I can finally sleep. Maybe I won't have that dream again.

Shivering, I light the gas fireplace, then go to the closet to grab a blanket, but find it empty. I guess I shouldn't be surprised. Regardless, I curl up on the couch, and sleep comes easily, just as it did the very first time.

"Maddie, wake up," someone says, kneeling in front of me, shaking me. I feel a warm hand on my cheek and then in my hair. "Jesus Christ, you're cold. You're going to freeze to death. What are you doing?"

I slowly come back into myself and open my eyes. I don't know how long I've been sleeping, but it's light out now. It is still cold.

"What are you doing, Ezra?"

"I came to check on your crazy ass," he says. "Hi, Maddie."

"I didn't think you ever wanted to see me again. How did you know I was here?"

"Small town," he says. "You left a pretty big red flag in the front yard."

"Oh. Right. I'm not...completely insane. Do you hate me?"

"No," he says and kisses me on my mouth. "No, baby. I don't hate you. I love you so much. I'm so fucking sorry."

I climb onto his lap and wrap my arms around him. He pulls me into him and threads his fingers through my hair. "I missed you," I tell him.

"I missed you, too. I should have called you. It *was* a stupid standoff."

"Did you listen to my message?"

"Of course I did," he says, kissing my neck. "I'm sorry I didn't call."

"It's okay."

"Merry Christmas, Maddie."

"Merry Christmas," I tell him.

We stay like that for a while. I wipe my watery eyes before the stupid tears can run down my face, although I'm sure the makeup I slept in is a nightmare, and it wouldn't make a difference anyway.

"I bet I look like shit. I'm sorry."

"Never," he says. "You look beautiful. Come on."

He gets up from the couch, pulling me with him.

"Where are we going?" I ask.

"It's freezing in here, and there's no food," he tells me, then grabs my left hip and says. "You want to go with me, right?"

"Yeah, I do..."

"And later, you're going to show me that tattoo."

"How do you know about my tattoo?" I ask.

He shrugs. I bite back a smile.

Nervously, I get into the truck. I'm not so sure his dad and Liam will welcome me, but upon arrival, I quickly find my fears unfounded.

"Hey, guys," Ezra says when we step inside. "Maddie's here."

His dad gets up, walks over to me, and pulls me into a hug. "Hey, Sweetheart. It's good to see you. Are you doing okay?"

"Yeah," I tell him. "I'm okay."

It's mostly true. Just being here, I feel better than I have in a while.

"You got something against 'For Sale' signs?" he asks.

Liam and Ezra both laugh.

"I've got something against that one," I say. "I guess I may have overdone it, though."

"You think?"

"Anger issues," Ezra says, shaking his head. "How you haven't ended up on the local news yet is beyond me. I didn't care much for it either, though. I can't tell you how many times I wanted to run it over myself."

"Get some food and some coffee, Maddie," Ty says and walks off.

So, I do. I fill up a plate and the biggest coffee mug I can find and eat on the couch. I text my parents and tell them Merry Christmas and that I'm in Oregon. They don't ask questions. Ryan comes over, too, and Ezra and I curl up under a flannel blanket and watch Christmas movies together. It isn't uncomfortable; it feels like a normal day. It feels like I never left, and no one asks me about that, either.

At some point, I must have fallen asleep on Ezra's shoulder. When I wake up, it's dark outside, and we're alone in the room. My shoulders and neck hurt; I think whiplash has started to set in from the sign incident this morning.

"Where did everybody go?" I ask.

"Liam and Ryan went back to his house; my dad went to bed," he says.

"You should have woken me up," I tell him.

"Nah, it's fine. You were tired. We have time. You want to go upstairs?"

I nod and follow him up the stairs, then down the hall to his bedroom. The minute the door closes behind us, he closes the space between us, and his mouth crashes into mine.

"I missed you, Maddie," he says. "Every fucking day, I missed you."

He backs us up to the bed, and I lie back, pulling him down on top of me, clutching his shirt and inhaling him like my life depends on it while he rolls his hips against me. His hard dick pushes into me, and even through my jeans, it makes me moan as I arch my hips up against him.

He breaks away from me and pulls his shirt over his head and then my own and my bra. I lie back and he pulls my jeans and my underwear off of my body, then his mouth makes its way down my neck and my chest, lingering to nibble and suck on my nipples before dipping lower, down my stomach until his warm tongue slides over my clit and his fingers work their way inside me.

"Oh, god," I call out, fisting his hair. "Fuck, I missed you."

"You're so fucking wet," he says. "How long have you been thinking about this?"

"All the time. Every day. Ezra..."

"What do you want?" he asks, still fucking me with his fingers. "Ask nicely."

"I want you inside of me," I tell him. "I mean, please. Please, fuck me."

His fingers are quickly replaced by his thick cock. I gasp, stretching to adjust to his size again. His hands run up my body, over my chest, and then one grips my hair hard at the roots while he thrusts into me. It isn't gentle; it's rough and desperate, and I feel desperate, too. He drills into me, holding me in place with the hand pulling my hair while my heels dig into the bed, feeling the building orgasm about to rip through me.

I scream before I come.

"That's it," he says. "I love feeling your tight, messy pussy squeezing my dick when you come. Fuck..."

The orgasm is still ripping through me when he collapses on top of me, groaning while his dick pulses inside me. I pull him toward me and bite into his chest when he does, just wanting to get closer somehow, to have more of him in me.

I realize it's kind of fucked up. I also think he'd understand.

"Look at you," he says, kissing me after. "This is exactly how I like you. Remember?"

Yeah. I do.

"How can you be like this? Aren't you mad at me?" I ask.

"I was," he says. "I was really mad at you. You shouldn't have left like that. Not without saying anything."

"I know."

"But after you called, I just missed you. I wish I would have done things differently, too."

"Where's your guitar?" I ask. "I'll play you something—not a love song, though."

"I don't have it," he says. "I stopped playing for fun, too."

"I'm really sorry."

"It really is okay, Maddie. We don't have to talk about it unless you want to. I could be mad at you—drag it out and make us both suffer, I guess. So could you. I just don't see the point. We've wasted enough time, don't you think?"

I nod, because I'm afraid if I try to speak, I might cry.

And he's right. We could punish each other—make it diffi-cult to make sure the other one was sorry. He could pretend I don't exist to punish me for leaving the way I did, and I could act like I don't care because he didn't call. We could keep it going until a future date when we both feel like we've hurt the other enough to make it even.

But it already hurt. And the future isn't real.

Eventually, we get up and shower together. I try not to think about the last time I was in that shower—when I was sitting in the tub after my aunt died, and he didn't say he loved me back. I feel loved now. I felt loved then, too.

Afterward, when we're lying in bed in the dark, he finally asks, "Maddie, how long are you going to stay?"

I don't answer immediately. I'm going to stay—at least for a while. I think maybe this was always my plan, even before I was willing to admit it to myself. This is where I want to be, and he is who I always wanted to be here with. I think that's the real reason why I dropped my major and signed up for online classes next semester. I always wanted to come back to Lost Hollow. I just didn't know if it would feel right if I did.

"If you have to go back to school, Maddie—that's okay. I still want to be with you. I can't replace you. I can't forget about you, either."

"All of my classes are online next semester," I tell him. "I won't be able to do that all the time, though. But...I can stay for a while. I'm not going to sell the house. I thought maybe I'd stay and see if Lisa needs any help at the store. Be with you...if you want."

He sighs and pulls me into him, kissing me on top of my head. "Thank you."

"I'll have to go home and get some things, though. I didn't bring anything with me."

"I'll go with you," he says. "I'll drive."

"You don't have to."

"Maddie, I don't even think your car is driveable. And I'd want to go with you, anyway."

"I love you," I tell him.

"I love you, too."

I know the next part won't be easy. When I wake up tomorrow, everything will be different. I'll have to go home and face my parents. I'll have to pack up and really leave, and hopefully, I'll do a better job than I did in that hasty eight minutes while my aunt waited in the driveway back in May. Everything will be different, and it will be hard, but it will feel better, too.

The days won't be numbered, and I won't have to count them. The sun will rise and set, and I'll watch them all slip through my fingers, knowing I'll be able to have as many as I want.

EPILOGUE

"Maddie, wake up."

"I don't want to," I tell Ezra. "I was up all night."

"Doesn't matter," he says. "You have to. It's Christmas. And your mom's coming."

"Ugh, shit. You're right. I better text her and see how far away she is. Do you think they'll be okay together?"

"It's Christmas," he says again. "Why wouldn't they be?"

I shrug. "They fought at the wedding."

"Well, I'm sure that was your mom's fault."

I don't argue because I don't disagree. I'm sure it was her fault.

I get dressed and head downstairs, the scent of coffee and cinnamon rolls hitting me before I get to the landing.

The old cabin hasn't changed much in the past six years. I did repaint the walls in dark blue and covered them again with Emma's work. We replaced some of the furniture and appliances, but it still has the same small, cozy, comfortable feel to it that it always did. There's a treehouse in the backyard, even though she won't be able to play in it for a while. It's still my favorite home, even though it's been a couple of years since we lived here full-time.

I never went back to Berkeley. I finished my online classes that spring with a 4.0 GPA and transferred to the University of Southern Oregon with Ava and Ariana. It was still about two hours from Lost Hollow, but we saw each other almost every weekend and made it work for three years. Sometime in the middle of those years, I let the pink grow out of my hair, returning it to its original blonde. I stopped dreaming about drowning. I learned how to stand still again. I added two more tattoos. I changed my major to music and, after I graduated, got a job teaching in Ashland, and Ezra moved there with me. We still spend as much time as possible in Lost Hollow—every holiday and most of our summers.

Our house isn't anything like the one I grew up in. I still drive the same car my parents bought me when I turned sixteen. And I'm happy, just like I wished for the first summer I was here.

Shortly after I graduated, we got married, and my parents divorced. They sold the house, my dad got a girlfriend, and my mom got an apartment on the beach in Monterey.

I tried not to be too upset about it. It doesn't change who they are to me in any way. And they did the best they could—I believe that. I believe they loved each other, too, even if they're better like this now.

"Oh my god, Ezra. You did not give her a cinnamon roll!" I grab a handful of baby wipes and pull our 8-month-old, who is currently covered in vanilla icing, out of her highchair. "She can't have stuff like that."

"It's not going to hurt her," he says, shrugging. "She liked it."

"She won't nap now," I tell him.

He hugs me from behind, planting a kiss on top of my head. "She probably wasn't going to nap anyway."

I shake my head. "I'm going to go get ready. You have to get her ready."

"No problem," he replies as I hand her off.

I stuff a cinnamon roll in my mouth and head upstairs with my coffee, then shower and get ready for the day. Liam and Ryan moved to Portland last year, and they aren't coming home until New Year's Eve, so it'll just be the five of us.

An hour later, we get into the car and make the short drive up past the village to Ezra's dad's house. I'm relieved that we get there before my mom, even if it's just barely. Getting ready and going anywhere with Poppy always takes ten times longer than I expect it to.

We're there just long enough to set down our things and grab a couple of drinks before I hear my mom's car coming up the driveway. Ezra sits on the sofa and starts flipping through channels. I join him and let Poppy crawl around on the floor. Ezra's dad sits down next to her, and she wastes no time getting to the tree and instantly starts removing anything she can reach and throwing it across the floor.

"Feel free to move her away from there," I tell Ty. "She'll just keep tearing it apart."

"I don't mind," he says. "I did all of this just for her, anyway."

The doorbell rings, and I start to get up.

"Don't. Sit. I've got it."

"Amelia," Ty says. "Come in. Merry Christmas."

"Merry Christmas," she says.

"Let me take that bag for you," he says. She hands him the bag of presents in her hand, and he sets it down next to Poppy under the tree.

"Hi, Mom."

"Hi, Madison."

She walks through the door, past the living room, and into the kitchen, then sets the dish in her hands down on the counter. "Um, it's cheesecake."

"Sounds great," he tells her.

She walks over to the tree and picks Poppy up from the floor. "You shouldn't be down here tearing this stuff up," she says and kisses her on the forehead.

"Tell your grandma you can do whatever you want while you're here."

"I am *not* Grandma," she tells him. "I'm Mimi. I'm way too young to be a grandma."

"Maybe, but here we are anyway, Grandma," he teases.

"Thanks for inviting me. I know you don't...like me very much."

"I like you just fine," he says. "How could I not? Look what we made."

She smiles and looks at him in that way that makes me uncomfortable. I shoot Ezra a wide-eyed glance, and he just shrugs like I expect him to.

We weren't like them. Not at all, and I was glad. Maybe they didn't have to be like them anymore, either.

"She is pretty great," Mom says.

"Yeah, Maddie did good. Can't even tell she's inbred," he says.

My mom's jaw drops; she punches him playfully in the arm.

"That's never going to be funny," I tell him while my husband laughs.

Christmas ends up being perfect, just like the other six that I've spent in this house. No one fights. Our daughter gets more than enough attention and presents, though she's more interested in playing with the trash than anything else. She even ends up napping after all; she falls asleep on my mom's lap before we go home.

"You ready to go, Mom?" I ask after I pack everything up.

"Why don't you let me take Poppy for a walk in the village? What do you think, Mel? You want to go? We can give them a little break, show her the Christmas lights and the ice sculptures. It's changed a lot down there. You might want to see it."

"Um, sure. Yeah. That sounds nice, actually...if it's okay with you guys."

"Fine with us," Ezra answers. "Let me grab her car seat and stroller out of the car for you."

I'm a little more apprehensive than he is, but I go along with it anyway.

We take home too much food and spend our free hours fucking and watching a horror movie. I know it's Christmas, but I explain to Ezra that it *has* to be horror to offset how G-rated the rest of my life has become with teaching and the baby.

Besides, I still like to be scared.

Three and a half hours later, my mom returns with the baby. She's oddly quiet; she hands her off to me and announces that she's exhausted and is going to go to bed.

"Everything go okay?" I ask.

"Oh, yeah. It was great. Poppy had fun. She was wonderful the whole time."

I knew the baby wasn't going to be a problem. That wasn't what I was talking about. Still, I accept the answer, thank her for taking her, and tell her goodnight.

Shortly after, we turn off the lights and the fireplace and head upstairs, too.

I get into bed with my husband and my daughter in what used to be Emma's room and think about how much I wish she could be here to see this—how I wish she could have met her.

But I know she's here with us anyway, in pieces. And they were good ones—the kind you hope to leave behind.

I remember when I came here that first summer and my mom told me I wouldn't resolve my crisis of character or find the answer to all of my problems in Lost Hollow—that whatever I was looking for, I wouldn't find it here.

I'm glad she was wrong.

I close my eyes and fall asleep. Still and quiet. Whole. And not dead inside at all.

THANKS FOR READING!

Enjoyed this book? Please leave a rating and/or review! Reviews are the lifeblood of indie authors and hearing from readers means everything to me!

ABOUT THE AUTHOR

Elle Mitchell is an avid reader, daydreamer, and devourer of knowledge. When she isn't existing inside her own head, she enjoys spending time with her husband and children, traveling, hiking, and finding joy in the ordinary.

She writes realistic NA romance centered around flawed, morally gray characters.

Slide into my DMs! @ellemitchellbooks on IG

ACKNOWLEDGEMENTS

First off, I would like to thank my husband for picking up the slack and waking up with the kids when I was up until 3:00 AM writing and editing this book, and for always being my first reader. None of this would be possible without his support, and for that, I am eternally grateful.

Thank you to my lovely friends and beta readers, Shelbie and Genesis. Your love and support means the world to me. The incest jokes, Shelbie, are especially for you.

Shoutout to Sunnybabe PR for their expert handling of my ARC team and for tolerating the absolute chaos that lives inside of my head. Also, to my Baby Authors Support Group for not kicking me out yet, a decision that I'm sure weighs heavily on you regularly.

And to everyone who took the time to leave a rating or review—again—I can't put into words how much it means to me. I'm just a girl with a dream.

ALSO BY ELLE MITCHELL

A Little Unstable
Broken People (Broken, #1)
Broken Apart (Broken, #1.5)
Broken Reverie (Broken, #2)

Made in the USA
Las Vegas, NV
14 August 2023

76098402R00184